S

Beach Strip

Beach Strip

JOHN LAWRENCE REYNOLDS

HARPERCOLLINS PUBLISHERS LTD

HarperCollins books may be purchased for educational, business, and
sales promotional use through our Special Markets Department.

HarperCollins Publishers Ltd
2 Bloor Street East, 20th Floor
Toronto, Ontario, Canada
M4W 1A8

www.harpercollins.ca

Library and Archives Canada Cataloguing in Publication
Reynolds, John Lawrence
Beach strip / John Lawrence Reynolds.

ISBN 978-1-44340-814-1 (paperback)
ISBN 978-1-44341-095-3 (library hardcover)

I. Title.
PS8585.E94B42 2012   C813'.54   C2012-900616-5

Printed and bound in the United States
9 8 7 6 5 4 3 2 1

To the memory of Wayne Ewing,
who understood the souls of the beach strip and of Lester Young,
and who celebrated both in his quiet and dignified style

It is not in giving life but in risking life that man is raised above the animal.

That is why superiority has been accorded in humanity not to the sex that brings forth life, but to the sex that kills.

—Simone de Beauvoir

Brevity is the soul of lingerie.

—Dorothy Parker

Beach Strip

I.

When I climb the stone steps my husband built to reach the path that separates my house from the beach, I am on the shore of a Great Lake. If I look east, down the length of the lake, I imagine I can see all the way to the St. Lawrence River. If I turn to look behind me, beyond the high bridges and their incessant traffic, I see the things my mother called the devil's appliances, meaning the steel mills and refineries that line the shore of the bay. And if I turn to look at the lake again, but closer now, at the grove of high caragana bushes on the beach in front of my house, just beyond the boardwalk, and if I visualize the open space within them, I see my husband lying on a blanket we brought from Mexico. He is naked. One arm rests across his chest and the other is flung out as though reaching for the gun just beyond his grasp, the one that fired a bullet into his brain.

MY HUSBAND WAS GABRIEL ENFIELD MARSHALL, and he was a police detective. Gabe was impressive but not truly handsome. He was tall with a voice that carried a hint of abrasiveness, like talcum sand. He spoke to me in bed often, sometimes reading from a book or magazine, sometimes telling me tales of his childhood or his work, and he did it because he knew how much I loved hearing his voice while my head rested on his shoulder. Men never appreciate the value of words spoken to a woman in bed. I loved it, and I loved him for doing it. Gabe could be reading the label on a bag of fertilizer. I wouldn't care.

Gabe would read to me in bed, and I would say silly things to make him laugh. It was our version of give and take. I've used laughter all my life to deal with things I don't like or can't face. I couldn't stop when I met Gabe. I couldn't stop after Gabe died. I can't stop now. I would rather laugh in bad taste than cry in good taste.

GABE AND I MARRIED FIVE YEARS AGO, the second time for each of us. My first husband now lives in Alberta with his wife, who teaches aerobics. She is twelve years younger than him, has hair the colour of lemons, and he bought her breast implants for her birthday. Do you need to know more about her than that? I didn't think so.

We left each other, my first husband and I, the way jockeys and horses part at the end of a race. The jockey mounts another horse and leaves the first horse facing a wall bathed in sweat and running the race over in her mind, trying to figure where she stumbled and why she lost. I spent a good deal of time staring at my stable wall. This is all I need to say about my first marriage.

Gabe's wife left him for an advertising executive, taking their two children with her. Gabe discovered she had been cheating on him for almost a year. When he asked her to choose between him and the advertising man, she chose the advertising man because he was not a cop, because he had a large house in a ritzy neighbourhood, because he owned three cars and part of the advertising agency, and maybe because she loved him.

She and the children moved out between Christmas and New Year's, leaving Gabe in an empty house in an empty Toronto suburb. Gabe's son called his father on New Year's Day, and Gabe told me they cried together as though both were eight years old, but only one was. Three weeks later, while the advertising man and

Gabe's wife and the children were on their way to the Laurentians for a skiing holiday, the advertising man's expensive SUV skidded around a turn and rolled down a stone embankment. No one survived.

Gabe spent a year getting over that. When he asked for his job back, he was advised to find other work. He didn't know other work. So he moved here, where the city police department hired him to manage files and push papers around. When they were satisfied that Gabe was not likely to break into tears while directing traffic, they gave him first a duty officer badge and later a detective badge, which is when I met him. We were introduced by a girlfriend of mine who had dated him and thought he was boring. She suggested that he and I were meant for each other. Some friends are like that. I don't miss her.

"Did you always want to be a cop?" I asked Gabe on our first date.

"No, I always wanted to be an entertainer," he said. He looked at me, his head bent, his eyes raised. "I wanted to sing and dance. I wish I had tried it. Singing and dancing for a living."

It was laughable, Gabe as a Vegas act, but I did not laugh. Instead, I said, "Do you know what I have always wanted to do? The one thing I have wanted to do more than any other?"

He shook his head.

"I have always wanted to live in a house on the strip of beach that separates the bay from the lake. I want a house facing east toward the lake, where I can watch the sun rise up out of water in the morning. That's what I have always wanted to do. Watch the sun rise over water every day of my life. I don't know if I have any other ambition. What do you think of that?"

"I think," he said, "it sounds like a wonderful place to live."

We married three months later, and moved into his apartment in the city, where we lived for almost a year until we found this house facing the lake on the beach strip. I had been single for almost five years and had known several men. Gabe had been single for three years, and I knew of no women other than his wife from his past, nor did I ask.

ON THE NIGHT GABE DIED, I had finished my bookkeeping at the retirement home where my mother lives, in a private room overlooking the lake. Two afternoons each week, Tuesday and Thursday, I did the books for Trafalgar Towers, which was owned by a corporation headquartered in Kansas. The company's policy said if Trafalgar Towers delivered a fifteen percent annual return on their investment it would be satisfied. If profits dropped below ten percent, it would change management. And if the retirement home began to lose money, serious thought would be given to demolishing the building and erecting a wall of condominiums. This was a business philosophy Charles Darwin would endorse. Maybe more of life's rules should be so simple. Probably not.

I don't know how much the company in Kansas earned each year, because we never heard from Kansas except when Christmas cards filled with warm Midwest greetings arrived for each full-time staff member.

Keeping the books for an organization that housed fifty-seven residents and a dozen staff was easier than it may sound. Monthly fees for almost all of the residents were paid from private and government pension plans. My job was to confirm receipts, issue salary payments, and pay utilities and repairs. Everything was routine. Surprises were rare and small. I finished my work in five hours, from one to six, two days a week.

I took half my pay in cash. The other half I gave back to ensure that Mother would enjoy the privilege of her private room, something her pension income alone wouldn't cover. When I arrived for work, she would be about to have lunch. When I left for home, she would have finished her dinner and said goodbye.

Trafalgar Towers is north of the canal, just beyond the marsh where herons stand in water and poke for fish. It is an easy walk to the retirement home from our house. I can make it there in less than half an hour. When the weather is pleasant, I follow the path to the canal, cross the lift bridge over the canal, skirt the marshland, and there I am. I did this on the day Gabe died.

In summer, the lift bridge rises every half-hour, permitting sailboats to leave the bay and enter the deeper, cleaner, more dangerous waters of the lake, or return to the bay and sail past the steel mills on their way to the yacht clubs and marinas west of the factories. The bridge also rises for cargo ships, which signal their approach from either direction with a blast of their horns, but there are few cargo ships now.

In summers when I was a teenager, and if my boyfriend had a car, I would ask him to drive me to the canal that cuts through the beach strip, joining the Great Lake to the bay. We would watch ships enter and leave the bay, floating past like moving mountains of steel, travelling to and from places that would always be names on a map to me, places I would never visit. Bremerhaven. Le Havre. Cadiz. Ships that sailed across the Atlantic, up the St. Lawrence River, and a thousand miles inland.

Hard-looking men stood at the railings of the ocean freighters, cigarettes hanging at an angle from their mouths. When the ships drew close, I would step out of the car to wave at the men. I would be wearing tight white shorts and a T-shirt, and they would smile and wave back, and sometimes grab their crotches or mutter something that would make other men standing near them laugh. As the ships passed, I would look at the sterns of the vessels to read their home ports, cities in Sweden or Yugoslavia or Greece or Taiwan or Panama, rusting hulks on morose journeys. I wondered if the men would picture me while lying in their beds that night, if they would remember the girl in the tight sweater, with long hair and good legs. I liked to think they would. The men looked dangerous, and I was near enough for them to absorb all they needed to absorb and too far away to reach it.

When it grew dark on the beach strip, boys wanted to do what boys always want to do with girls in cars at night. Sometimes it was a thrill and sometimes it wasn't. But it was always exciting to watch the ships pass, and see the lonely men at the rail staring at me, a girl they would know only in their fantasies.

The lift bridge carries beach strip traffic across the canal, people in cars and people on bicycles and couples who walk along the beach for exercise. Twice every hour, an air horn blasts a warning before the bridge rises, and a man behind a high smoky glass window in a building next to the bridge changes the traffic lights from green to red, and pushes a switch to lower wooden arms over the road and walkway to hold back cars and people. When all is clear, the bridge begins to rise. If only pleasure boats are waiting to go through the canal, the bridge stops a few feet in the air and the boats pass beneath it quickly, the people in the boats waving at those strolling along the edge of the canal. If a freighter is passing through, the span rises to its full height, groaning like an old man lifting weights, all the way to the top and staying there, sometimes for a half-hour or more, until the ship passes through the canal.

You can walk along the canal beneath the lift bridge and stand there as the span first rises above you, then settles back down again. Boys used to leave pennies on the flat surface of the footings when the bridge was up. They would return after the bridge rose again half an hour later and retrieve the coins, pressed to paper-thin blotches of copper, until a fence was installed to keep them away, although the boys would climb or even tear down the wire fence to get to the footings. That's what they're called, the concrete pads that the bridge settles on. Footings. Gabe told me that. Gabe told me many things, and he avoided others.

High above the canal on the bay side, twin steel bridges carry traffic along the freeway. The highway bridges begin their rise a mile back on either side of the canal, and are more than two hundred feet above it at their peak. The traffic they carry is distant and uninteresting, which is how I suspect the people in those cars view us who live below them on the beach strip. The high bridges are on the beach strip, but they are not of it. I ignore them, like everyone else who lives on the strip. We develop blind eyes and selective ears. We ignore the high bridges and pretend not to hear the noise of the traffic they carry. We turn our backs on them, and on the oil-slicked bay and the steel mills with their slag and steam and smoke, and we look east across the lake extending to the Thousand Islands, lovely green and granite jewels that, in the pictures I have seen, look like pieces of paradise.

On the beach strip, we live between a distant heaven and a smoky hell.

MOTHER SUFFERED A STROKE TWO YEARS AGO, a knife-edge rupture, the doctors called it. The stroke left her mind intact but destroyed her ability to speak, and weakened her sense of balance so badly that she can't walk safely. That's when I found her a room at Trafalgar Towers and worked out an arrangement to do their books in return for her private room and some cash for me. This took an hour of negotiation with Helen Detwiler, who manages Trafalgar Towers. Helen has hair like steel wool, wears print dresses and drives a Buick. I could learn more about her, I suppose, but I have never had the inclination.

Mother sits and moves in a wheelchair, and needs special medication to hold the next stroke—the doctors talk about it the way people in California talk about the next earthquake—at bay. Otherwise, Mother is aware and alert, perpetually silent, sometimes angry, and always happy to see me. She appreciates what I have done for her.

Her room with a view of the lake is akin, I am told, to having a hotel room in Paris with a view of both the Eiffel Tower and Notre Dame Cathedral, on a smaller scale. Mother takes pride in that. I have called her a View Snob, and she agrees. This is why she refused all of my invitations, half-hearted as they may have been, to come live with Gabe and me.

My visits with Mother at the end of each working day were usually brief. Perhaps once a month, or when Gabe would not be home in time, Mother and I would have dinner together. I would describe my day and talk about friends and relatives. My sister, Tina, and her husband in British Columbia. A cousin in New York. An aunt in Toronto. If Mother had a comment to make, she would write it on a small blackboard I bought her, tracing her comments with chalk in the lovely cursive handwriting that had won her awards in public school. She would write, *Your hair is very nice today, but you should get a manicure.* Or, *You put too much salt on your potatoes.* Mother will always be a mother.

She has her sense of humour as well. She described a staff member who kept butting into other peoples' lives by writing, *She's so nosy, she'd peek over a glass wall.*

The night Gabe died, Mother made no humorous comments because she knew I was troubled. She did not know why I was troubled. But she realized later, as did I, that had I not been so troubled by what I needed to do that evening, Gabe would still be alive.

2.

I carried Mother's empty dinner tray to the commissary, then returned to her room. At this point I would usually say goodbye and return home. But that early August night I told Mother I wanted to stay with her for an hour or so. We could watch television together or just absorb the view out her window facing the lake.

Sitting in her room, you can see the small white lighthouse at the end of the canal on the lake side. There is nothing special about the lighthouse. It is white and slim and functional, with a red metal roof and a light that beams across the lake. Lighthouses don't need to have a unique design to be romantic or picturesque. They are romantic and picturesque by definition. You say the word "lighthouse," or picture one in your mind, and something within you relaxes because it feels good. Just the idea, even without the reality, feels good to you. Like hearing a railroad whistle in the distance. Or being married to a strong and gentle man.

On summer evenings, people stroll along the pier to the light-house or sit fishing on the walls of the canal. You can watch them from Mother's room. The pleasure boats and freighters come and go on the canal, passing through the beach strip from the bay to the lake or from the lake into the bay. Birds soar through the sky visible from the window—cormorants black and determined, herons silent and haughty, seagulls gliding and screeching, and Canada geese honking in formation. There are worse views in the world.

We sat watching the lake grow golden in the light of the sunset. It was a muggy evening with no breeze, and many people walked along the pier to the lighthouse, where they stood looking east down the length of the lake or chatted with fishermen before walking back to the beach strip.

When it became too dark to see the people clearly, we turned from the window and I switched on the television. We sat for a while, Mother in silence and me commenting on the silliness of first one comedy show, then another, until Mother wrote on her blackboard, *Why aren't you going home?*

"Gabe's not home yet," I said. "He's on an investigation. Told me he'd be late." Which was a lie.

Mother erased her first message and wrote, *What's bothering you?*

"Nothing is bothering me," I said, annoyed. "Tonight I'd rather sit here with you than hang around our empty house, waiting for Gabe."

She watched me with an expression that said she didn't believe me, then turned back to the television. We sat quietly until Frieda, one of the night nurses, knocked on the door to say that someone wanted to speak to me on the telephone in the reception area. I don't have a cell phone. It's part of my clinging to tradition. I don't own a computer, either. I use the retirement home's computer for bookkeeping, but I don't have one in my house. It's not that I believe technology is evil. I just believe it encourages evil things.

I followed Frieda to reception and picked up the receiver. It was Gabe.

"Come home and let's do it," Gabe said.

"Do what?"

"Get naked in the bushes."

"Have you been drinking?"

"A glass of wine. Maybe a couple. Been home for over an hour waiting for you."

"There are people around."

"Hardly any. Besides, once we're in the bushes you can't see anything. It's dark out. Soon it'll be pitch black."

"I'm with Mother."

"I know." He sounded relieved. "I know. I love you, Josie."

"Gabe—"

"Please come home. It's not just . . . there's something else."

"I know."

"How can you know? I love you so much, Josie—"

"Gabe—"

"I'll get the blanket. It's good wine. Chewy Merlot, the kind you like."

"Gabe—"

He hung up.

I wanted fresh air. I walked down the hall to a set of French doors that opened onto a small balcony overlooking the lake, where I stood clenching the rail and staring at nothing. Sometimes we make fools of ourselves without intending to, and sometimes we do it with full knowledge of our foolishness. I counted cars passing on Lakeshore Road. I counted the jokes Gabe had told to make me laugh. I counted the places we had made love. When I felt foolish enough, I returned to Mother's room.

"Gabe wants me to come home," I told Mother.

She frowned and waved her hand at the door, meaning, *Go, go.*

"He's been drinking." I settled in the chair.

Mother shrugged.

"I'll go when this program is over."

Mother sat watching me, not the television set. I stayed to the end of the silly comedy, and through three commercials, almost half an hour. Then I rose and walked to Mother's chair. I kissed her forehead and squeezed her arm. "I may be back tomorrow," I said. "Everything's fine."

She looked at me with concern. I have never been able to fool Mother.

I WALKED OUT OF THE RETIREMENT HOME into the summer evening's warm, damp darkness, something I have always enjoyed. My sister, Tina, hates humid weather, especially at night. She tells me that anybody who likes warm, humid evenings is longing for a womb, and she's too old for wombs, including her own.

I crossed the road to the beach trail I had followed from my home and walked south. It is almost a mile along the lakeshore to the canal, where I crossed the lift bridge on the pedestrian walkway, traffic flowing past me, then turned onto the lakeside lane. It's shorter along the road, but that would take me home sooner. I didn't want sooner. I wanted later.

Ahead of me, small white lights were moving in patterns both random and logical, like a cloud of insects, and red and blue flashes reflected from trees on Beach Boulevard. The location of the lights was as distant as our house, Gabe's and mine.

Someone had fallen from their bicycle or their in-line skates onto the boardwalk, I thought. Crazy kids, out too late at night. They move so fast, tearing along in darkness. Perhaps they struck someone walking.

Two larger white lights shone on the lake side of the boardwalk. Their beams moved and broke erratically, making sudden flashes through arbitrary darkness, and I realized they were shining from within the caragana bushes where Gabe and I had made love last summer, and where we had promised to return some warm night.

I began running, past other people attracted to the lights, coming from their homes and their cars, and some from the water's edge. As I approached, I saw a mass of onlookers standing behind yellow plastic tape and uniformed police officers, the crowd whispering among themselves, the younger ones adding low laughter to their words. I elbowed my way through them all until I reached the yellow tape, and when I stepped under the tape a uniformed cop approached with his hand raised.

"I live here," I said. "This is my house. Where is my husband?"

"Josie." A man in shirt and tie, his large body topped with an almost hairless head, oversized nose, and thick lips, walked toward me.

"Walter," I said, "where's Gabe?"

Walter Freeman was the chief of detectives, a man neither Gabe nor I liked very much. Walter held a notebook in one hand, and he placed the other on my shoulder. "Josie," he said, "go and wait in the house."

"No." I pulled away from his touch. I wanted no one touching me, especially Walter. "Where is Gabe?"

"You don't need to see this," he said.

"See what? Is it Gabe? I want to see Gabe!" I began shaking with fear. "Please let me see Gabe. Please take me to him . . ." I would have begged Walter, if that's what it took. I was already crying. I was already expecting what I would see.

Walter's voice grew more commanding, like a father dominating a child. "Josie, just go into the house. Now."

That's when I forgot about begging. I forgot about everything. "*I want to see my husband!*" I screamed the words and flailed my arms to push Walter Freeman's hand away, and ran for the circle of high caragana shrubs. I was beyond fear and sorrow. I wanted to know, I wanted to be with Gabe, Gabe needed me, we needed each other. We didn't need Walter Freeman, who treated Gabe with disdain, and who once made a pass at me at a charity barbecue.

Two officers were erecting blue plastic sheeting around the bushes, an unnecessary shield because the growth was so thick that everything within their embrace was already invisible. A uniformed cop stood at the opening in the circle of shrubs facing our house. He was young with a bland face, the kind of cop that enrages me with their good looks and intransigence. He stepped in front of me, staring at me without blinking like some damned stone statue, like a granite robot.

"Is my husband in there, you son of a bitch?" I shrieked, and people behind the yellow tape snickered.

"You can't go in, ma'am," the cop replied.

"I'm his wife!" I seized the young cop's shining black belt. It smelled of fresh shoe polish. Of course it would, because the kid was ambitious, the kid wanted to be promoted, the kid kept his belt shined, the kid was an asshole. "If my husband is in there, I want to see him!"

"Josie," a voice behind me said. "Josie."

I knew that voice. I released the young cop and turned to face Mel Holiday, Gabe's detective partner. "Is it Gabe?" I asked.

"I don't know," Mel said. "I just arrived." Then: "I think so. One of the guys out front, in a cruiser, said . . ." Mel started over again. "He said it's Gabe."

"I want to see." I kept my eyes closed. Maybe it would help to keep the tears in. "I need to see him, Mel."

I felt Mel turn to look back at Walter Freeman, and heard Walter say, "Quickly."

Mel pushed away to look at me, hands on my shoulders. "You don't have to," he began.

"Yes, I do." I twisted out of his grip. "Yes, I do."

The young cop stepped aside at a gesture from Mel, who returned his hand to my shoulder, keeping me from bursting through the opening in the shrubs. I saw the corner of the blanket first, the blanket we had purchased in Ixtapa on our honeymoon, its orange and green pattern lit by the flashlights of two police officers and two medical technicians in white coats. The blanket covered the area of sand enclosed within the circle of shrubs rising almost ten feet around it. One light lifted to shine on my face, then returned to the scene it had been illuminating: the naked body, the eyes open, the face calm, the head framed in an obscene pool of blood.

I screamed Gabe's name as though he could hear me. Perhaps if I screamed loud enough, if I raged madly enough, he would rise from the blanket and duck his head like he did, and smile, asking me to be quiet, to speak softly. I could not believe that the man who had saved me, as I had saved him, was dead. But the child in me believed it, the one who always wanted to live on the beach strip, the one who had lain here with Gabe, both of us as naked as he was now but alive in the darkness, making love while voices passed on the sand along the water's edge and on the lane behind the houses, while traffic raced noisily over the highway bridges and boats moved in silence through the canal.

I saw red, I saw anger, I saw blood beneath Gabe's body, I saw two men in blue uniforms approach and felt someone seize my arms from behind. I gave up. Actually, my consciousness gave up and abandoned me.

3.

Glass, glass, glass. Stay away from broken glass. Don't run with a glass in your hand. Never take glass containers to the beach. Glass in the sand beneath bare feet. I am a child on the beach. No, I am a woman on a sofa.

Glass, glass, glass. My arm ached. I wanted to throw up.

Oh, glass. And a man's voice: "I think she's awake."

Open your eyes, I told myself. I did not want to.

Not glass. Lass. "Lass, lass, lass." A voice like porridge. Warm, rich, soft. My neighbour Maude Blair was speaking to me. Fifty years out of Glasgow and she still wore her soft highland burr like a tartan, like a brooch in the shape of a thistle. Maude and her husband, Jock, are two of the few friends I have on the beach strip. Not "How are ya?" friends you pass on a walk or in the supermarket. I have many of those. I mean friends who know and care about you. They're more difficult to find. The beach strip is made up of individuals who prefer to remain that way.

Maude was stroking my head, and when I opened my eyes she smiled at me but spoke to someone else, out of my view. "Aye, she's fine now," Maude said. "She's awake. You're awake and all right, aren't you, lass?"

Two medical attendants entered from the kitchen. They looked purposeful, the way professionals do when they're allowed to demonstrate their training and use their tools. They took my blood pressure, shone lights into my eyes, gave me a pill and some

16

water, asked if I needed a blanket, and left, satisfied that they had practised on a living person.

I rose from the sofa, helped by Maude Blair. I stumbled into the kitchen and sat slumped in a chair, drained in the manner you have when your body's supply of tears is exhausted. Nothing ached, but everything pained me.

"Should I be staying with you?" Maude asked. Her hands were touching my head, my shoulders, my arms, as though she wanted to assure herself or me that I wasn't falling apart physically as much as I appeared to be mentally.

I hugged her to me, burying my face against the printed pattern of her dress, and permitted myself to wail while Maude patted the back of my head gently, saying, "There, there."

When I sat back, I saw Jock, Maude's husband, peering around Mel and two uniformed officers, all three making notes on small paper pads.

"We need to question Mrs. Marshall," Mel said to Maude, then added "privately," and Maude nodded and stood, looking from me to Jock and back again, dabbing at her eyes with a small lace-trimmed handkerchief. Jock raised a hand to me, then took Maude's arm and walked toward the back door, into the garden.

Mel followed them, returned to speak to the two uniformed cops, who nodded and left, and sat facing me.

"Who did it?" I asked him.

Someone had brought coffee in paper cups and set several on the kitchen table. Mel placed one in front of me.

"He did. Gabe shot himself."

"No, he didn't."

"Josie—"

"My husband did not shoot himself in the head. My husband did not tell me to meet him out there just so I could find him dead. My husband was not that mean or that selfish. I spoke to him, he called me on the telephone, he was fine, he was Gabe . . ."

"When did he call you?"

"An hour ago. Maybe more."

"Where were you?"

"With Mother. Just down . . ." My throat tightened. "You know where she is." I shook my head. My words emerged between sobs. "Gabe did not kill himself. Where was the gun? Why wasn't it in his hand? How could he shoot himself without a gun in his hand?"

"The gun was there. He was kneeling when he shot himself. He fell to his left, his arm . . . when he died, all the muscles relaxed, Josie. That's what happens. The arm drops, the gun is released. It was there on the blanket. The weapon does not always remain in the hands of a suicide, Josie. I've seen it a dozen times. The recoil, the kick of the gun—"

I didn't want to hear about it. "You've seen it a dozen times. Good for you. I've seen it once and I hate it. I hate it and I don't understand it. I don't believe it, either."

Mel rose from his chair and walked outside, leaving me listening to sounds I had rarely heard on other evenings: traffic on the twin high bridges, feet shuffling along the boardwalk, muffled noises from factories along the bay. When he returned he said, "There's an open bottle of wine with him."

I told him I knew that. I knew all about it. Merlot. Rich, red, chewy Merlot. That's what we drank.

Walter Freeman entered the kitchen with authority and without knocking. "Josie," Walter said, "I need a statement."

"About what?"

"About Gabe calling you tonight."

"Who told you that?"

"I did," Mel said. "Somebody has to put the facts down."

"Then put down the fact that my husband did not commit suicide." I was crying again. Tears must be inexhaustible.

Walter gestured to Mel, who rose from the chair and walked

outside. Walter took his place at the table, watching me as he set his wire-bound notebook in front of him. He reached for a pen in the pocket of his cheap shirt. Walter always wore cheap clothes. Walter had no class. "Walter Freeman is a man," Gabe said to me once, "who is confident enough in himself to be an ass and not care about it. You have to admire him for that." I did not admire Walter for anything.

"You see this?" Walter said. He took a small page of lined paper from inside his notebook. Two pieces of sticky tape extended on either side, like coiled transparent wings. On the note was, *I'm in the bushes. Get naked!* It looked like Gabe's writing. It *was* Gabe's writing.

I shook my head.

"It was stuck to the door, the back door," Walter said. "Look like Gabe's writing to you?"

I nodded.

Walter inserted the note between the pages of his notebook. "What did Gabe say when he called you tonight?"

"He asked me to come home. You saw the note. He wanted me to go with him into the bushes."

"Why?"

I looked at Walter, who was staring at me with the same expression he wore, I suspected, while reading a telephone directory. I did not want to speak to Walter, and I wanted him to know it, so I replaced my despair with anger. It made a good substitute. "Why the hell do you think?"

Walter blinked. "We didn't find his clothes. It appears he left the house naked, wrapped in the blanket. Once you're inside those bushes at night, nobody can see you."

"Do you suppose that's why he wanted to make love there?"

Walter wrote something in his notebook, and as he wrote he said, "Tell me what time your husband called you. At a retirement home, was it?"

"Trafalgar Towers. My mother lives there. I work there twice a week. You already know that. It was around nine."

Walter's eyebrows moved up his forehead and stayed there. "It's past eleven now. You haven't been here for, what? Half an hour? What took you so long?"

"I walked."

"Which way? Along the highway?"

"Along the lake to the bridge."

"Any reason you came down the lake tonight, didn't walk along the road?"

I shrugged.

"Coming back along the road should have taken you twenty minutes. Half an hour at the most. You took over an hour to get here. Why so long?"

"I was not aware that a wife needs to drop everything and run home just because her husband wants to screw her in the moonlight."

I watched Walter's eyebrows descend slowly into place. "What was the state of your marriage?" he asked. He was making notes again.

"The state of our marriage? What the hell kind of question is that?" I looked away, then back again. "The state of our marriage? I don't know. Michigan? No, Florida. Gabe liked Florida. How's that for a state of marriage? If Florida is a state of marriage, is Nevada a state of divorce?"

"Josie—"

"Call me Mrs. Marshall. That's my name. My husband is dead, so I'm the widow Marshall now, but it's still my name, and you damn well better use it."

It was a tantrum, but I thought I deserved to throw one and Walter Freeman deserved to catch it. He drew a deep breath and started to speak, but I wasn't finished. "Did Gabe leave a note? Where's his note?"

"There is no note." Walter nodded at his own words as though confirming something. He looked up at me. "Was your marriage happy, Mrs. Marshall?"

"Delirious."

"Are you certain?"

"I know when I'm happy."

"Did your husband give you any gifts?"

"Of course he gave me gifts. And I gave him gifts."

"Expensive ones? Recently?"

"I don't know what the hell you're talking about."

"Were there conflicts in your marriage?"

"Conflicts? Like arguments? Sure there were. We were married."

"I was thinking of other partners. I was thinking of that kind of conflict."

I shook my head. "Think about something else."

"Neither of you was having an affair?"

"No."

Whenever I lie, I'm convinced something happens to inform the other person that I am not being truthful. I blush, I look away, I stutter, my mouth gets dry, maybe my nose grows longer, I don't know. Walter Freeman knew I was lying, and he sat looking at me, saying nothing, which made me so uncomfortable that I spoke first. "Who found Gabe's body?"

Walter pushed both lips forward like a man playing a trumpet, a habit he had when thinking deeply, or as deeply as Walter's intelligence could take him. "Couple of kids. Down on the beach. They heard the shot and thought it came from your house. One of them called us on his cell phone, and a bunch of them came up here, looking around. They found the opening into the bushes. Stomped all over the place. Screwed up a lot of things, but . . ." Walter shrugged.

"If I heard a gunshot, I'd run the other way."

"So would most people over the age of twenty." He stood up just as Mel entered the room again.

"They're ready to take Gabe away," Mel said. "Is there anything I can do, Josie? Somebody I can call?"

I could only shake my head. I could think of nobody I wanted to speak to. Only Gabe. "I want to go with him," I said. "I want to see him and hug him."

"I'll arrange something," Walter said. "You can follow the coroner's vehicle in a cruiser. It'll be out front. The officer will call you." He walked out of the kitchen through the back door, and Mel took his place in the chair facing me.

"I know it's hard to accept." Mel looked back over his shoulder to confirm we were alone, then reached for my hand and held it as he spoke. "It always is. Gabe did it. He had reason to. We both know that. God, I feel terrible. Gabe was . . ." He dropped my hand and turned away.

"He wanted to make love to me." I was crying again. Damn it, damn it.

"He carried his gun out there with him, Josie." Mel turned back to me. "Maybe he planned to do something else."

"Like what?"

He wiped his eyes and looked at me.

"Bullshit," I said. "That's bullshit, Mel. He wouldn't do that. Gabe loved me."

"He knew things."

"He suspected them. Unless you told him. Did you tell him, Mel? Jesus, did you tell him?"

Mel shook his head. "How could I? Why would I?" He knelt to look directly at me. "It's his weapon, Josie. They'll retrieve the bullet, and when they match it to his gun, what else can they think?"

I walked to the cupboard next to the refrigerator and opened the top drawer. Then I walked to the pantry and looked behind the sugar. Gabe always followed the same routine with his weapon when he was off duty, removing the ammunition clip and placing it in the drawer near the refrigerator, and keeping the gun itself in the pantry behind the sugar. All the cops had their own way of dealing with their guns. Gabe told me they joked with each other about it. One put his ammunition clip inside an empty cereal box. Another hid his behind his wife's box of tampons.

Neither piece of Gabe's gun was where he would hide it. I leaned against the kitchen counter, staring into the sink.

"It's his gun, Josie." Mel was watching me, his head tilted to one side.

"He wouldn't take it with him," I said. "Not to meet me. He knows I hate guns."

Someone called Mel's name from the door to the garden, and he left me alone for the first time since I arrived home. Gabe disliked carrying a gun, and he disliked police officers who expressed a desire to use their weapon. "If I didn't have to carry one, I wouldn't," he told me once. "Anybody who collects weapons or loves to fire them or says he loves them—I've heard guys say that—well, they're sick." Gabe was always late for his tests at the firing range, and he always dismantled his gun as soon as he arrived home because he knew I hated the sight of it. He would not have taken it with him to the caragana bushes for that reason. Not to meet me. Not to use it on me. He loved me that much. I knew he did.

When Mel returned, he closed the door behind him. "The coroner wants to move the . . . to move Gabe," he said. "The officer in the cruiser out front is ready to take you to the morgue. You're sure you want to do this?"

I nodded.

"You could ride with me, but . . ."

Riding with Mel was the last thing I wanted to do. No, seeing Gabe on a slab in the morgue was the last thing I wanted to do. I could avoid one, but not the other. I wanted no one to accompany me to see Gabe. I wanted to speak with no one. I didn't even want to look at anyone. I buried myself in myself. I didn't want to do that, either, but I had no choice.

4.

I don't know how long it took the officer to drive me to the morgue, or the route he took to get there, or even what he looked like. I just made myself as small as possible against the corner of the back seat of the cruiser and kept my eyes closed, wishing at times that someone was with me and wishing at other times that I would see no one for days.

The car pulled to a stop and the officer driving it said, "We're here." Through the windshield I saw a small, frosted door with MORGUE stencilled across the glass, and I followed the cop inside.

We entered a room that looked like the reception area of my dentist's office. Clean, antiseptic and grey. Chrome and vinyl chairs. Dated magazines spread across a low table. I steadied myself against a wall while the officer disappeared through a metal door and emerged a few minutes later with a woman dressed in a green top and trousers who said I should wait for a few minutes and that she could bring me coffee or water. I think I said, "Just bring me my husband," and sat alone on one of the vinyl chairs.

I waited ten minutes. I know because I looked at a clock on the wall and was surprised to find it was three minutes after midnight. At thirteen minutes after midnight the woman returned and asked me to follow her, please, and I did, down a corridor and into a room that was all stainless steel, like the inside of a dishwasher, and there was Gabe, on a stainless steel table. Someone had laid a white towel across his groin. Another towel covered his head above his eyebrows, where the wound would show. His hands were wrapped in plastic bags. A man in a white coat stood with his back to me, preparing something on a counter, and the woman in green took my arm and held it, and I think she said she was sorry as we walked to the table.

I took Gabe's arm in my hands, and it was my turn to say I was sorry, over and over again, telling Gabe while the woman stood at my elbow watching and the man in the white coat fussed over his instruments, his tools of dissection.

I have no idea how long I stood speaking to Gabe. I know I looked up to see the man in the white coat, an older, sweet-faced man who looked as though he mourned for every person he encountered on the slabs, watching me over the top of his glasses. I saw him flick his eyes from mine to the woman beside me and felt a slight tug on my arm. It was time to go. I pulled away from her long enough to lean over Gabe and kiss him lightly on the lips, whispered goodbye, and walked away.

The officer who had driven me to the morgue was waiting in the reception area, talking with Mel Holiday, and as I emerged from the morgue the two men separated. Mel asked me to sit down, took a chair beside me, and asked if he could get me anything. All I could do was stare at the floor and shake my head.

"Walter wants to get things started," Mel said, "do the tests as soon as possible, get the autopsy results, get a report issued, and wrap everything up." When I said nothing, he added as though I had asked why there was such a rush, "When this happens to an officer, people speculate, they talk, the media makes it a big deal, you know that. The longer it takes to settle things, to get the official word out, the more they talk."

I remained silent.

"You sure you're okay?" he asked, bending to look at me.

"No," I said. "I'm not okay. But I will be eventually. I hope."

"You shouldn't be alone tonight," he said. "Who can you stay with?"

I shook my head. Wherever I was, I would not sleep.

"The woman who was talking to you, she and her husband," Mel said. "Your neighbours, next door. They say you can stay with them, or the woman, she'll come in and stay with you. It's late, but we could call her. She's waiting for us to call her."

"The Blairs. Tell them no. Tell them thanks, but no."

"You can't stay alone. I can have a female officer sent over."

I had been the emotionally crippled victim long enough. I no longer felt emotionally crippled. I began to feel anger at what had been done to Gabe, what had been done to me, what had been done to us. "Lovely," I said to Mel. "We'll sit and do embroidery together."

"Damn it, Josie!" Mel snapped. He looked around. The uniformed officer had left to wait for me in the police cruiser, and the woman in green had returned to be with Gabe and the sweet old man with the knives and saws. "Gabe's dead. I'll miss him too. We worked together nearly a year. You know how close we were. And all you can do is come up with smart-ass comments?"

"No!" I shouted loud enough for anyone to hear. "No, I can't keep playing the broken-hearted widow, because I don't know how, Mel. Do you have something that will tell me how to behave? Is it in the police procedures manual? Do I dress in black and wear prayer beads? The hell I will. Take all your compassion and crap about sending female cops to sit with the grieving wife and shove it. I don't need them. I need Gabe."

I sat with my head in my hands and felt my rage dissolve. I heard Mel walk outside and speak to someone. When he returned, he stood in the middle of the room and said, "There will be two officers at your house all night, keeping things secure."

I looked up to see him standing with his hands in his pockets, his eyes avoiding mine.

"We'll have more forensics people there in the morning, when the light's better," he added. "If you need something, just ask the officers."

"Tell them to stay outside," I said. "Tell them I don't want them knocking on my door, checking up on me or wanting to use the john."

"The constable outside will take you home. You should stay with somebody tonight, but it's your choice. I'll be back at my place in a couple of hours." Mel walked to the door and stood with his hand on the knob. "Call, just to talk or whatever, all right?"

"Mel?"

He looked back.

"Why did Walter Freeman want to know if Gabe had bought me any expensive gifts recently?"

Mel looked puzzled. "He asked you that?"

"Yes."

"He must have something on his mind. I'll find out." Mel glanced out the window in the back door, then walked toward me. "Did he, Josie?"

"Did he what?"

"Buy you something expensive lately? Between you and me, so that when Walter explains why he asked you . . ."

I shook my head.

"Okay." Mel told me to call whenever I wanted. He did not tell me his telephone number. He didn't need to.

THE OFFICER DROVE ME HOME in the same silence as before. A handful of police and forensics people milled about the caragana bushes under intense lights. I permitted the constable to walk me to the door, thanked him, and entered the house, where I sat alone in the darkness, on a living-room chair, facing the window that looked west, away from the lake and toward the bay.

I watched the sky to the west, above the steel companies along the shore of the bay, begin to glow with the colour of peaches that changed to a redness like roses or perhaps of blood, and I began to relax at the sight, familiar from my childhood.

Those explosions of light had appeared in the night sky above my parents' house, the one my father would pay for with his life, when I was a child. Their radiance would flood the room I shared with my sister, making the walls blush with a strange, roiling redness. I had no word for that colour, but I thought it might be the same shade of red as blood on the floor of an abattoir.

My grandfather had worked in an abattoir. For thirty-three years, five days a week, he slit the throats of cattle and hogs, calves and lambs and suckling pigs, sometimes a hundred or more each day. What does that do to a person? What does it say about his view of life. Or, more important, of death?

My grandfather did not die in the manner that the animals died. He died asleep on New Year's Eve. In his own bed, totally sober. On the morning of the first day of 1967, my grandmother awoke and my grandfather didn't. There was no slitting of throats, no rope of red blood shooting from the carotid arteries, no gasping realization. Just a dream that ended with his death.

Dad showed me his father's killing knife, which represented most of my father's inheritance. I remember the scimitar blade, worn with years of honing and stained with blood, like rust. It was all I knew of my grandfather, that knife and the job he held for all those years. Did he not want another job? Was he not qualified to do something besides killing? This bothers me. It did not bother my father, my mother, or my sister. But it bothers me, and I will never know the answer.

When I see the glow blossoming into the night sky from my house on the beach strip, the sight is comforting in the way that snapshots of old friends and lovers can be comforting. The friends have changed with time, and so has the light. It appears less frequently now, and is weaker. Like the people in the snapshots.

My father told me the red light in the sky was caused by molten slag pouring from the blast furnaces of the steel companies along the shore of the bay. Slag, he explained, was liquid stone as hot as the sun. The glow of the molten rock reflected off clouds of steam billowing from the coke ovens nearby. "Hot as lava, the slag is," he said, "pouring from the blast furnaces like water when you open the tap in the bathtub. Melted limestone and other stuff they don't want in the steel, all running into pits where it cools. And right next door are the coke ovens, where coal is heated to a thousand, two thousand degrees in sealed ovens, and it turns into coke. That's what they use to fire the blast furnaces. Sometimes they open the coke ovens at the same time as they tap the slag, and they spray the hot coke with water . . . see, there it goes now."

It was a cold day, and I was ten years old, I suppose. Not much older, because my father died on my twelfth birthday. As he spoke, a white cloud ascended into a faded blue sky to the north of our house, along the shore of the bay.

"They spray water on the hot coke so that it won't burn up when it hits the air, y'see." He was pointing at a rising white cloud that seemed to be powered from within, rolling as it climbed into the air. "That's what makes the steam, the water they spray on the coke. That cloud'll go up maybe a thousand, two thousand feet, and when it gets high like that at night, and they tap the slag in the blast furnace at the same time, it's the firelight from the hot slag that bounces off the cloud and lights up this whole end of town." He nodded his head and placed a cigarette in his mouth, watching the cloud of steam. "That's what wakes you up at night sometimes. That's the light that shines through your window, all right?" He looked down at me, patting his pockets, searching for his lighter. "All right? So there's no reason to be scared when you see that light."

He was wrong. The light never frightened me. It frightened my sister, Tina, but merely annoyed me because it reminded me of where we lived, amid the soot and the noise of the furnaces and mills that made the steel for the factories that were our neigh-bours. The crimson colour that shone in the night sky fascinated me because when he was a boy my father had visited the kill-ing floor where my grandfather worked each day, standing ankle-deep in blood and water. My father had seen the liquid floor and described it to me, saying it was red, but not as red as blood itself because so much else was mixed with it from the animals that hung by their hind legs and writhed while dying. The image of the writhing, dying animals frightened me. My grandfather's killing knife frightened me too. But not the hellish glow in the night sky above our house.

Few things frighten me today.

Which is not to say I am brave.

So maybe I'm a coward.

Men fear being labelled cowards in the same way they fear growing impotent, and I suppose Sigmund Freud would say "Precisely!" as though it should be obvious. It has never been obvious to me.

Women escape that particular silliness. Call me a redhead or call me a coward, what does it matter? So it is not difficult for me to use the word, and I felt no shame at my cowardice.

I had not wanted to meet Gabe on the blanket within the shrubs, the ones growing between the water's edge and the board-walk behind our home, because I feared what I had promised myself I would do that evening.

I had promised I would confess to Gabe that I had made love to Mel Holiday. That I could count the times and identify the locations and describe the positions, if that was what he wished to hear. That I had been more than foolish, I had been stupid and selfish. That I was sorry, more sorry than I could ever explain. That I promised I would never do it again because I loved Gabe and I would always love him, and I had never stopped loving him. That I wanted to tell him because I could no longer stand the guilt I felt each time we made love, or the fear I felt when Gabe looked at me in a certain way, as though he suspected the truth. I had told myself to deny, deny, deny if he asked, but every denial, I knew, would be another betrayal. Lately, every day that passed without telling him felt like a betrayal.

The truth is, I was still being selfish. I couldn't stand the pain of guilt anymore, so I would pass it on to Gabe by confessing.

I would never have said it in that manner, in those words. I would have confessed through tears. I would also have confirmed suspicions that I feared Gabe already harboured. He had wanted, I knew, to dissolve those suspicions in the adolescent act of making love in the summer night air, smothering our giggles to avoid alerting passersby, drinking wine, and watching the moonlight and our hands pass over each other's skin.

Would I have told him as soon as I arrived, there among the shrubs, me in my pants and T-shirt and him naked? It was unthinkable; it would have been unbearable. I wanted him dressed and sitting with me in our living room. I wanted him to see my face and understand how sorry I was, and how much I needed his forgiveness. I wanted to tell him that I would understand if he left me, but I did not want him to leave me. I never wanted him to leave me. So I had delayed returning, hoping he would decide I wasn't coming to meet him on the blanket and he would wrap himself within it and return to the house and get dressed, and I would arrive home to tell him.

I believed Gabe would forgive me, and I had almost looked forward to the anger, the tears, the shouts, and the cleansing of confession.

But what if, I wondered, and this was why I needed to spend hours alone in the darkness of the house we shared: What if Gabe's anger knew no bounds? What if his suspicion and rage were stronger than I knew? What if he had taken his gun with him to the blanket, not to kill himself but to kill me? And why did Walter Freeman ask if Gabe had given me any expensive gifts lately? Because he had, of course. And if anyone but Walter had asked, I might have admitted it.

I thought of all these things and more as the steam above the mills dissipated in the evening air, the glow of the slag vanishing with it, leaving the beach strip in its familiar darkness.

A HUNDRED YEARS AGO, when immigrants were arriving from Italy and Croatia and Ireland and Poland to work in the steel plants and the factories along the bay, the wealthy families who owned the mills and the factories built summer residences on the beach strip. The strand was clean and uncluttered, the bay and the lake were teeming with fish, and air conditioning was an impossible dream. The August breezes that swept off the water and into the windowed towers of the cottages, each several times larger than the crowded homes of the immigrant factory workers who lived in the city, provided natural cooling, and this was where the wealthy families spent each summer. The rich factory owners sailed dinghies on the lake, their privileged children flew kites on the strand, and their pampered wives gossiped beneath parasols in their gardens. Irishwomen cleaned the rooms and laundered the linen, Scotswomen made the cucumber sandwiches and sliced the ham, and Welshmen tended the gardens. God bless the Empire.

They moved to the beach strip, these rich families, every June with their children and servants and steamer trunks, and remained until September. The husbands were here only on weekends. As I grew older and learned about the beach strip and about men, I wondered if the absence of the husbands from their families during the week permitted them to spend time with their mistresses back in the city, or spend money on the girls who worked the side streets near the factories. I suspected the men would tolerate the city air, heavy with smoke and heat and humidity, in return for the freedom to entertain young girls alone in their mansions.

About a dozen of the original Victorian cottages remain on the beach. These gingerbread-trimmed fire traps, restored and winterized, sit crowded between houses like the one Gabe and I purchased, a frame bungalow with a lawn in front and a garden in back. Our house shares nothing with the summer mansions of the Victorians except location. It is dull in design, square in shape, predictable in layout. "Amorphous," Mother called it when she first saw it, back when she could speak. Mother's vocabulary was always elaborate and surprising, and the nature of the hell she finds herself in now can be defined by that fact. She used that term herself when she wrote, on the small blackboard, *I live in an unspeakable hell!!!* When she handed it to me, she smiled at the pun.

Air conditioning changed the beach strip, and perhaps the morals of the wealthy men who deposited their families here for the summer, but that's a doubtful notion. As the factories grew larger and dirtier, their smoke and dust were carried on the west wind down the shore of the bay to the strip of sand separating it from the lake. In time, the soot and smells became unbearable for wealthy families with cottages on the strip. Luckily for them, air conditioning arrived just as the soot began turning the strip as black as the rest of the city. With air conditioning installed in their mansions, located upwind from the factories and mills, no one needed twenty-four-room Victorian cottages on the beach strip and the cooling breezes from the lake to get a good night's sleep in summer. Many of the massive summer homes were first converted to rooming houses, then demolished and replaced by spindly three-room frame cottages with screened porches, and these became the belated palaces of factory workers who rented them for a week or two each summer in the years after the wealthy families abandoned the beach strip. The men would sit on their porch and listen to insects buzz against the screens while their children played in the sand and their wives prepared summer salads and lemonade in the kitchen. The men sat like that, their backs to the factories, for two weeks each year, living fourteen days each summer in the manner they wished to live every day of their lives.

I huddled in the living-room chair thinking of the wealthy families who once lived here on the most desirable side of the strip, facing the lake. I was thinking of the wives, and what they thought of their husbands back in the city. I decided they thought very little of them, intent as they were on operating a household free of the interference of men.

I have never been free of the interference of men, and I would not be for some time.

That is what I thought after the red glow in the sky faded and I heard police officers speaking in low voices outside my window, talking about what had occurred that evening among the shrubs, about the naked cop who had shot himself on a blanket beneath the moon.

5.

I slept in the living-room chair and awoke remembering. I remembered hearing the sound of the transport trucks on the high bridges behind me as I was falling asleep. I remembered thinking of the men who drove them, and how strange it must be to be constantly moving, without a choice of destination. I remembered what woke me up.

It was our telephone in the kitchen, where telephones belong. Not in cars or purses or pockets or attached to your ear like jewellery. Telephones should be in the kitchen, where lives are lived, and I followed its sound. I had refused to get a cell phone, but I gave in to Gabe's idea of getting a cordless phone that we could use in the garden, if we chose, although why anybody would want to use a telephone in the garden was beyond me. I called people in the kitchen, and I answered the phone there. Am I stubborn? Do I cling to old ways? Does a shark have teeth?

The kitchen was bright with light from the sun, already high above the lake and shining through the windows facing the water.

It was Mel calling, as I knew it would be. "Did you sleep at all?"

"Yes. In a chair in the living room."

"I'm going back downtown. I was there until past two."

I said nothing. I didn't care where or how long or with whom he had slept.

"There'll be an inquest. It's all over the news. People from the newspapers, the TV stations, will want to talk to you."

I heard voices on the boardwalk along the beach. When I pushed the curtain aside, I saw two television trucks in the lane next to our house, and a woman pointing a microphone like a weapon. I closed the curtain. "They're here," I said.

"You don't have to talk to them."

"I know." Someone had seen me and was ringing the doorbell. "I won't." Now there was rapping at the back door. I squinted at the clock. Twenty minutes to eight in the morning. How did the woman with the microphone get her hair and her makeup so perfect this early in the day? It was obscene. She didn't even need it—she was maybe twenty-five years old. Women like me, we need . . . I began to cry.

"Josie?"

"I'm here." I thought I would never eat again, and that I would never cease crying.

"Refer them to Reg Gilmour. He handles media downtown. That's all you have to tell them. They can talk to him at . . . you got a pen there?"

I opened the kitchen drawer, the one next to the drawer where Gabe kept the ammunition for his gun when he was home, pulled out a pencil, and looked for the notebook we always kept on the counter, the wire-bound book he had torn a page from and written *I'm in the bushes. Get naked!* It wasn't there. Gabe and I wrote shopping lists and telephone numbers and messages to each other in the notebook. I had bought it at a drugstore. We could have used one of the police-issue pads, like others did, Gabe bringing home a couple at a time, but Gabe said no, that's not what they were for. Using them for our personal use would be theft. So we paid two bucks for the same damn pad from a drugstore. That's how honest Gabe was. That's what my husband was like.

When I couldn't find the pad on the counter, all the anger, guilt, and frustration from the evening before welled up in me again. I opened all the drawers, then turned to look on the kitchen table and in the cupboards where the dishes were kept, all the places I knew the pad would never be. I began shaking with rage and anxiety and something else. "I can't find it," I said to Mel. "I can't find it, it's not here."

Mel asked what I was talking about, but I couldn't say. I just hung up the telephone, walked to the rear door, and screamed, "Go to hell!" at everyone—the television reporter with the perfect hair and makeup, two guys with TV cameras, a photographer who took my picture over and over. Hans and Trudy, the German couple down the beach who were still building their oversized house to resemble a castle, complete with parapets, were walking their dog, and both they and the schnauzer stopped to look. They all saw the grieving widow at her worst.

I returned to the chair in the living room, where I curled into a ball and thought about Gabe, and how he wouldn't even steal a two-dollar wire-bound pad from the police department, and fell asleep there.

I DID NOT DREAM FOR THE NEXT TWO HOURS. I woke to the ringing telephone, to people knocking on my door, to the sound of cars arriving and leaving in the lane next to the house. Each time the noise ceased, I slept again. No dreams. No organizing of thoughts. No dealing with facts I did not understand, like why my husband would carry a gun with him to a blanket in the bushes and wait for me there and, when I did not arrive, why he would shoot himself in the head.

Around ten, I walked to the bathroom and showered and combed my hair and put on some lipstick and cried a little more. I dressed, made coffee, and listened to my telephone messages. Two were from Mel. He was concerned, he was sorry, and he honestly wanted to do whatever he could for me. I believed him. In everything we had done, as wrong as it might have been, Mel had been gentle with me, and concerned about Gabe. Men can do that—sleep with another man's wife and worry about the couple's marriage. Mel had worried about Gabe. Had Mel been married, I would not have given a damn about his wife. Why should I? That's a man's job.

Three neighbours and an old friend, Dewey Maas, had called to say they had heard the news about Gabe and to express their sadness. Helen Detwiler from the retirement home passed along her condolences and told me not to worry about work because they would make other arrangements for as long as it took me to get over my loss, and that I might consider calling Mother as soon as I was able. Two radio stations and a local newspaper reporter wanted to talk to me.

I phoned Helen, was told she was in a staff meeting, and asked that she assure Mother that I was all right and I would visit her later in the day. Then I drank three cups of coffee and considered drinking a glass of whisky, just to gather nerve to call my sister, Tina.

NEITHER MY SISTER NOR I HAVE CHILDREN. Some people see this as a tragedy. I see it as evidence of genetic selection.

I was unable to have children, although I was informed that my problem, if that's what you wish to call it, could be cured with a combination of drugs, surgery and petri dishes. When my first husband and I learned we could not be parents, everyone we knew suggested adoption. I replied that adopting a child was like buying a used car through the mail. The truth is, we weren't devastated by the news, although my first husband, in one of our last fights before our divorce, accused me of lying about being unhappy that I could not bear his child. By that time he was at least half correct.

Tina, on the other hand, is almost abnormally fecund, which is a word that looks and sounds uglier than it should. The way

Tina explained it, she could get knocked up by folding a man's underwear. Tina got pregnant twice, with two consecutive boyfriends, before she was eighteen. She claimed she'd had sex with each of them only once. She aborted both, and the second time was so painful she decided never to go through childbirth. And she didn't.

I sat with my hand on the telephone, knowing it was early in British Columbia and thinking perhaps I should wait until she was fully awake before calling her. As if she would hesitate to call me, I realized, and dialed her number.

She was awake, probably having made eggs Benedict for the neighbourhood after leading them in an hour of yoga. Tina lives in Kitsilano, a part of Vancouver that tries to pretend it's Beverly Hills, just as Vancouver wishes it were Los Angeles. She lives there with her husband, a surgeon who inherited a reasonably sizable fortune from his father's lumber investments. Andrew, Tina's husband, had enough cash on hand to buy the southern half of Vancouver Island and dine on pheasant every day without lifting a finger, if he chose to. Instead, he married Tina, purchased a small mansion in Kitsilano, and spends his days cutting people open and examining their innards, and I have no idea why.

When I visited Tina and Andrew before marrying Gabe, Tina introduced me to her country club friends. They were so gracious and warm that by the third day I feared I would throw up on the next woman who gave me an air kiss before handing me a glass of Chardonnay. On the fourth day, I flagged a cab near the university and had the driver take me to East Hastings Street, the skid row of Vancouver. I sat in the cab, parked at the curb, for twenty minutes while I watched hookers stumble into alleyways to give twenty-dollar quickies, and guys with vomit on their sweatshirts wash windshields at stoplights, and druggies pick up their fixes, and people in tourist buses stare open-mouthed at the carnival freak show. Then I had the driver take me back to Kitsilano for canapés and pretension. The few minutes on the other side of town set me up for the rest of the week. Everything, my father used to say, needs to be rebalanced from time to time. My father was rarely wrong about anything.

Now, at the sound of my sister's voice on the telephone, something terrible happened to me: I became my mother, unable to speak.

She said "Hello?" three or four times, growing angrier with each delivery, until I finally got the words past the lump in my throat. "It's me," I said.

"Who's me?" Tina said. Then: "Josephine Olivia? Josephine?"

Some people hate their names. I don't hate mine. I just think Josephine Olivia is perfect for somebody else. Anybody else. By the time I reached puberty, I insisted that everyone call me Josie. Not Josephine. Not ever. Tina would tease me about it, calling me Josephine and then saying "Oops!" as though she'd forgotten how much I disliked it. She said "Oops!" so often she began calling me Josephine Oops until I poured a can of turpentine in her underwear drawer and told her why. Her full name, by the way, is Christina Abigail. The second time I called her Abigail, she hit me on the head with a book.

"Gabe's dead," I managed to get out.

"Oh my god. How? At work?"

"Outside our house. On the beach last night. They say . . ." I swallowed the lump. "They say he shot himself."

"Oh my god." Tina is not much on originality about anything, including her expressions of surprise. "Are you okay?"

"Well . . ." I didn't have an answer for that.

"Oh my god. I'm coming down."

"That's not necessary, Tina—"

"I'm catching a plane this morning. I'll call you from the airport. Oh my god. What are the funeral arrangements?"

"The what?"

She was losing her patience. I was supposed to be the co-operative victim, I guess. *"The arrangements.* Who's taking care of them? When'll he be buried?"

"I have no idea."

"That's what I figured. I'll be there tonight. Don't bother coming to the airport to pick me up." The thought had never entered my mind. "I'll take a limo. We'll stay up and talk all night if we have to. Gabe's killed himself. Oh my god. Love you."

"Me too," I said. And she was gone.

I slumped back in the chair. My husband was shot to death practically in our own backyard, and my sister was coming to stay with me, maybe for a week. How much punishment could one woman take?

6.

One of my neighbours has a helicopter on his front porch. It has sat there for more than a year. Not the whole helicopter, just the part you ride in that looks like a large white plastic egg on skis. The rest of it, the blades that spin on top and the long tail with the small propeller on the back, are missing, but Gabe assured me it's a real helicopter. We would pass the house with the helicopter on the porch during our walks along Beach Boulevard on summer nights, when we wanted to avoid the boardwalk crowded with skaters and skateboarders and bicyclists and joggers and retired people and vagrant hoodlums. We would stroll past the few remaining Victorian-era cottages and the tar-paper shacks and the new prefab homes with goldfish ponds in the front yard and hot tubs in the back, and we would be happy doing it.

The neighbour with the helicopter on his porch also keeps a Florida swamp buggy in the lane next to the house, in front of an army machine that Gabe said looks like an APC, which he translated as Armoured Personnel Carrier. I don't know what the man who keeps this stuff looks like, because I have never seen him.

The beach strip is peppered with misfits and eccentrics living among young professionals winding themselves up and retired people winding their lives down. They start out in Porsches and end up in golf carts.

If misfits and nonconformists can be catalogued, I do not know any faction that is not represented among our neighbours.

Hans and Trudy, the German couple down the beach with the schnauzer, have been building their stone castle since Gabe and I moved here. Along with the rooftop parapets, it includes narrow windows set deeply into the walls—the better for archers to aim their arrows, I guess—and a heavy oak door studded with rivets. I expected to see gnomes in lederhosen at work on a moat some-day. Most of the neighbours think it's quaint. Nobody considers it out of place.

A motorcycle club converted a cottage at the south end of the beach, the scuzzy end, into a clubhouse, adding steel bars to the windows and drawing weekly visits from the police. Near them, over the dusty upholstery shop, lives a woman who for the past month had been stalking the boardwalk and glaring into our gar-den, her mouth moving without any words emerging.

Compared with the people, the homes on the beach strip are almost conventional. Some are abandoned, others nearly so. It is a community, as the sociologists say, in transition. A few cus-tom homes are being built among the decaying cottages. The new homes feature cedar shake shingles, bay windows, and something called a great room, which is what you get when you don't put a ceiling on the living room. They sit among the cheap frame cot-tages and the trailer park and the retirement homes. There are many distractions on the beach strip. There is little boredom.

AFTER SPEAKING TO TINA, I looked out the kitchen window and into my garden, where two police officers were standing near the gate. The news reporters had moved on to some other disaster, I assumed. The air was already warm and heavy. It was going to be one of those August days they invented air conditioning for.

I opened my door and almost tripped over two jars of marma-lade and a plastic-wrapped loaf of banana bread with a note taped to it. *Call us if you need to,* the note said. It was from Maude

Blair, of course. There are many people like the Blairs living on the beach strip. They keep no helicopters on their front porch or bars on their windows. They always nod and smile, and they do not gossip. They care for you, but they find no need to tell you about it except when necessary.

I set the bread and marmalade in the kitchen and returned to look out at the garden shed. The door was closed, but I could see the hook dangling free. "Somebody's been in our garden shed," I said to Gabe the first time I found the hook unlatched earlier in the summer. "We should start locking the door."

"What's to steal?" he said. "If we're lucky they'll take the old lawn mower, maybe the rusty rake and the bag of topsoil."

"You'll do anything to get out of gardening," I muttered.

The shed door was normally held closed with a simple hook and eye. "How much will a padlock cost?" I asked when I found the door open again a day or two later. "Three dollars? Five dollars?"

Gabe said if we hung a padlock on the door we would have to keep the key somewhere, and he was always losing keys.

"Get one with a combination," I suggested.

Gabe said we would forget the combination and never be able to get back in. So the garden shed remained unlocked. Someone had been in there last night. It might have been a police officer. Or one of the reporters. Or someone could have been hiding in the garden shed when Gabe came out the garden door wrapped in the blanket and carrying the bottle of wine. They could have followed him into the bushes and shot him there.

I walked to the shed and looked inside. It was, of course, empty except for some dusty garden tools.

Why would anyone, assuming they had a need to kill Gabe, follow him onto the beach? It didn't make sense. Nothing made sense. Gabe was gone, whoever had been in the garden shed had gone, and I needed time in the sun. I needed to heal.

I sat in one of the garden chairs, my back to the beach. Traffic soared along the high bridges spanning the canal, and beyond them the steam and smoke of the steel companies rose through a still-clear sky. I heard the warning blast from the lift bridge down the strip, and geese calling to each other as they passed overhead. I smelled the roses growing against the fence. None of the sounds and smells reached me the way they might have a day earlier. I was untouchable. I was distant. I was in free fall, waiting to land on solid ground. I was something else as well, but I didn't want to think about that at the moment. I tilted my head back and closed my eyes, feeling nothing except a sudden hand on my shoulder.

I jumped at the touch, spilling my coffee. I screamed as well, and I'm sure I swore before looking around to see Mel Holiday holding his hands up in surrender. "I'm sorry, I'm sorry," he said. "I should have said something—"

"You should have knocked at the damn door," I said.

"I did." Mel lowered his hands. "Then I came around the side and saw you out here—"

"And decided to scare the hell out of me."

"How are you doing?" Mel looked toward the shrubs behind the house. The two cops, their attention attracted by my scream, turned away.

"My sister is coming to stay with me. She's arriving tonight."

"That's good."

"No, it's not. You asked me how I was doing. I just told you that my sister is coming to stay with me, probably for a week. That's how badly things are going. And it looks like somebody was in the tool shed last night." I pointed at the open door. "One of your guys?"

"I doubt it." Mel walked to the shed and looked inside. The shed has two small windows. One faces the garden, the other faces the house. I watched Mel scan the interior, then the shed's wooden floor. He bent to examine the area beneath the window facing the house, then stepped inside and looked through the window and up at the house. "Have you noticed anybody in the shed?" he asked when he returned.

"No, but I come out here some mornings and find the door opened or unlocked. I told Gabe about it. He didn't think it was a big deal."

Mel looked back at the shed. "It might be." He looked at me. "You have a secret admirer. A pervert. Somebody's been standing at that window and masturbating. That's what it looks like."

"Some mornings I lie on the cot over there," I said, nodding my head toward the corner of the garden. "Sunbathing. People going by on the boardwalk can't see into the corner because the trees and the shed block the view."

"Anybody standing at the window in the shed could watch you," Mel said.

"Great." I felt sick.

"I'll have a technician take samples from the stains on the floor. We might get his DNA profile from them."

"See if you can get his phone number too. My sister's on her way."

Mel knelt next to the chair. "I know why you're making jokes. Makes it easier to handle things."

"You think it's a joke? You've never met Tina."

Mel took a deep breath and closed his eyes. "Josie, there are only so many things I can do for you."

"One thing you can do for me is tell Walter Freeman that Gabe did not shoot himself with his own gun."

Mel stood up. "We'll send the bullet that the coroner took out and another one from Gabe's gun to forensics, and the paraffin test from his hand. We'll get the results back next week."

"Won't prove a thing."

"Hey."

I looked up at Mel and was reminded how good he looked when he was angry. Some men are like that.

"If it makes it easier to believe somebody murdered your husband, go ahead and believe it," he said. "But the rest of us, the people who have to deal with this stuff every day, we know a suicide when we see one. And I'm sorry if it's painful for you." He walked to the gate opening onto the boardwalk. "The technician should be here this afternoon. I'll tell him to knock first."

After Mel left, I went inside and had a slice of Maude's banana bread with a spoonful of her marmalade on it. It made me feel so much better that I had another one. I had resumed eating. I had not ceased crying.

I answered the messages from friends who had called, beginning with Hans and Trudy, building their German castle on the beach strip as though it were on the Rhine. Gabe and I had enjoyed their company the few times we got together. Hans likes the same kind of jazz as Gabe, and Trudy bakes a killer strudel, which she always brought along. What wasn't to like? "You come by, have strudel and tea," Hans said in something between a command and an invitation. I promised I would.

Debbie, a friend from my days at the veterinary hospital, called from Toronto, inviting me to stay with her in her high-rise condo on Bloor Street, thirty-six floors above the muggers. I politely declined.

I called Dewey Maas, the last man I dated before I met Gabe. Dewey burst into tears at the sound of my voice. He had heard the news about Gabe and called once, but didn't want to bother me by calling again until . . . well, until I called him. Dewey is a sweetheart of a guy for whom I felt every attraction but sexual. I have never fully understood that. Neither has Dewey, whose name is actually Byron, which is silly enough to make a nickname like Dewey preferable.

I met Dewey while working at a veterinary office, as receptionist and bookkeeper. Dewey was an animal groomer, working out of a storefront beneath his condominium. In the morning, people brought Dewey their dogs to be washed, trimmed, brushed, and manicured, and Dewey spent his day talking to animals and listening to opera. Most people assumed Dewey was gay, which made some of the older women warm up to him in ways they wouldn't if they believed he was straight. Dewey was neither gay nor straight. He dated both sexes, which made him more interesting but, as far as I was concerned, somehow less appealing. I mean, a divorced woman in her thirties has enough competition as it is from her own gender. Why double the odds against you?

Dewey had cried on the telephone when he heard I was marrying Gabe, which was the last time I had heard from him, and he cried into my ear now that Gabe was dead. "Please tell me you'll let me help you through this," he said between sniffs.

I told him I would.

"I'll come and see you whenever you say," he added.

I explained that my sister was on her way, and that she would be all the company I needed. Then I thanked him for his concern and said goodbye.

Humans engage in a lot of silly things, but platonic relationships between two single people of similar ages and different genders has to be among the silliest. Or maybe just the most uncomfortable.

THE FORENSICS TECHNICIAN ARRIVED after three o'clock, an overweight man with a fringe of hair that, in his dreams, might have been as thick as his moustache. I led him around the house to the shed. He snapped on a pair of rubber gloves, scraped the floor in front of the window, sealed the shed door with a strip of plastic tape with CRIME SCENE printed all over it, and left me alone to face Tina.

7.

That afternoon I made tea and walked through the house with the cup in my hand, looking at things that reminded me of Gabe. They were everywhere, especially in our bedroom. A piece of jade I had bought to help him relax. He was to rub it in the palm of his hand when he was tense. I picked it up and stroked it now. It may have worked for Gabe. It did not work for me.

A favourite mug for his coffee, garish yellow and red, with a picture of a hand-painted chicken on the side and a small chip on the rim. His collection of jazz CDs, a nail clipper he had owned since he was sixteen years old, and an earthenware plate we had brought from Mexico. Gabe used the plate to hold spare change from his trouser pocket when he got undressed at night. I counted the amount in the plate, penny by penny, nickel by nickel. Eight dollars and sixty-three cents.

And his shirts and his ties and his underwear, hanging in his closet and folded neatly in the drawers of his dresser cabinet. I touched them all with one hand and held my teacup in the other, alternately smiling and crying at the memories and images they created. What was I to do with them now? I would decide some other time. Maybe in some other life. Then I returned downstairs, poured the cold tea in the sink, climbed back up to our bedroom and fell on the bed. I believe I cried before falling asleep. Yes, I did.

I woke in the summer dusk greyness that I have always considered poignant, thinking of Mother and remembering I was to visit her and explain what happened. The clock said it was almost eight. It wasn't guilt about not seeing Mother that had awakened me. It was knocking, fast and light, like a drummer in a marching band. But I awoke feeling guilty anyway.

I managed to stand up, fluff my hair, and open the front door. Tina gave me barely a glance before turning to the limo driver, whom she had left standing at the open trunk of the car, and said, "She's here. Bring them up." Meaning her luggage, four matched pieces in caramel-coloured leather. "Oh, Josie." She hugged me and I counted to three before she released me. "Are you sure you're okay?" She stood back, glanced over her shoulder to ensure that the limo driver was on his way with her luggage, smiled her approval at his progress, then looked at me again, tilted her head, and let her eyes fill with tears. Tina is several interesting people.

"Sure." I walked back to the kitchen, aware that the house Gabe and I had loved so much, the bungalow we believed looked funky and real, was basically shabby and plain. "Want some tea?"

"Oh, that's wonderful, Alex," Tina said from the front door.

I turned to see the oversized limo driver, handsome in the way an oak armoire can be handsome, enter with Tina's luggage, carrying one piece under each arm and another in each hand. "Is the guest room upstairs?" Tina asked.

"There's a pullout couch in the room on your left, just off the landing," I said. Tina was already climbing the stairs, swinging her ass at Alex, the limo driver, who was following her. From the expression on his face, Alex was enjoying the view. There is comfort in continuity, I suppose, and Tina, bless her cold Prada heart, was providing some for me.

I have never seen an airport limo driver carry luggage into a house and up the stairs. From the expression on his face, it was apparent that Alex had never seen a woman quite like Tina either.

When they came downstairs, Tina and Alex returned to the limo, where, I assumed, they discussed his fee and the price of tomatoes.

"HOW CAN YOU MAKE IT HERE from Vancouver so fast?" I said. We were seated in the kitchen, sipping tea from earthenware mugs dating back to my first marriage. I refused to apologize for the absence of Royal Doulton. "I talked to you barely eight hours ago. It takes me that long to pack. And how did you get to know your limo driver so quickly?"

I knew how. Tina is an outrageous flirt.

"I always talk to limo drivers." Tina dampened her lips with the tea. She had changed from her black pencil skirt and pink blouse into rhinestone-encrusted jeans and a cotton sweater that ended precisely halfway between her hips and her knees. I had to admit she looked terrific in both outfits. "I refuse to sit silently in the back of a car, like cargo. I asked him about his life. Alex is a hard-working guy from Lebanon with two sons and a shrewish wife. Do you have cream for the tea?"

"No." I rose and walked to the bar in the living room. "But I have some brandy for it." I returned with the bottle and offered it to Tina, who shook her head.

"You really should cut your hair, you know," Tina said after I had poured enough brandy in my cup to kill the taste of the tea. "You're getting too old for long hair."

My hair is toffee-coloured with a natural wave and a hint of red. It, plus the fact that I inherited our mother's bosom, has always made Tina jealous. Tina inherited our father's thin black hair, which she keeps short, and more of his chest than Mother's. Maybe even the hair on it. I haven't looked lately. Until a few years ago, Tina's revenge had been to suggest I was adopted.

"Gabe likes it this way," I said.

I waited for her to correct me, telling me I should be using the past tense now. Instead, my sarcastic older sister was replaced by a solicitous friend, who reached her hand across to enclose mine as her eyes flooded with tears. "Tell me what happened."

I told her. I told her almost everything. When I had to pause and release my own tears, Tina placed her arm around my shoulder and dabbed my eyes with a tissue. When I gathered myself together again, she sat back and watched me.

"You guys did it on a blanket?" she said when I finished. "The two of you out there on the sand? Were you drunk?"

"A little."

"I mean, teenagers do that stuff, but at your age . . ."

"My age? Thanks, Tina."

"Actually, it sounds kinky and romantic."

"The truth is, I got bitten by mosquitoes and washed sand out of my hair for a week."

Tina looked out the window toward the lake. "Gabe was nice. I didn't know him as well as what's-his-name." Meaning my first husband, the one married to Miss Lemon Hair, the aerobics instructor.

"His name was Danny. My first husband's name was Danny."

"What's he doing now?"

"Probably saving his money to buy his wife new tits when the old ones wear out."

"Why do you do that?" She fixed me with a look on her face that I hadn't seen since I was sixteen and dating Dale somebody, a boy on the next block with perfect teeth, curly hair, and the personality of a tree stump. Tina lusted after him, tried to hide her jealousy when he ignored her, and covered it with the look of distaste she wore now.

"Why do I do what?"

"Make wisecracks all the time. Your heart is breaking, I know it is, and you act like you're . . ." She pursed her lips and shook her head, looking for the analogy. She found it. "Like you're a stand-up comedienne in Las Vegas."

"I cry in private, Tina. I laugh, or try to, in public because it protects me."

"From what?"

"Whatever you've got. Look, Tina, I love you for coming here, I really do. Gabe and I . . ." The lump was rising from my heart into my throat, squeezing tears from my eyes on the way, making a liar of me about not crying in public. "Gabe and I kept to our-selves down here. So I don't have many people I can call on, and I'm just glad you came. Really."

Tina rose from the chair and held me in her arms. I cried this time not for the absence of Gabe but for the presence of Tina and the touch of her arms on my back, pulling me to her. Sometimes the worse-tasting the medicine, the more you need to take it.

"WE'LL GO SEE MOTHER and then eat at one of those cute little res-taurants down by the lake." Tina had planned our evening for us. A week ago I would have resented it. Now I welcomed it.

I had had a bath, put on a blouse and skirt, tied my hair back, slipped on a ring Gabe had given me, and returned downstairs. Tina had unpacked her clothes and moved a chair from the dining room into the downstairs bathroom to hold her perfumes, sham-poo, nail polish, blush, skin cream, anti-fungal spray for her feet, and cosmetics.

"Your hair looks nice," she said. "Maybe you shouldn't cut it after all." Then, looking down at my hands, "Where did you get that ring?"

"Gabe bought it for me," I said. "A long time ago." Which was a lie, unless two weeks is a long time on your calendar. It was on mine.

She lifted my hand and looked at the ring, then at me and back

to the ring again. "It's a black opal," she said. "They're expensive."
She twisted my hand to catch the light from the lamp. "Looks like
diamonds around it."

That's what they were. Twelve perfect diamonds positioned
around the opal in a yellow-gold setting, the stones elevated on a
series of round concentric steps. I knew every facet of every stone
and the swirl of every mark on the opal.

Tina brought her eyes back to mine. "This ring cost a fortune."

"Maybe new."

"He didn't buy it new?"

"I don't know." I withdrew my hand and began twisting the
ring to take it off. This had not been a good idea. I had been child-
ish, the kid wanting to show her older sister something more
spectacular than anything Tina's wealthy husband had given her.

"Was it a special occasion?" she asked. "Your birthday?"

"No." I removed the ring and walked to the stairs. "I don't
think I'll wear it."

"He just shows up one day with a ring like that and says,
'Here's something for nothing'?" She was speaking to my back.

"Yes." I began to climb the stairs.

"How much do they pay cops in this town anyway?" she
shouted, but I had turned the corner on the landing, heading
for my lingerie drawer, where I had hidden the ring after Walter
Freeman asked if Gabe had purchased anything expensive for me
lately.

"SHOULD'VE PUT IT IN A POPCORN BOX." That's what Gabe said
the night he gave me the ring, sitting on a bench on the beach,
facing the lake. He pulled a tiny brown felt bag from the pocket of
his windbreaker, the blue one with the police department crest,
withdrew the ring, and handed it to me. "Let's see if it fits."

When I found my voice, I asked where he got it.

"A jeweller," he said. "Here." He took my right hand and slid the ring onto the third finger. It was a little loose, but I didn't care. Gabe had given me a small diamond solitaire before we were married. I loved it and never asked nor even thought about owning more jewellery beyond it and my wedding band. I detest the idea that jewellery and clothes and expensive shoes make a statement. I didn't want to make any damn statement. I wanted to wear that ring, though.

"Gabe," I said, "we have a problem."

"What's that?" He was sitting back with his arms resting along the top of the bench, watching the cormorants pass. It was early evening, the time of day when the black cormorants return from their journey to the lake, when they come home to the bay and nest on the north shore, across the water from the factories and the steel mills.

"We can't afford it."

"Yes, we can."

"This ring is worth thousands."

"Probably."

"Where did you get the money?"

"It didn't take much."

I closed my eyes. "Was it stolen?"

I felt Gabe's hand grip my shoulder. I opened my eyes and saw him watching me with an expression I had not seen before, one that made me think either he had not considered that possibility or he had not prepared an answer. "No, Josie," he said. "It is not stolen. I gave it to you because you are a beautiful woman. That's why a man gives jewellery to a woman. Because she is beautiful and because he loves her."

I EXPECTED MORE QUESTIONS ABOUT THE RING from Tina when I came downstairs, but Tina, as she often does, surprised me by not mentioning it. "Did you make the funeral arrangements yet?" she asked.

I sat at the table. Funeral arrangements? That's what you do for dead people, isn't it. "No," I said. "I'm still getting used to things."

"We'll need to find out when the body will be released. Where's your computer?"

I told her I didn't have a computer.

Tina looked at me as though I didn't have a nose. "Don't you know about the Internet?" she said. "Don't you use email?"

I explained that yes, damn it, I knew about the Internet and email, and we even had a toilet and running water in the house, if she cared to notice, and that Gabe used a computer at his office and I used one at the retirement home to keep the books and at the library whenever I wanted to look up the name of the last king of Albania, but we didn't own one because . . . well, because Gabe and I liked the idea of being contrary, I guess.

Tina shrugged and began opening cupboards. "Have you got a pad and pencil somewhere?"

"I think so." I held my head in my hands. No, we didn't. Not anymore. Not one I could find. Gabe would know where the pad was, the one we used to write things down. Shopping lists. Telephone numbers. Notes to each other.

"Where is it?"

"Don't know."

"I have one upstairs." Of course Tina would travel with a notepad in her luggage. Tina is always prepared. When she returned, we began making a list of things to do. My life was getting organized.

TINA DROVE OUR HONDA TO VISIT MOTHER, crossing the lift bridge and skirting the water's edge to Mother's retirement home, where she and Mother greeted each other like two soldiers from an old war who had nothing in common beyond their regimental badges, and staff members came to tell me how sorry they were to hear about Gabe. When I approached her chair, Mother clung to me and we both cried over Gabe.

"MOTHER LOOKS GOOD," Tina said when we left. "I feel like pasta. Where's a good place for pasta?"

"Italy."

"I didn't realize new widows overflowed with humour."

"It's not humour, it's irony. Tina, this is WASP country. They only know two spices here: salt and pepper. Pepper is the exotic one."

"Every town has at least one good Italian restaurant."

"Yes, and a war memorial and a whore."

She found a strip-mall Italian bistro with red-and-white-checkered tablecloths on small tables and a waitress who, together with the restaurant decor, made me think we had encountered two out of three of every town's traditional attractions. After she ordered for both of us—spaghetti bolognese for me, veal parmigiana for her—Tina leaned across the table wearing her listen-to-your-older-sister expression. "Sweetheart," she said, "I want you to consider something." When I did not respond, she said, "I want you to consider moving to Vancouver when it's over."

"When what's over? My life?"

"This. Do you want to keep living where you are? Breathing smoke and dust from the damn steel companies? Living under a couple of expressway bridges, tracking sand into your house every day?" She sat up again. "Do you know that one of your neighbours keeps a helicopter on his porch and a swamp buggy in his driveway? We passed it on the way in."

"I'll bet you don't see that in Kitsilano."

"I'm not suggesting you live in Kitsilano. I mean, you can if you want." She meant I could if I could afford it. "It would just be nice to have you nearby, downtown or Burnaby or somewhere. What's wrong with wanting to have your sister live near you?"

"Mother too?"

I had caught her off guard. It had taken her twenty minutes to forget about Mother. Her jaw tightened. "Mother could have another stroke, a major stroke, any day."

"Then better she has it here, with me near her. When Mother goes, I'll consider coming to Vancouver. How's that?" I had no intention of moving to British Columbia.

Tina thought about that. Then, "How long had Gabe been depressed?"

"He wasn't depressed."

"It tends to be depressed people who commit suicide."

"Gabe did not commit suicide. He did not put his gun to his head and kill himself."

"Isn't that what the police are saying? Aren't they saying it was a suicide?"

"They're wrong. I know they're wrong. Gabe never put his gun together unless he was going on duty—"

"What's that mean, 'put his gun together'?"

"You take your weapon apart . . ." I sounded like a police procedure manual. " . . . when you're at home. You put the clip with the ammunition in one place, making sure there's no bullet in the firing chamber, and put the other part somewhere else. So the gun's never ready to fire, in case somebody finds it or . . ." I wasn't sure of the other reason for making a gun unable to fire. I just felt better about it. "Everybody puts their weapon in kitchen drawers. It's a cop thing, around here at least. You put the weapon in the kitchen drawer and the ammunition clip beside the cereal boxes, or some other place. Cops joke about it. Cops joke about everything. Don't reach for the cornflakes and come up with the Glock. Gabe would not put his gun together and carry it out to the blanket when he knew I was on my way to meet him."

"Unless he planned to use it."

"I don't believe it. I'll never believe it."

"What's a Glock?"

"His gun. I don't know what happened to Smith & Wesson. One made cough drops and the other made cooking oil." It was Gabe's joke. Most people don't get it. Tina was most people, so she thought it over before reaching across the table and putting her hand on mine.

"Okay, I understand," she said. "About the gun." The waitress arrived with two glasses of Chianti and a basket of bread sticks. "What's with all that yellow tape wrapped around your tool shed?" Tina asked when she left. "Wasn't Gabe found on the beach?"

"Some pervert's been in there playing with himself," I said. "That's what Mel thinks."

"Mel? Who's Mel?"

"A cop who used to work with Gabe."

"What's he like?"

I shrugged. "A nice guy." I had to say *something*.

I looked up to see Tina staring at me with one eyebrow raised. The waitress brought our food, and when she left I expected Tina to say aloud what I had just read in her expression, but we ate in silence until Tina began reminiscing about Dad and various aunts and uncles. I ate barely half of my pasta. Tina devoured her meal, then flashed her American Express card, and we drove back to the beach strip in silence.

TINA WAS STANDING AT OUR KITCHEN WINDOW, looking out at the garden. Beyond the fence and above the boardwalk, the horizon was lit with the white silken promise of a moon preparing to rise over the lake. "I can see the attraction of living here on the lake," Tina said. "Except for everything else."

I was sitting at the kitchen table. I had poured a finger or two of brandy into an old glass but had not touched it yet. I was waiting for my sister to leave. Some sins need solitude. "What's 'everything else' mean?"

Tina waved her hand. "The traffic on the bridge, the stuff from the steel companies, some of your neighbours . . . and, you know, it's not the cleanest beach in the world."

"That's why Martha Stewart keeps turning down my invitations."

She turned from the window, her arms folded across her chest. "Did Gabe appreciate your sense of humour?"

"As a matter of fact—" I began.

"Does Mel?"

Someday, Tina will have a verbal ambush named after her. In high school, Tina claimed she joined the debating club because a couple of cute boys were members, which was a lie. The only man in my lifetime who was both cute and a good debater was Bill Clinton, and the combination was so rare that it got him elected president. Tina joined the debating club so she could learn to cut people up with her comments. If she had joined the choir and learned to sing as well as she learned to win arguments, she'd be Céline bloody Dion.

Hearing her mention Mel was enough to overcome my reluctance about the brandy. I took a long swallow and closed my eyes while it burned its way toward my stomach. When I opened them, Tina was still staring at me. "What do you want to know about Mel?" I asked.

"What makes him a nice guy?" She began walking and talking, moving around the kitchen, closing cupboard doors and picking crumbs off the counter. "When women like us, you and me, when we say a man is a nice guy, it means more than he opens a door for you or buys his wife expensive trinkets, stuff like that. That's what I think."

"He's not married."

"Why doesn't that surprise me?"

"He's also younger than me."

"How many years?"

"Four or five."

"Tall?"

"Kind of."

"Lots of hair?"

"A bunch."

"Wavy?"

"Sure."

"Blue eyes, right? You always fell for guys with blue eyes."

I refused to give her the satisfaction.

"Am I going to meet this Mel?" She sat across from me.

"Probably." I looked up at the clock. It was past ten. "I'm going to bed. Hang your breakfast order on your doorknob."

"Josephine."

My sister had become my mother. I hadn't changed. I refused to answer and climbed the stairs to my bedroom, finishing the brandy on the way.

I HAVE A THEORY that time moves at different speeds in darkness. I don't know if it moves faster or slower when the light is out. Only that its pace changes. The first night with a new lover always passes at a speed you never expect, sometimes long and leisurely, sometimes swift and fleeting. Never normal.

Lying in the darkness, I heard the television set in the living room below me and the traffic passing on the highway bridges above the roof. From out on the lake, I heard a freighter's horn announce that it was approaching the canal, and a moment later the air horn on the bridge warned everyone it was about to rise. From another place, I heard Gabe in the bathroom, brushing his teeth and then whistling under his breath in that tuneless way he did. Lying on my side, my back to the bathroom, I heard him pad across the floor and felt the bed sink behind me with the weight of his body, and I awoke.

I rolled over. No one was next to me. The house was silent, the traffic from the highway bridges distant and intermittent. I rested my arm across my eyes until the tears stopped. Then I rose from the bed, wrapped myself in my bathrobe, and crossed the hall to the guest room, where I stood at the open door and called Tina's name until she stirred and said, "What?"

"I want you to know . . ." I began. There was an old steamer trunk near the door. I'd bought it from the junk shop down the beach strip last year. There was nothing inside. I sat on it now. "I want you to know that whatever happened, or whatever you think happened, I never stopped loving my husband. Okay?"

"Why are you saying this?" Tina's voice floated at me from the darkness.

"I just want you to know." I was clenching my fists so tightly in my lap that they hurt. "I never stopped loving Gabe. Not for one minute, okay?"

"Okay." Tina's voice was sleepy and frightened. I had intimidated my older sister. It did not make me feel good about myself.

I think I mumbled something about seeing her in the morning. Then I returned to bed.

8.

The first hour after sunrise was the time my father believed he was most likely to see angels. My father was not a religious man, so he didn't mean it literally. He simply loved mornings because mornings held promises, and evenings held something else. I agree with him. If angels exist, I expect to meet one at sunrise.

I was up with the sun. Tina would remain sleeping for hours, still on west coast time. I made coffee, poured myself a cup, and carried it to the back door, where I stood looking out at the lake. Joggers were already passing on the boardwalk, some alone and wearing headphones, others in groups of two or three, chatting as they bounced past, a couple with dogs trotting alongside. I watched them all, silhouetted against the sun, and I looked up to see cormorants flying east across the lake. I looked at the tool shed last, wrapped in yellow plastic tape printed with CRIME SCENE. I imagined a man inside, watching while I moved about the kitchen or dressed or undressed in the upstairs bedroom with its window overlooking the lake, where Gabe and I slept and talked and made love.

Some people saw angels in the dawn. I saw perverts.

I finished the coffee and morning paper and almost walked to the telephone to call Gabe at Central Station. That's what I did after I finished my coffee and the newspaper. I would call Gabe to talk to him, if he was available. When I reached him, Gabe and I would discuss everything except the case he was working on at the time. When the case was closed and Gabe had moved on to the next one, he might reveal some of it to me, leaving out the gory details. But when he was in the middle of an investigation, especially a violent homicide or child abuse case, he left his feelings on the beach. If he were involved in something horrific, he would park the car at the side of the house when he arrived home, walk to the boardwalk, and stand looking at the lake. Then he would come through the garden to the back door and into the house, leaving life's crap outside.

He learned how to do this while getting over the death of his children. A therapist taught him about places where he could leave things he didn't need or want. He had a place like that in his mind while he lived alone. He called it his white room. Wherever he was, he would close his mind and erase images of all the furniture, the pictures, the books, the carpets, the lamps, everything. In his mind, the room around him would be totally plain and white. Nothing could intrude. He would be Gabe Marshall for a while, without connections or pain.

After we married and moved to the beach strip, he found another place, which was the lake. He did not need to be Gabe Marshall, free of everything including pain this time. Just free of things he didn't need, and he would stand staring at the water long enough to leave the things he didn't want to burden me with out on the water until they sank from sight. I'm a little sceptical of that stuff, but then I've never been in therapy or worked at a job that involved stepping over somebody's intestines. All I know is that Gabe never failed to walk through our back door with a smile for me, no matter how upset he might have looked when he got home and parked the car at the side of the house, before he walked to the beach and stood looking at the lake until all the bad stuff was sent out there to sink to the bottom with the other pollution.

I was sitting at the kitchen table, remembering that smile,

when I sensed someone coming through the garden from the beach, as Gabe might have, and I held my breath until he reached the door. It was Mel. He wore his blue police windbreaker over a white cotton T-shirt that wrapped around his chest like skin on an apple, tight jeans, and white Reeboks. He stood staring at the garden shed, his hands on his hips, and I opened the door before he could knock. We looked at each other, not speaking. I was wondering how Tina knew Mel's eyes would be blue.

"How're you doing?" Mel asked finally.

"Surviving. My sister's here. From Vancouver."

Mel looked over my shoulder.

"She's sleeping," I said. "You want some coffee?"

"No, it's all right. I'm on my way to the station. Just dropped in to see how you were. And I've got news."

Two people going by on the boardwalk stopped and leaned toward each other, watching us and whispering. There's the widow, I could imagine them saying. I didn't want them seeing or saying anything about me.

"Come in," I said, walking back to the kitchen table.

Mel closed the door and leaned against it, inside the house but not in the kitchen. "I called the station this morning," he said. "The lab says that's definitely semen from the floor of the garden shed. They'll do a DNA analysis for identification purposes in case they come up with a suspect."

I didn't want a suspect for perversion. I wanted a suspect for the murder of my husband. More than that, I wanted the murderer himself. I wanted Mel to help me find him and help me kill him. I honestly had that thought, staring across the garden at the boardwalk and the beach beyond, where Gabe had died.

"Is it possible . . ." I began. I started over. "Is it possible that whoever killed Gabe—"

"Josie—"

"Let me finish. Is it possible that whoever killed Gabe might have hidden in the shed and followed him to the beach, into the bushes?"

"The guy whose semen we found?"

I shrugged.

"First, we don't know if anybody was in there at the time. And second, Josie, Gabe did it. It's clear as hell—"

"No, he didn't."

Mel looked up at the ceiling, rolled his eyes, and spread his arms in a gesture of defeat. "There's something else," he said. "The body . . . Gabe is being released today."

I sat staring at the wall, my chin on my hand.

"They need to know what you want to do, Josie," Mel said. "Have you made arrangements for burial? Have you chosen a funeral parlour, an undertaker?"

"No."

"You have to."

"I'll wait for Tina. My sister," I added when he stood scratching an eyebrow and looking puzzled. "One of us will call later. Who do we talk to?"

Mel removed his notepad, scribbled a name and telephone number on the top sheet, tore it off, and walked to where I sat, placing the paper in front of me. "I'm worried about you," he said.

"Good." I reached for his hand. "So am I."

Mel said nothing. Then, "I'll call later," and he walked to the back door.

"Do we need that damn yellow tape around the garden shed?" I asked.

"Not really," he said. "You want me to take it off?"

I nodded and followed him into the garden.

Pulling the tape from the door, he called over his shoulder, "Walter Freeman's arranging a ceremony for Gabe next week."

I told Mel I didn't want one.

"Doesn't matter." He carried the yellow tape to the trash pail.

"A cop dies, there's a ceremony for him. You can do what you want about a funeral, but cops like to have a ceremony." He brushed his hands together and looked at me. "Even when it's a suicide."

I told Mel it wasn't a suicide.

"I wish you'd see it that way. Anyway, he'll want you there. For the services."

I told him to tell Walter if I wasn't there he could start without me. Then I turned and went back into the house.

I didn't need a place to visit Gabe. I didn't need a block of marble in a cemetery to tell me who and where and what he was. And I didn't need an undertaker selling me a five-thousand-dollar coffin either. There would be no ceremony with me present. Walter Freeman could do whatever the hell he wanted. I would have Gabe cremated and scatter his ashes on the lake.

TINA CAME DOWNSTAIRS AN HOUR LATER wearing a peach-coloured robe and L'Air du Temps. She walked to me without a word and placed her arms around me, more of an embrace than a hug.

"You missed Blue Eyes," I said when she straightened up and poured herself a coffee.

"Who?"

"Mel. He was here this morning. Gabe's body is . . ." I swallowed the lump and started again. "They're releasing Gabe's body today. They want me to choose an undertaker. How the hell do you choose an undertaker?"

Tina set her coffee cup down and asked where my telephone book was.

I chose the funeral parlour nearest to the police morgue. That way, they wouldn't have to drive very far. Maybe hearses have meters. I figured the shorter the distance, the lower the fee. It might be a silly reason for choosing an undertaker, but it was the only one I could think of.

Tina was appalled. Tina likes ceremonies, including funerals. They are an opportunity to wear new clothes. I didn't tell her what I planned. She heard it for the first time after driving me to the funeral home and listening to me inform the undertaker that I wanted Gabe cremated and the whole procedure done for the lowest price they offered. The undertaker, or at least the guy who took the orders at the office, was young enough to believe that his own mortality was merely a rumour. It was easy to picture him as the class nerd in high school, which was probably last year. He nodded, closed his eyes, and smiled when I said I wanted no ceremony, just cremation in a plain wooden box, and I could pick up the ashes myself if it saved a few bucks.

"Returning the remains to you," he said with his eyes still closed, "is included in our services."

I signed the order, used my credit card, and we left.

"You're just going to . . ." Tina said as we drove away and, after waiting for the courage to say it aloud, " . . . cremate him?"

"He has no other family," I said. "He was an only child and his parents are gone. I'm it. And I'll remember him my way."

"But he was a police officer. Won't they want to do something for him? I mean, when a police officer dies on duty, cops show up from all over the country—"

"He didn't die on duty. And the police have decided he wasn't shot by somebody else. They'll have some ritual. A bunch of out-of-town cops will show up, march around wearing white gloves and a serious expression, and spend the night at a Holiday Inn playing poker and telling dirty stories. Or maybe they'll forget the whole thing, considering it was suicide."

"So you also think Gabe killed himself."

"No, I don't. The cops do."

"Shouldn't you have a funeral anyway?"

"For you and me? Listen, Gabe and I talked about this last year, when an officer was shot while checking a warehouse. They really went overboard on that one, two thousand cops marching behind the hearse, tying up traffic all across the city. Gabe said if he was ever killed on duty I should comb his hair, dress him in a sweatshirt and jeans, and set him on a bench looking out at the lake."

"Men can never talk about death seriously." Tina folded her arms and glanced at me. "That's why they have affairs."

"To avoid discussing death with their wives?"

"No, because they're afraid of dying. They want one more lay before they go, and they think the next might be their last."

"You're such a romantic."

"It's true."

"Why do women have affairs?"

"Because their men let them down."

That hurt. Gabe never let me down. Well, maybe once.

WE WERE OUT OF THE CITY and driving along the south end of the beach strip, the low-rent section studded with small cottages whose residents gathered at Tuffy's Tavern on the days their welfare cheques arrived. Tina wrinkled her nose at the sight of people sitting on their front steps smoking and drinking beer out of long-necked bottles. "You really like living here?" she asked.

"I love it."

"Will you love it without your husband?"

"Not as much. But I'm staying anyway."

"Daddy always said you were stubborn."

And he always said you were a spoiled little bitch, I thought.

"There's a car in your driveway." Tina looked apprehensive.

I recognized Mel's red Mustang convertible. When Mel was on duty, he drove brown and grey Chevrolets, but he refused to drive anything so mundane on his own time.

"Don't panic," I said. "You'll enjoy this."

I parked at the curb, and we walked down the driveway to the rear of the house and into the garden, where Mel stood looking out at the lake. I called Mel's name and he turned and smiled. "Hey," he said. Mel had a way of combining two expressions in one, his brow furrowing and his eyes narrowing as though he were somewhere between confusion and anger. He wore that expression when he wanted to make you feel good about him, or maybe just good about yourself for being near him. He wore it now.

Behind me, Tina made a pseudo-orgasmic sound in her throat.

"Mel, this is my sister, Tina. Tina, Mel Holiday."

Mel extended a hand large enough to lift a watermelon. "Pleased to meet you," he said. "I'm glad you're here to help Josie."

Tina said that's what sisters were for, which caused my eyes to roll.

"We just made arrangements for Gabe's funeral," I said.

"I'll be there," Mel said.

"Well, you'll be the only one. There's no ceremony."

"That's how you want it?"

"That's how Gabe would want it. The force won't send anybody if I ask them not to, right? Not as long as they believe he killed himself."

"The results came back from forensics," Mel said. He glanced behind me at Tina, and I sensed the rest of his words were directed at her. "The bullet is from his gun. The guys in Toronto reviewed it, and they're the best. So there's no doubt about it. The paraffin test was positive, and there was alcohol in his blood—"

"How much?" I asked.

"Zero point five, something like that."

"You can legally drive with that much." I kicked at the garden shed door. "He could have been behind the wheel of his car, and you guys couldn't have touched him. Don't tell me he was so drunk he decided to kill himself, Mel. He had maybe a couple of glasses of wine—"

"Josie—"

"No suicide note, Mel. How do you explain that? Gabe would leave me a note when he went for a walk on the beach. Why doesn't he leave me a note before he shoots himself in the head?"

"It's not me, Josie." Mel was looking from Tina to me and back to Tina again. Tina—I know because I checked—was looking at Mel's eyes. "Look." He lowered his voice. "Everything you say is true. Nothing about this makes sense. But Walter and everybody else at Central, they look at what we have as evidence, and they believe he did it. There'll be an inquest, but unless the coroner decides criminal action was involved, Walter's not going to assign a bunch of cops to look into Gabe's death. He'll have no reason to. He'll say that Gabe wouldn't be the first cop to fold under pressure, and he'll be right. Maybe Gabe was working on something that got him so damned depressed—"

"Have they looked into that?" I interrupted. "What he was working on? Gabe never talked to me about the cases he had going, not until everything was settled and the trial started. So has Walter, has he and everybody else, taken a look at Gabe's cases, the ones he was working on?"

Mel dropped his arms and nodded. "They looked and I looked. They found nothing in his files. If Gabe killed himself, they don't have a motive for what he did."

"No, they don't," I said. "But maybe we do, right?"

I turned and began walking back to the house, then stopped and looked back at Mel. "What are you doing here anyway?"

"We want the pervert who's been sneaking into your garden shed," Mel said. "These guys, they start with this kind of thing," and he waved at the shed, "then move on to other things. Anybody standing at that window has a perfect view into the kitchen, and upstairs to your bedroom window."

"Yeah, well, apparently he liked what he saw." I resumed walking back to the house.

"What will you do?" I heard Tina ask Mel. "How will you catch him?"

Mel said something about spreading crystals on the floor that would cling to the suspect's shoes, and alerting bicycle patrols on the boardwalk. I didn't hear the rest. I walked to the rear door, unlocked it, let myself into the kitchen, and had a good cry. A long one. I figured I had the time. Tina would stand out there and listen to Mel recite the entire police procedure manual if he chose, the sunlight on those damn deep blue eyes of his.

9.

Men want to be eagles. Women wish they were swans. I prefer cormorants. It's my working-class upbringing.

Gabe and I talked about this one day while sitting on the pier that extends beyond the mouth of the canal into the lake, the one with the lighthouse at the end. We were watching birds, a pleasant thing to do on warm evenings along the lake. We saw a vee of Canada geese fly over the strand, so lovely in the air and so crappy on the ground. We were always stepping into their droppings, and the damn birds would lunge at you if you approached during their nesting season. Geese, Gabe and I agreed, are best when served with sage dressing.

Gulls flew past, all wings and noise. Flocks of these garbage birds hang around the drive-in restaurant at the far end of the strip and fly up to the canal when they get bored, which they are when they're not eating. Gulls are the scuzzos of the bird world. Nobody would want to be a gull.

I liked the little terns that scurried in and out of the water's edge, snaring insects in the sand. Cute, like puppies, but not model material. Gabe liked the herons that lived in the marshlands to the north of the strip. Herons have a lot of class, but they're ugly. Not just look-the-other-way ugly, but disgustingly ugly. I didn't need to be a swan, but I refused to be a heron.

That evening, we watched dozens of black birds flying toward the shore from the lake, looking as though they knew exactly where they were going, and why. With graceful necks and tapered wings, they appeared more independent than the geese, who flew in military precision, or the gulls, who would fly into a furnace if they thought food was there.

"What are they?" I asked Gabe. I had seen the birds before but given them no thought.

Gabe said they were cormorants, which sounded exotic. Gabe told me they flew out over the lake in search of food each morning. At the end of the day they returned to nest in trees along the shore of the bay, facing the fires of the blast furnaces and mills. Neither scavengers like gulls nor beggars like geese nor timid souls like terns, the cormorants took charge of their lives. Out of sight of shore, they dove underwater and became submerged predators, swimming after their food like feathered barracudas. When their workday was over, they gathered with their buddies and flew home to snuggle on their perch and watch the sun go down. Blue-collar birds.

On summer mornings, I would step through the rear door of our house on the beach strip and into our garden and watch the cormorants fly east toward the sun, still hanging low over the water. The more I learned about the birds, the more I liked them. Cormorants work hard and mate for life. They're not as pretty as swans, but not every man I slept with was Hugh Grant, either. They can dive into water cold as ice, they fly twenty miles back and forth to work each day, and they look good in black. To hell with swans. I'd rather be a cormorant.

Cormorants could not live anywhere else nearly as well as they do on the beach strip. Nor could I.

I needed Tina to understand this, but I never tried to explain it to her. The only blue collar Tina knows about is the one on her Chanel jacket. And the only birds she can identify are flamingos. Seen at a distance. From a yacht in the Caribbean.

HERE IS THE DIFFERENCE between Tina and me that you need to know: when we were kids, Tina wanted to grow up and marry a doctor, and she did; I wanted to grow up and become a doctor, and I didn't.

When Tina announced that she had met the man she was going to marry, after their first date, Mother said, "Tell me about him."

Tina met him while volunteering at a charity lunch in Toronto, probably raising money for underprivileged poodles or needy brain surgeons. She didn't say, although she told me she had been wearing an absolutely stunning new Donna Karan suit and Anne Klein pumps that made her feel like Julia Roberts on a good day. Tina has always believed she resembles Julia Roberts, but only her mouth does. It's her largest, most notable feature. A former boyfriend of hers told me that whenever he kissed Tina, he swore he heard an echo.

Anyway, Tina raved about her new man, who got his medical degree at Harvard, trained as a surgeon at McGill, was next in line to become head of surgery at Vancouver General, won a provincial junior tennis championship while an undergraduate, drove a silver BMW 535, had a mild case of eczema on his right elbow, and wore a size 42 Tall suit.

"And his name is?" Mother asked.

Tina said, "Andrew Golden."

"Golden?" I said. "Is he Jewish?"

I might have asked if he wore boxers or briefs. Tina shrugged. "I guess so. Never asked." A small thing like her future husband's religion wasn't important to her. Not as important as becoming the next head of surgery or driving a silver BMW. Over the years since, I have regretted not asking if Andrew wore boxers or briefs. I'll bet Tina would have known.

So Tina married Andrew and I made it to pre-med before realizing that some dreams are better left that way. I dropped out after the first year. My marks were not good, and I was convinced they would not get better. While Tina pranced through college and Junior League, I worked at pharmacies, commercial art studios, food caterers and veterinary hospitals, always on the front desk, away from the action in the back rooms. I have a voice made for answering the telephone, I've been told, and a face for greeting men. Along the way, I developed a knack for bookkeeping. It's my pension plan. Someday both the voice and the face will have faded, but as long as we pay taxes we'll have tax collectors, and as long as we have tax collectors we'll need bookkeepers.

TINA SAID NOTHING when she came into the house after Mel left. I told her I was going for a walk, and I spent the afternoon sitting on a bench facing the lake, waiting for the cormorants.

IT WAS ALMOST DINNERTIME when I returned home, walking through the garden and looking up at the bedroom window that Mel said the pervert might have watched from the garden shed. He would not have seen much. At forty, most women show as little flesh as possible, even to themselves, although I have managed to keep my body trim. I tend to stay away from windows and stay wrapped in silk robes. Still, I didn't know what this season's perversions were.

At a commercial art studio where I worked with a dozen other women, one of the artists would buy our old shoes from us, preferably high-heeled pumps. He preferred well-worn shoes and would almost salivate when we brought them in. We knew why he wanted them—he was a shoe pervert—we just didn't know what he did with them or how he did it. Some of the women thought about it to the point where they refused to sell their shoes to him anymore. He almost cried over the vision of those smelly old shoes being tossed into the garbage. He looked so miserable that I felt sorry for him and sold him any old shoes I could find. I even sold him a few of my mother's old shoes, although her feet were two sizes larger than mine. If he noticed, he never mentioned it. Sometimes I think perverts are the most misunderstood people in the world. Of course, I also think they should stay that way.

Tina was nibbling crackers and watching television in the living room. "We should go and visit Mother," she said, keeping her eyes on the screen.

I said that was a good idea.

"Before or after dinner?" Tina asked.

I said after dinner was better, because then we wouldn't be interrupted by Mother's meal.

"Do you want to eat out or make dinner here?" she said.

I said I didn't feel like cooking, but could make us sandwiches if that's what she wanted. Tina's questions, I knew, were stepping stones to the real goal, which we finally reached when she said, "What's he like?" She still hadn't looked directly at me.

"What's who like?" Of course I knew.

"Your friend Mel."

"You saw him. You talked to him."

"I mean, what's he like in bed?" This time she turned her head to stare at me.

"Go to hell."

"Did your husband know?"

"There was nothing to know."

"Yes, there was. He knew, didn't he? He took the gun with him to the blanket because he knew, and maybe he was going to kill you and then himself, or maybe he just wanted to hear all the details, because that's what men do. They torture themselves with the details. When you didn't show up, he shot himself. Isn't that what the police think?"

"Did Mel say that?"

She looked away, then back at me. "Come on, Josie. A blind woman could figure out you two had something going."

"Tina, whether he and I . . ." I began to speak to her through clenched teeth and hated the sound of my own voice, so I started over. "Whether or not Mel and I had something going, as you put it so poetically, Gabe . . . Gabe knew nothing about it and even if he did, Gabe . . ." I kept stumbling over his name. "Gabe would never do what you said he might have done, okay?"

Tina actually smiled at that. "That's what Mel said. He told me that even he was finding it hard to believe that Gabe would kill himself. He said he's beginning to think somebody else killed Gabe with his own gun, and maybe the police should start investigating it as a murder. Just like you've been saying all along." She stood up and walked past me toward the front door. "Close your mouth," she said, like Mother used to say when we were kids, "or you'll catch flies. And I don't want a sandwich. I want a real meal."

WE ATE AT A RESTAURANT ALONG THE LAKE, one of those places where they serve drinks in old preserves jars and the menu looks like a page from the Sunday comics. But the salads were edible and the view over the water was attractive. We watched sailboats skim across the lake, their sails and spinnakers shining against the low light of the setting sun. I have never liked sailing. Too much work and seasickness. But I have always liked the idea of sailing, the way I have always liked the idea of travelling to other planets. I think it's a wonderful idea. Just don't invite me to join in.

"Look," Tina said when our food arrived, "I'm not going to ask what you and Mel were up to—"

"Good," I said. "Because I would tell you to mind your own business."

"He seems to be a nice guy. And he cares about you. I could see that." She was picking at her food, grilled chicken over Caesar salad. "And he's cute. Younger than you, too."

"You jealous?"

"Damn right." She patted her mouth with her napkin. "I've always been jealous of you. I used to tell myself that you got the body and I got the brains, but that doesn't work anymore, either."

"Well, you got the money, anyway."

She looked across the water. "I take consolation in that. Did I tell you that Andrew and I have booked a cruise to Hawaii for Thanksgiving? We have a suite with a private balcony. Should be fun. Andrew wants to spend Christmas there, too."

"I'm pleased for you, Tina. I really am."

Tina poked at her salad as though a mouse might be hiding in it, then asked, "Do you think I lead a shallow life?"

"Does it matter?"

"That I lead a shallow life?"

"No, if I think you do. I don't worry about your opinion of my life, Tina. Each of us is responsible for her own happiness, right?"

"That's what Daddy used to say." She smiled and looked down at her lap.

I have an opinion of forty-four-year-old women who still call their fathers Daddy. "He used to say a lot of things, most of them true."

She nodded. "Do you think Mother still misses him?"

"I think," I said, "that after all these years, she misses not being able to speak more than she misses our father."

I pushed my plate away, and both of us sat in silence until Tina began talking about Mel again.

"He's worried about you, did I say that? Mel, I mean. He's really concerned about this guy who was in the garden shed, watching you."

"Or watching Gabe."

Tina blinked. "Why would he be watching Gabe?"

"For god's sake, Tina, they can get married now."

Tina said, "Oh." Then, "Anyway, Mel was telling me that he's checking the records for confirmed perverts who live on the beach strip. You know, people who've been convicted of doing what this guy was doing, and other stuff. So far he's come up with over a dozen. Listen, there can't be more than eight hundred, a thousand people living there, and at least a dozen are convicted perverts. Now you're all alone and—"

"I'll buy a big dog."

Tina returned to her food. "Maybe you should just start getting a little more friendly with Mel again." She looked up, saw the expression on my face, and said, "I mean, when all of this is over, of course. This stuff with your husband. You know, maybe six months, a year from now. Damn." She put her hand on mine and looked away, embarrassed.

WE SAT WITH MOTHER FOR AN HOUR, Tina and I answering questions she wrote in her lovely cursive penmanship on the blackboard. *Did Gabe shoot himself?* she wanted to know, and I said, "Absolutely not."

"She's either crying or making wisecracks," Tina told Mother about me, and Mother smiled and wrote, *As long as she's making jokes, she's okay.* That's one reason I love my mother: she knows me better than anyone else.

When we ran out of things to say and write, Tina and I remained to watch television with her. After suffering her stroke, whenever Mother tried to speak and could not she would cry. This lasted a couple of months. Mother did not stop trying to speak, but she stopped crying over it. Instead, she would get angry at the words she formed but could not deliver. She would make a fist, bringing it down on her knee or on the table, if she were sitting at one, then stare into space, biting her lip. I loved her for that. I loved her for getting angry at the unfairness of life. It proved what I have known all my life, that I am my mother's child, and maybe Tina is the adopted one.

Mother did not become angry this time. She looked from Tina to me and back again, as though trying to choose between us. Or, and this chilled me, trying to remember exactly who we were and why we were in her room.

When we left, Tina hugged her briefly. I held on to her longer. Then I leaned back to look into her eyes. "Are you all right?" I asked her.

She frowned, pointed at her lips, and shook her head.

"I know you can't speak," I said. "But you know us, right? Tina and me?"

She nodded, then pulled me to her again.

"HOW LONG DO YOU THINK MOTHER HAS?" Tina asked on the way back to my house.

I was driving. "Until what?"

"Until the next stroke, the one that'll kill her."

"Jesus, Tina."

"Don't get angry with me. It's a legitimate question. Andrew told me that when someone Mother's age has a stroke like that, she'll have another, and we had better expect it. The difference between you and me is that I'm a realist and you're a dreamer."

"Yeah, well, the reality is that my husband's dead and yours isn't."

"Which reminds me. I should call Andrew."

She pulled the smallest cell phone I had ever seen out of her purse and dialed it, right there in the car. "Got his voice mail," she said. We were crossing the lift bridge over the canal, the tires growling against the textured steel road surface. When we were children, crossing the bridge in Dad's car, he would tell us a troll lived under the bridge, and the troll grew angry whenever anyone drove over him, and it was the troll we heard growling, not our tires on the rough steel. I smiled at the memory and would have mentioned it to Tina, something we could share between us, but she was continuing her extended conversation with her absent husband.

" . . . know you're busy, but I want you to look at that dining-room suite I mentioned at Dorsey's. I left you a note on it—did you get the note? Stop in on your way home from the hospital tonight. I think we should have it for Thanksgiving, but it may be a special order, so we should do something about it now, all right? Josie says hello. She's driving, or I would hand her the telephone. She's bearing up so well, the sweetheart, and I'll give her your love. Call me when you get time, and speak to the landscapers, will you? They still haven't trimmed the hedge at the back the way I like it. You're going to have to give them hell, Andrew. You're too nice to them. I think we should change them, the maintenance people, I mean."

She pecked a few kisses into the telephone and snapped it shut just as we pulled into the driveway. I switched off the engine and lights and sat staring at the darkened house and the eastern sky behind it, over the lake. The high clouds were lit in that dying pink shade of summer dusk.

Tina spoke my name twice before I looked at her.

"What are you going to do?" she asked.

"About what?"

"About . . ." She waved at the house. "This. Your life. You stayed home while Gabe worked, right? Except for afternoons doing the books where Mother lives?"

"That's how Gabe wanted it," I said. I stepped out of the car and walked toward the house, Tina trailing me. "And so did I. We paid cash for the house—"

"Why?" Tina asked.

"It didn't take that much money. Real estate prices here are cheap. You can probably buy our house for the same price you'd pay for a parking spot in Vancouver."

I unlocked the front door, tossed the keys on a table, and turned to face Tina.

"Why didn't Gabe want you to work?" Tina asked. "At a full-time job?"

I didn't like her tone. "Hey, I didn't want to work either. Not full-time. I'd been fired from my job just after we moved here—"

"Is that when you worked at the veterinarian's?"

"As a matter of fact—"

"And you told some woman who brought her little dog into the animal hospital that the dumbest bitch in the room wasn't the one with four legs and an infected paw but the one wearing the cheap dress and the dumb hairdo?" She'd always enjoyed telling that story. I'd assumed she was proud of her little sister's wit. Now I thought it was something else, and it made me angry.

"What the hell, Tina?" I said. "You haven't worked a day since you married Andrew, you tramp."

"Of course not!" she shouted. "Unlike you, I have social commitments." That almost inspired me to pour turpentine into her underwear again, this time while she was wearing it, but just then the telephone rang. I seized it as an opportunity to end the battle, or maybe as a weapon, and barked, "Hello!"

"Josie?" It was Dewey. "Should I call some other time?"

"Yes," I said, then "No," because this seemed like a good way for Tina and I to stop arguing gracefully. "Hi, Dewey," I said and looked across at Tina, who mouthed "Dewey?"

"I've been reading about Gabe and you in the papers," Dewey said, "and feeling terrible, but I didn't want to make a pest of myself, you know, unless you wanted to see me."

I thanked Dewey and said I would love to see him, I needed

all the friends I could get, and asked him to call me next week. He promised he would, we said our goodbyes, and I hung up and turned to face Tina, both of us calm.

"Dewey?" Tina said, aloud this time. "As in Huey, Louie and?"

"He's a friend from way back," I said.

"How far back?"

"Before Gabe."

"And now he thinks the coast is clear?"

"There's nothing romantic about it," I said. "I haven't seen him since Gabe and I were married. Now give me a hug, shut up for five minutes, and I'll tell you about him. If you're interested."

Tina lowered her head, looked at me with a smirk, and said she was interested in any man who had known me for years, who wasn't a gnome, and who had never parked his shoes under my bed. Then she opened her arms and we hugged and patted each other's back. What would I do without the little snip?

I explained that I had met Dewey while I was working at the veterinarian's. His business name, Dewey Does Dogs, was the least attractive thing about him. All day long, while he washed and clipped and manicured hairy little creatures, his stereo belted out Mozart and Beethoven or Renée Fleming and Maria Callas. At the end of the day, when the dog owners had rescued their little sweetums and paid Dewey, he pocketed a couple of hundred dollars and smelled like a cocker spaniel.

"That's two things I can imagine you not liking about him," Tina said. "His name and his aroma."

"There's more," I said. "He's bisexual."

"I hear it doubles your chances of getting a date on Saturday night."

"What," I said, "were we talking about before we started fighting?" I didn't want to talk about Dewey. I wanted only to think about Gabe. I wanted to wallow in the memories of him. And I wanted Tina's shoulder to cry on when I needed it.

"We were talking about your finances," she said. "Unless you've got a big stash of money hidden away somewhere, or Gabe qualifies for a bank president's pension . . . I mean, what are you going to live on? You'll need to get a real job."

"A real job?" She might have said I needed to buy a camel.

"Do you have any savings?"

"Like I said, the house is paid for. I guess there'll be pension money . . ."

"So, what are you going to do, even if there is? Sit here the rest of your life, looking out at the lake?"

It was a classic big sister question. One I hadn't thought of. Now that Tina had spoken it aloud, I chose to answer it aloud, and I answered it with the reply I had kept hidden since talking with Mel that morning. "Yes," I said. "Yes, I think I will. I think I'll sit here and stare at the lake, and when I get tired of doing that, I'll look for whoever killed Gabe. I'll look for the rest of my life, if I have to."

10.

Tina left two days later, catching an afternoon flight to Vancouver. She rushed through breakfast and sat in the living room, looking beyond Beach Boulevard through the arches of the highway bridge toward the bay and the steel factories, waiting for her limo to arrive.

"Here's Alex," she said, standing up. Her luggage was at the front door.

"You called the same limo driver?" I asked.

"He asked me to. He's lonely."

I looked out the window. Alex was lumbering toward our front door, straightening his tie and beginning to suck in his stomach, which promised to be an extended journey. "He's horny, Tina."

"Being lonely and being horny are the same thing with men." Tina leaned to look at herself in the hall mirror, smoothing her hair. Then she hugged me, and another Tina, the concerned sister, spoke in the concerned sister's voice. "I hope I helped. I hope I wasn't a problem."

"You're never a problem," I said. "A pain in the ass sometimes, but never a problem."

I kissed her on the cheek and looked over her shoulder to see Alex peering through the door window at us. "Your lonely driver's here," I said, and she turned and showed him Tina number three. This one smiled with wide eyes and squealed with an eight-year-old's voice when she opened the door, "Alex, you're so *good*. Here they are," pointing at her honey-coloured luggage. She glanced at her watch. "I've got three hours before my flight, so we can drive slow and talk."

Alex showed a series of gapped teeth and touched the brim of his cap.

"You two go straight to the airport," I called from the door as Alex carried Tina's luggage to the limo. "And don't forget—"

I stopped at the sight of a small, shiny black van stopping in front of the house. In place of windows it had a silver hinge-like affair, as though the top could fold back like a baby carriage. A grey-haired man emerged from behind the wheel. He carried a plain metal box in one hand and a clipboard in the other. While Tina, Alex, and I watched, he glanced down at the sheet of paper on the clipboard, up at the house again, nodded to Tina and Alex—I almost thought of them as a couple—and walked toward me.

"Mrs. Marshall?" He had a voice acquired by older men of a certain stripe, as though they had been smoothing their vocal cords with paste wax for forty years.

"Yes," I said.

He handed me the clipboard and a pen. "May I ask you to sign here, please?"

I signed the bottom of the sheet of paper and handed it to him. He thanked me, bowed his head, and with two hands gave me the box, which was about the size and weight of three pounds of coffee. Then he bowed again, took three steps backward, and returned to his shiny black car.

Tina walked toward me, concerned. "What's that?" she asked, pointing at the box in my hand.

"This," I said, and I was so glad I did not begin to cry, not there, not then. "This is Gabe." Then I turned before Tina could hug me and closed the door, waving through the glass at her and nodding when she blew me a kiss.

THEY COULD HAVE PUT GABE'S ASHES in a china urn "suitable for placing on a mantle or in a display case," the young undertaker had told me. He had shown me a sample: deep blue, with small white flowers at its base and white birds soaring near the rim. It cost seventy-five dollars and qualified as a piece of china because that's where it was made, which meant it was probably worth eight-five cents when it was crated on a ship out of Shanghai.

I wasn't being cheap when I said the metal box would be fine. I didn't want Gabe on a mantle, which I don't have anyway. I wanted Gabe in my bed. I wanted him holding my hand while we strolled the beach strip. I wanted him inside me on winter nights when we could hear the lake water crashing against ice-coated rocks along the pier.

Tina was gone and Gabe was in a small metal box, and neither event was making me happy, so I poured myself some brandy neat and drank it while staring at the metal case. I had a little cry, poured myself more brandy, and drank it too. Then I curled up on the sofa and slept, waking when the telephone rang. I refused to get up and answer it until it rang four times. Telemarketers never wait longer than that. Sisters do.

"I'm at the airport," Tina said, a little breathlessly, I thought. "I'm taking a later flight, got a couple of hours to kill. Listen, I'm worried about you. I wish you would come and stay with me and Andrew."

"We'll see."

"What are you going to do with . . . you know."

"No, I don't know."

"That package the man in the black car delivered."

"Gabe's ashes? I'm going to look after that tonight."

"What do you mean, look after it?"

"I'm going to deal with it. Do what is right. Do what I want to do, which I know is not always the same thing, but I've made up my mind."

"Josephine, you have to tell me."

"No, I don't."

"I'll keep calling you until you do."

I said, "Goodbye, Tina," added, "Goodbye, Alex," and hung up. Then I curled myself into a ball and went back to sleep.

I WOKE AGAIN in that same melancholy greyness of summer dusk that never fails to make me nostalgic. It made me feel that way even when Gabe was alive and we were walking along the boardwalk to Tuffy's for hamburgers and beer. I have never been afraid of the dark. There is beauty to be found in darkness—the moon rising over the lake, making diamonds on the water, the shimmer of northern lights, the lights of ships in the distance. It is not darkness I fear. It's greyness, the in-between, the dying.

I made coffee and sipped it, feeling the caffeine doing battle with the alcohol and winning, until the telephone rang again. It was Mel.

"Just called to see how you're doing," he said.

I told him the widow Marshall was doing fine.

"Why do you call yourself that?" he asked.

"Because it gives me intrigue. Widows are always more intriguing than married women, don't you think?"

"I think you have always been intriguing."

"And I think you're a nice guy. So does my sister, by the way."

"Tina's an intriguing woman. She still there?"

"No, she's either in a Boeing over Manitoba or in a limo under the chauffeur." I heard a truck in the background. "Where are you?"

"On a watch."

"What, a Rolex?"

"I was sitting here and I started thinking about you, wondering how you were doing."

"I don't need you to come and see me."

"That's not why I was calling."

"Sure it is. I'm alone in the house. We don't even need a motel room now, do we?"

I heard him breathe out slowly.

"Okay," I said before he could speak. "I appreciate you calling, I really do. But there's something I have to do tonight." I looked at the clock. It was almost ten. "Call me from your place at midnight if you're still up."

"You're not going out." It was a command, not a question.

"I have to."

"Did your sister tell you how many convicted perverts we've identified living on the strip? We've been interviewing them—there must be a dozen of them."

"Mel, I can find more than that on the bus into Toronto."

"One of them has been watching you from your garden shed."

"They're tied in, aren't they?" I said.

"What are?"

"The guy in the tool shed and Gabe's death."

He thought it over. "It could be."

"I knew it."

"We don't know for sure. Just don't go out until I get there."

"You're not coming here, Mel. Not tonight. Not anymore."

"Then wait for the morning."

"No." I knew what I wanted to do, and I wanted to do it now.

He grunted. Something had distracted him.

"What?"

"Nothing."

"Nothing? Something going on where you are?"

"Yeah." He lowered his voice. "I'll call you later."

"Sure."

I was used to this. Gabe would call me while he was on a stakeout, or a watch, as Mel called it, especially late at night.

He would tell me he was calling to see if I was safe, alone in the house on the beach strip. I knew that was a crock. Gabe had seen something that had shaken whatever faith he had in the goodness of human nature, and he needed to talk with someone he cared about. Someone, I suppose, he trusted. He would call and ask how I was, and I would say I was fine, I was watching television or reading a book, and ask when he would be home. And he would say, "Oh, soon. I have a couple of things to do yet, a couple of reports to write." And I could tell from his voice, from the amount of shake in it and the way it sounded pinched and higher than normal, that something had upset him.

"You're a cop," I said to him once. "You spend time around murder scenes. You should be used to it by now."

"I'll never get used to some things," Gabe said. "Some cops do, but I never will."

"Then find something else, Gabe," I told him. "You don't have to be out on the street all the time."

"Yes, I do," Gabe said. I remember he smiled at me in the way that could break my heart, and he reached his hand, one of his lovely bear-paw hands, toward me and curled it around the back of my head. "How about a coffee with some brandy in it?" he said. "And then I'll tell you the joke about the bald-headed Swede who worked in the pickle factory."

There was no joke about a bald-headed Swede and a pickle factory. Talking about a non-existent joke was a joke in itself. We were silly like that. His mention of the joke about the Swede was our signal that we would fool around later, starting on the sofa in front of the television and finishing in the bedroom. Or, as we had done one warm evening, among the caragana bushes on the beach. God, some of us remain children when it comes to sex, as though we can restore its mystery and fascination to the same level as when we were teenagers. Perhaps that's what Tina meant when she said men have affairs because they are afraid of death.

The only way to hold off dying is to grow younger, not older. Maybe sex fools men into believing they are growing younger.

I pictured the way Gabe looked when he made me smile, how pleased he appeared when he saw me laugh at his jokes, his fun. That's the expression I remembered, along with the strong body and the bear-paw hands. I looked at the metal box delivered to me that afternoon. Gabe was not in there. I didn't know what the hell was in there, but it was not Gabe, and I didn't want it with me.

The onshore wind would be cool, I knew. I slipped on a sweater, picked up the box, took my keys from the hall table, and left the house, locking the door behind me.

SOON AFTER WE MOVED HERE, I told Gabe about the amusement park, the one that had stretched from the canal along the bay side of the strip across Beach Boulevard from our house. It had been built as an attraction for the wealthy families from the city who spent summers on the strip, Victorian classy with lawn bowling, a concert stage, and elaborate wrought-iron benches set beneath willow trees. When the wealthy people left for their air-conditioned mansions in the city and the workers moved in, the park became cheap and tacky the way amusement parks are supposed to be, with neon signs, carnival rides, arcade games, greasy french fries, and even greasier guys with cigarettes in their mouths and combs in their back pockets. The park was still operating when I was a teenager, although most of the rides were closed and things that once had been merely shabby were now a little scary.

My father said that when he was a boy in the 1950s, excursion boats steamed across the bay from the city during the summer, carrying people to the beach strip amusement park, where picnic tables were set among trees near the shore and kids played on a safe, sandy beach. No one we knew went to Florida in the winter or to the northern lakes in the summer. No one we knew could afford it. Everything they needed for fun was on the beach strip. I suspect many of the old people who live on the strip today were once kids who rode the excursion boats to the amusement park back then, giddy with anticipation for rides on the merry-go-round, the ponies, the Octopus, and the Ferris wheel. The rides are gone, but the people remain, maybe because their goal as children was to always be near those long-gone amusements on the strip, and living here in rented rooms and peeling-paint cottages is the only ambition they truly achieved in their lives.

The amusement park had been separated from traffic by fancy cast-iron fencing set between concrete posts lining the shoulder of the road. Each post was topped with an electric light inside a white globe, and the line of posts and lights extended all the way from the canal to the farthest end of the amusement park, across from the house that Gabe and I shared. I remember how attractive the line of shining globes appeared in the night air when I was a child, glowing soft against the glare of the neon and fluorescent lights of the rides and arcade. When the amusement park was demolished, so was the string of lights. The cast-iron fence was carried off to be melted down in the blast furnaces across the bay, and the light standards were shattered and carted away.

All but one. The last one in the line, the one opposite our house, had been merely decapitated, and whenever Gabe and I walked on that side of the road and passed the waist-high stub of the post I would touch it, trailing my fingers along the pebbly surface. I don't know why this one was permitted to remain. Perhaps because it marked the most distant corner of the parking lot that the amusement area had become. Boaters, dragging their toys on trailers behind their SUVs, drove through the parking lot to a launch ramp beneath the highway bridges, and others parked their cars there while they strolled the boardwalk or fished in the canal. There were always cars in the parking lot, and there were several now as I crossed Beach Boulevard with the box containing

Gabe's ashes under one arm and walked to the stubby post and dragged my fingertips along its surface.

Ahead of me, the lift bridge grumbled with each car passing over it. To my left and two hundred feet above me, the high bridges roared with traffic. The steel mills flared, the waves on the lake whispered, and I walked in silence, my head down, carrying the ashes of my husband in my arms.

I had planned to scatter them on the lake, but not in daylight. It would look like littering, which is what it would be. And this late in the season, bathers ventured into the lake to swim in the warm waters. I was unsure how someone might feel emerging from the water with Gabe's ashes clinging to his Speedo. Besides, there was something socially unacceptable about the idea of scattering your spouse's ashes while others watched, as though you were performing some private act in public. No, it would not take place in the glare of day. Nor would it happen, I decided, on the beach in an onshore wind that would blow Gabe back onto the sand and—a hideous but somehow appropriate thought—onto me as well.

So I chose to scatter them from the lift bridge over the canal, whose waters flowed from the bay into the lake and would carry him toward the ocean like some sort of heaven-bound commuter. Gabe hated the idea of commuting. This trip would be different.

I was not maintaining the correct sombre attitude here perhaps, but I have always clung to anything that makes me smile in the midst of tragedy, even if it comes with a side helping of guilt.

Approaching the canal, Beach Boulevard rises to meet the lift bridge, creating room for people to stroll along the canal edge beneath the structure. I walked up the incline and almost across the bridge, a breeze off the lake teasing my hair. Cars passed and the glare of their headlights caught me, a lone woman with a metal box standing on a bridge late at night, prepared to—what? Leap into the water? Dump her garbage in the canal? Two cars slowed as they passed, their drivers staring at me, and when they did I resumed walking until I was at the far end of the bridge, waiting for a break in traffic.

When I saw no cars ahead of me and none approaching from behind, I lifted the box to the rail and rested it there. With one more look around to ensure that I was alone, I glanced up to see the bridge operator, a balding man in a white shirt, suspenders, and thick-rimmed glasses, watching me from the window where he worked, pulling levers and pushing buttons. His office in an ugly metal structure painted the colour of an avocado was brightly lit and set thirty or forty feet above the roadway, giving him an unobstructed view of road traffic and approaching ships. He was looking down at me with curiosity and perhaps suspicion. I didn't want an audience, so I lowered the box and began walking back along the bridge toward home, preparing to set my alarm for an ungodly hour like three a.m. But I knew, I just knew, I would not rouse myself to do this. I had to do it now.

When I reached a point near the edge of the canal where the heaviest steel beam of the bridge blocked the operator's view of me, I stopped. The steel beam was as wide as a small car, and in its shadow I could scatter Gabe's ashes unseen by the bridge operator. I would have to hold the box to one side and ensure that Gabe's ashes fell into the water and not on the canal ledge. It helped that the wind had shifted to my left. The breeze would carry the ashes toward the centre of the water if I lifted the box high enough above the rail.

No traffic was in sight. Out on the lake, a ship was approaching. I raised the box to the bridge railing and began prying off the lid. My hands were shaking so much that the lid slipped from my grasp and dropped directly beneath me, landing on the concrete wall of the canal with the sound of a cheap cymbal.

Gripping the edge of the container with both hands, I inverted the box and shook it until, in the glow of reflected light from the bridge, from the stars, from the hot radiance of the slag pits across the bay, I could see Gabe slip away in a grey cloud of sorrow, first rising with the breeze and hovering above the canal waters, then falling forever into darkness.

After all of him had vanished, I remained with my hands and my head lowered, waiting to cry. I felt sadder than I had ever felt in my life, but there was another emotion as well, and I recognized it as relief. I missed Gabe and I loved Gabe, and I would never in some way cease missing and loving him. But scattering his ashes to the wind and the water had marked something, an end or a beginning, or maybe both, and I was glad of it.

I stood with my head bowed until I realized tears would not be coming. This surprised and comforted me, although it appeared to be accompanied by hallucinations, because I heard someone call my name.

It's Gabe, I thought for a heartbeat or two. No, it wasn't. Gabe never spoke in a hoarse whisper, and Gabe never called me Mrs. Marshall. But *someone* had called me Mrs. Marshall, and he did it again. The voice came from the darkness beneath my feet, its owner standing directly under me, on the edge of the canal. I looked down into shadow.

"Mrs. Marshall."

I looked around. No cars were approaching. The bridge operator was out of sight.

"Mrs. Marshall."

Because I saw no one, I believed no one was there, and I'd be damned if I would stand on a bridge late at night talking to no one.

"I know what happened," the voice said. "Listen to me. I know what happened."

I saw a shadow within shadows below me, faint light reflected off a fainter image of a man, craning his neck to look up at me.

I was about to speak. Or maybe walk—no, run like hell—off the bridge and return home. I'm not sure because, before I could do either, I was almost knocked backwards by a blast from a few feet away, aimed directly at me.

II.

A sign on the bridge warns: CAUTION—LOUD HORN MAY SOUND AT ANY TIME. The horn looks like the ones mounted on top of transport trucks that kids on highway overpasses want the truckers to blast on their way by, but it's bigger and louder, set about six feet above the walkway. The bridge operator sounds the horn to warn pedestrians, cyclists, and dawdlers that the bridge is about to rise. I hear it several times a day from our house a hundred yards down the strip and from almost anywhere on the beach, always at a distance.

It blasted at me within arm's reach, so loud it was painful and so startling that I dropped the tin box to bring my hands to my ears. My instinct was to run from the sound and off the bridge, and I did, even while the horn kept blasting. When it finally stopped, the near-silence was like the rush of a narcotic, a freedom from agony, and the softly ringing bell marking the lowering of wooden barriers to block traffic across the bridge was a soothing release.

I was off the bridge and stumbling down the incline. A pickup truck slowed as it approached the barrier, and the driver grinned at me when I passed and said, "What's your hurry, sweetheart?" I didn't stop running until I reached the bottom of the incline, where I leaned against a wooden bench to catch my breath and wait for my body to stop shaking.

The bell kept ringing over various metallic creaks, groans, and snapping sounds. The bridge was beginning to rise. I turned to watch and ensure that whoever had spoken to me from beneath the bridge was not following me. I saw only the driver of the pickup truck as he lit a cigarette and prepared to wait ten, perhaps fifteen minutes for the approaching ship, which looked like a village floating on the lake, to enter the extended mouth of the canal and move into the bay. Two more cars slowed as they approached the bridge barriers, and their presence, along with the steady ringing of the bell and complaints from the aged bridge as it rose high into the night air, were comforting.

My hands felt unnaturally empty. The tin that had contained Gabe's ashes was now out of reach on the rising bridge or out of sight in the shadows beneath it. Either way, I had no intention of retrieving it, and I turned my back just as the bridge reached its height and the freighter, about to enter the canal, sounded its horn, deep-voiced and friendly like a grandfather's greeting, and distant.

MY EARS WERE STILL RINGING and my hands were shaking when I arrived home and stood at the door, fumbling for my keys. I was no longer thinking of the voice I heard, or believed I heard, from the shadows under the bridge, or even the realization that Gabe's ashes were at that moment being stirred among the waters of the canal by some rusting hulk from Slovenia or Panama. I wanted only to be within my own house, our house, Gabe's and mine, with the door locked behind me.

And I was. I snapped the deadlock into place, switched on the living-room light, walked through to the kitchen, turned on the lights there as well, and slumped in a chair. I considered pouring myself a brandy. That's what people in movies do when they need strength or something to calm their nerves. But the idea of pouring neat brandy into my stomach, which continued to move as though it were a trampoline under a herd of gerbils, repelled me. Coffee might be good, but coffee meant walking to the cupboard and performing the rest of that ritual, which had once been comforting but now seemed risky. So I remained where I was, sitting with my arms folded and my chin up, for about as long as it took me to remember the song about whistling a happy tune whenever I feel afraid. Then I placed my elbows on the table, my head in my hands, and settled my mind in that uncertain space between fear and anger while the tears flowed.

Some creep under the bridge knew my name. What was he doing there so late at night? Looking up my skirt, if I had been wearing a skirt? And what did he want me to do, walk under the bridge and join him there? It was probably the pervert from the garden shed. If he knew enough about me to jerk off in the tool shed whenever I appeared at a window, he might know my name. If it was him. The pervert in the tool shed. Which made me curious.

I rose from the table and walked to the rear door leading to the garden. Gabe had installed lights shining from the house into the garden and toward the beach after we found kids drinking beer among the flowers and shrubs one night. On summer evenings we would turn the lights on before going to bed, persuading the kids to find some other garden for their drinking and puking.

I turned the lights on now and looked across at the garden shed, whose door stood open. The door had been closed that afternoon, locked with the simple metal closure Gabe had installed, long before Tina departed for the airport with Alex. Long before Gabe's ashes arrived. Someone had opened the shed door and no doubt entered, and left without closing it again.

The rear door was locked, but I had left the kitchen window open to catch the breeze. The screen was attached and intact, which meant little. Anyone could have entered from the garden and replaced the screen. I closed and locked the window, then remembered that the window in the dining room was open as well, and closed and locked it.

I sat on one of the dining-room chairs. Sat there in the dark. Sat thinking that I was alone in a house with every door and window locked. Sat and realized that if anyone had entered the house in my absence, he and I—it was always a man, wasn't it?—were now sealed inside a locked house together. And upstairs it was very dark.

I had never feared being alone in our house before, but I had always had Gabe to protect me, even from a distance.

I tried being logical. If someone was in the house with me, and it had anything to do with the open garden shed—because isn't that what triggered this whole panic thing?—it must be The Pervert. But wasn't he the guy who spoke to me, if anyone had spoken to me, from beneath the bridge? It had to be him. Maybe he had been in the garden shed. Maybe he followed me to the canal and hid under the bridge. Who was this little shit anyway, this creep who got his jollies peeping at me, and who had the nerve to call me Mrs. Marshall?

I went into the kitchen and took the flashlight from the shelf in the broom closet. Then, leaving all the lights on in the lower floor of the house, and taking care to lock the front door behind me, I walked across Beach Boulevard and toward the lift bridge. I had no intention of confronting some lecher who had called to me from the shadows under the bridge. I wanted the tin box back, the one that had held Gabe's ashes. If it had fallen onto the walkway of the lift bridge when the horn startled me, I would bring it home. If it had fallen onto the walkway of the canal, I would at least be able to see it with the flashlight. And if I spotted the pervert—if that's who had called up to me—I would satisfy my curiosity. Or maybe I just wanted to get the hell out of a darkened house where I no longer felt safe.

There was even less traffic on Beach Boulevard than before. I crossed the road and stroked the broken concrete pole as I passed it. I felt safer in the open air. Ahead of me, I saw the light shining from the bridge operator's high window. A car approached, crossing the lift bridge, its windows darkened and thumping with the bass beat of hip-hop music.

The bridge had settled back into place after the freighter passed through the canal and entered the bay, and I could see the ship's hulk across the bay, approaching the steel plants. At the foot of the incline leading to the bridge, I glanced up at the window, where the bridge operator was looking down at me with some curiosity. I wondered if his work was as boring as it appeared. He enjoyed job security, at least, because the federal government owned and operated the bridge. Another kind of security, I suspected, was being locked in a well-lit room, maybe with a radio or TV to keep you company. It all went together. Boredom and security. Salt and pepper. Love and marriage. Me and Gabe.

The sight of the bridge operator watching me made me feel better, and when I stepped onto the bridge I made a point of remaining where he could see me, instead of concealing myself behind the steel pillar as I had earlier. I turned the flashlight on and shone it into the shadows beneath the bridge, searching for the metal box.

Gabe had purchased the flashlight in the spring and, Gabe being Gabe, he couldn't buy an ordinary light. He chose one with a battery the size of a small loaf of bread, with something that looked like a headlight from our car mounted on top. Gabe wanted a powerful light that he could shine from our garden across the beach to the water's edge. He was always worried that somebody, some summer's night, would arrive pounding on our back door, screaming that someone was in trouble out in the water. "You need a serious light at times like that," Gabe said. "This is a serious light." It was also the weight of a large bag of potatoes, and my arm was aching when I lifted the light to the top of the walkway rail and aimed it at the edge of the canal, directly beneath my feet, expecting it to reveal the empty metal box or the shining eyes of our neighbourhood pervert. But it showed nothing beyond a crumpled paper coffee cup, a newspaper, and assorted cigarette butts.

The box might have fallen and bounced out of sight, so I walked toward the centre of the bridge, where, by leaning over the railing, I could look back beneath it. I swept the beam wider. Everything within the circle of its light appeared as bright as day. I passed it back and forth across the concrete walkway, from the edge of the wire fence to the painted yellow strip where the edge of the walkway met the canal waters.

Seeing nothing, I turned the light back to the edge of the fence itself, holding it on a place where the fence had been detached from the metal pole supporting it, creating an opening. I remembered the stories of boys clambering beneath the bridge to leave pennies on the metal platform when the bridge was raised, and returning after it had lowered and been raised again to retrieve the coins, flat and thin and misshapen. The fence had been built to keep them out, but I have always believed very little can keep twelve-year-old boys from entering anything they choose to enter.

I kept the light moving until I saw the metal box lying among the trash and gravel inside the fence, where it could not possibly have fallen. Someone had carried it there, and at the edge of the circle of light, I saw who it might have been.

Actually, I saw a pair of shoes, and I moved the light as far up the rest of the man, who was lying on his stomach, as I could. He was near the base of the bridge supports, which rose three or four feet above him. There was something awkward and unnatural about the way he was lying there. Nobody's legs stretched out at those angles, even in a deep sleep, although I couldn't tell if he was sleeping because I was unable to see beyond his shoulders.

I suspected it was the pervert, but even perverts deserve consideration. I kept shining the light back and forth to get the man's attention, without success. Leave him for somebody else to find in the morning, I thought. Or do something now. Which is what Gabe would do. Which is what I did.

I walked to the end of the bridge and aimed the light up at the bridge operator's window. He seemed to be reading a book or newspaper, and it took several sweeps of the light across the window before he looked down at me with more curiosity than before. I began waving at him, launching one of the more inane conversations I have had with a man.

Swinging the window open, he leaned out, and I shouted over the sound of the trucks passing above us on the high level bridges, "Hey!"

He, naturally, answered, "What?"

"There's a guy down here."

"A what?"

"Some man."

"A can?"

"A man. A guy."

"Who?"

"What?"

"Who is he?"

"I don't know. But I think he's in trouble."

"What kind of trouble?"

"I think he's sick."

"You think it's a trick?"

"Sick! Sick!"

"What, he's puking?"

"No, he's sleeping."

"Is he drunk?"

"Is he what?"

"Hey, are *you* drunk?"

"What the hell does *that* mean?"

"What're you doing all alone on the bridge at this time of night? You were just here half an hour ago. You gonna jump or what?"

"Thanks for your concern. Look, there is something wrong with this guy. At least call the cops or an ambulance."

The bridge operator gave that some thought. I saw him reach for what I assumed was a telephone. "Where is he?" he called down.

"He's inside the fence."

"Where?"

"Inside the fence. There's a hole there."

"There's not supposed to be anybody in there."

"Well, he's not supposed to be looking like he's dead, either. But he does."

"Like he's what?"

"Dead. I mean, maybe he isn't, but—"

"What's he wearing?"

"Blue plaid shirt, khaki pants—"

"He's not dead." The operator leaned back inside his office, brought the receiver to his mouth, said a few words into it, then stuck his head out the window again. "I've told that guy a dozen times to stay the hell out. Wait there. I'll be right down."

He emerged from a landing just beyond his window and trotted down metal steps that ended on another landing below the level of the walkway where I stood. He was older than I expected, with a fringe of grey hair above his ears and around the back of his head, making a fuzzy frame. His face was softer and friendlier than it appeared at a distance through the window. He stood at the edge of the stair landing, squinting toward the area beneath the lift bridge before looking back at me. "This place'd drive you nuts. Guys sleeping under the bridge, couples having sex, kids putting pennies on the platforms, last week some guy's shooting a gun down here." He dropped his eyes and lifted them back to mine again, having liked, I assumed, what he saw. "Lend me your light, will you?" he said, stretching a hand toward me.

I walked down the steps to hand it to him. He turned it on,

swept it across the rubble inside the fence until he located the man, then began descending to the level of the canal walkway, shouting, "Hey! Hey, you!"

I followed him. He had my flashlight, after all, and I felt safer with him than standing alone on the bridge.

"Watch yourself," he said, and he shone the light on the ground ahead of us. I stayed well back from the edge of the canal, following a few steps behind the bridge operator. When we reached the opening in the chain-link fence, he shook his head and made the same "Tch, tch, tch" sound my grandmother used to make when reading about disasters in the newspaper.

He knelt and shone the light through the opening in the wire fence and toward the bridge supports until it reflected back from the soles of the man's shoes. "Hey, Charlie," the operator called. Did this mean he knew the man's name? "Hey, asshole. Get up and get moving. The cops are on their way. I warned you about this, damn it." Bent from the waist, he duck-walked through the opening in the fence. As he stood erect on the other side of the fence, he winced and placed a hand at the small of his back before raising the light again. "You okay?" he said. His voice had lost its commanding tone. "Have you . . . holy shit."

He was standing between me and the man on the rubble, so I moved to one side to see whatever it was that made him respond that way. By the time I did, he had swung the light from the man to the bridge supports, each made of square concrete as wide and high as a refrigerator and topped with thick steel pads. The light climbed up the support directly in front of the man's body. Unlike the others alongside it, this one was shiny and red, the blood thicker and congealed among matter at the top, where the weight of the lift bridge rested on it, and I was just understanding what this was, or what it had been, when he swung the light back to the body. This time it wasn't the shadows, or the angle, or the thick rubble the light illuminated. This time it was clear to me and to the bridge operator, and eventually to the police, whose sirens announced their arrival on the lift bridge above us, that the man was not only dead but headless.

12.

"Okay, okay, okay." I kept repeating the words like a wind-up doll, although nothing was okay. Everything was crazy. Everything was out of control. A man who had spoken to me less than an hour ago was dead, his head crushed into a thin film of jelly beneath hundreds of tons of steel when the bridge descended. I needed time for my brain to catch up with the rest of the world.

I was in the back seat of a police car, my hands fluttering in front of my face. Tom Grychuk, for that was the name of the bridge operator, sat next to me, staring at the lake, his chin on his hand. Flashing red, yellow and blue lights from a dozen or so cars, ambulances and trucks crowding the parking lot next to the lift bridge lit up the area like a misguided bush party.

In the front passenger seat of the car, a detective waited for me to finish stuttering. He had introduced himself as Sergeant Harold Hayashida. I remembered Gabe mentioning his name. Gabe thought he was one of the better detectives. When Hayashida arrived ten minutes ago, he looked as though nothing much would excite him, and when he returned from inspecting the body beneath the bridge, he looked more sombre but still not surprised. Beside him, a uniformed patrolman sat at the wheel, writing on a wire-bound pad.

"Okay," I said one more time. "You're telling me that this guy, this man under the bridge, you think he committed suicide? By sticking his head on top of that piece of concrete and waiting for the bridge to come down and crush it like an egg?"

"I'm not saying that's what he did," Hayashida said. "I'm saying that's what it *looks* like he did."

"How . . ." I shook my head and started again. "How crazy does somebody have to be to do that?"

"You'd be surprised." It was the patrolman behind the wheel. All I had seen of him so far was the back of his neck. "Last month, out near Grimsby? Had a guy lie on the railroad track, right in front of the wheel of a boxcar on a freight train waiting for a signal to change." He twisted to look at me. The back of his neck was his best feature. "Lot of people who live near the tracks, they saw this guy. Couple of them ran out to stop him. Pulled on his legs and everything, but he hung on. Other people tried running up to warn the engineers, but the train was half a mile long, and before they could get there the thing started moving. Took his head off clean as a butcher's knife." He turned back to his report.

"I talked to him," I said. "Or at least, he talked to me. Just before he did it."

"Did you see him?" Hayashida said. "The man you spoke to?"

"No," I replied. "I told you I didn't."

"So it might have been someone else." Hayashida turned to Tom Grychuk. "How often are you here?"

Grychuk sounded as though it were an effort to speak. "Six nights a week. Six to midnight, every night except Sunday."

"You're sure the man under the bridge is the one you've been warning away the last few days?"

Grychuk answered without taking his eyes from the lake or his hand from his chin. "Looked like him. I mean, same shirt, I recognized that. Same size. Not a big guy."

"You called him Charlie," I said to Grychuk.

"Called who Charlie?" the detective asked.

"The man. Under the bridge. He called him Charlie. Did you know him?"

Grychuk looked at me as though I had revealed some personal secret about him. "I knew him to see him, that's all."

"But you called him Charlie."

"That's what I do when I'm pissed off at somebody and I don't know their name. I call them Charlie." He looked at Hayashida. "I don't know his name."

"What is his name?" I asked the detective. "Who is he?"

Hayashida thought that over for a moment before looking down at his notebook. "The ID in his wallet says he was Wayne Weaver Honeysett. Shows an address on Hutchings Lane—"

"That's near here," I said. "Down the beach strip, near Tuffy's, isn't it?"

Hayashida nodded. "Somebody's there now, searching for next of kin." He looked at Grychuk. "How old would you say this man was, the one you kept chasing away from the bridge support?"

Grychuk shrugged. "Maybe fifty. Around there."

"Height?"

"Five five, five six."

"Weight?"

"He was skinny. I'd guess 130 pounds. Maybe less."

Hayashida nodded. "It fits." He looked at me. "Does that sound like anyone you know?"

"No," I answered.

"But he knew you. You said he knew your name, and that he knew what happened to your husband."

"Maybe he knew who killed Gabe."

"What happened was, Gabe killed himself." It was the thick-necked cop.

"That's what you people think," I said.

"I've seen the report, Mrs. Marshall," Hayashida said. "In fact, I worked on it myself, the forensics and all. It looks pretty clear."

"You knew Gabe."

"Yes, I did. We didn't work together, but—"

"Do you think he could kill himself like that?"

Hayashida took a deep breath, scratched his head, and smiled without humour. "One thing you get used to in this job is surprise. You get so used to it that after a while, nothing surprises you, if that makes sense." He looked at me, the smile gone. "But you're right. Gabe Marshall was maybe the last guy I could imagine killing himself."

"Thank you," I said. "Thank you for that. Now how about this. You're saying you believe my husband killed himself less than a week ago, and now this poor man under the bridge, who told me that he knew what *really* happened to Gabe, because he saw it all, you're saying he killed himself too?"

"You don't know it's him." It was the uniformed cop behind the wheel, watching me in the rear-view mirror. "You talked to some guy, but you never saw him. Doesn't mean it's the one who put his head under the bridge, let it come down on him."

"Hey," I said, "I know it was him, and I know he damn well didn't kill himself. And neither did my husband."

That was too much for the cop, who had the bulk and attitude of a bear, and he turned and pointed a finger at me as though it were a weapon. "Look, lady," he said, "you're gonna have to stop jumping to conclusions and shooting your mouth off about things you know nothing about—"

Hayashida set a hand on the cop's arm, but not before I exploded at him. "*You arrogant bastard!* You didn't see my husband dead on a blanket, you didn't talk to the guy under the bridge, and you didn't stumble over a headless body, either. I'll jump to any conclusion I damn well want to, and I'm not a lady, you prick—*I am Gabe Marshall's widow!*"

I demanded that Hayashida open the door for me. I needed to breathe fresh air. Once he did, I walked quickly away from the car, my hands clenched into fists. The cop was saying something to Hayashida about getting me back in the car, but nobody was getting me back into that car, and nobody was going to talk to me that way.

"Mrs. Marshall." Hayashida had followed me. "I think we've got all we need now. Would you like a ride home?"

"No," I said. "But maybe you can walk with me. It's only two blocks."

"YOU LIKE LIVING DOWN HERE?" Hayashida was beside me, walking past the parking lot that had been the amusement park. Flames from the steel companies flared across the bay, and the transport trucks kept rumbling on the high bridges over our heads.

"I love it," I said. "Gabe loved it too."

"Some of us couldn't believe it, about your husband. Cops have been known to do that. What Gabe did, I mean. But it's usually uniformed guys, younger cops who start drinking too much or let the job get to them. Or older guys who've got nothing more to look forward to than a skinny pension. But not a guy like Gabe Marshall."

"Why not a guy like Gabe Marshall?"

"Because he always seemed, I don't know. Too grounded, I guess. Relaxed, contented. Liked his work, liked his life. That's who he was at work. What was he like at home?"

"He was relaxed, contented, liked his work, and liked his life. That's why he didn't kill himself."

"But he did."

"Bullshit." I started to cross Beach Boulevard.

"He did, Mrs. Marshall."

"You can believe it." Hayashida had fallen behind, and now he was walking briskly to catch up. "The whole damn police force can believe it, but I don't, and I never will."

"Mrs. Marshall—"

I had picked up my pace. Hayashida was still behind me. "That man, back there under the bridge, was going to tell me something. I know it. His words scared me so damn much I came home, and when I went back not thirty minutes later, he was dead. And you're telling me that he killed himself too?"

I was at the foot of the steps leading to the front door. I began looking for my keys.

Hayashida stopped at the end of my walk and called my name again.

"What?" I turned to look at him, the key in my hand.

"Somebody will probably want to talk to you tomorrow. It won't be me. Is there anything I can do for you now?"

"Yeah, there is." I pushed the key in the lock and twisted it. "Walk through my house and make sure there's no man inside, would you?"

"I HELPED PREPARE THE REPORT." Hayashida was sitting across from me at the kitchen table, both hands around a cup of black coffee. "About Gabe."

"The one that says he committed suicide."

"And the forensics report too, the lab tests. They all fit." He stared into the coffee as he spoke. "He's alone, some witnesses arrive within minutes of hearing the shot, the gun is there, recently fired, the coroner did a paraffin test and found gunshot residue on Gabe's hand, and the bullet . . . forensics confirms it came from his gun."

"How do they know that?"

"You compare the one that . . . the one that killed Gabe . . ."

"The one they dug out of his brain."

"Yes. Look, we worked on the forensics, Mel Holiday and I. We took the sample here, completed the form, sent it off to the lab in Toronto—and those guys are good, by the way. They compare both projectiles, put them under a microscope—"

"And match up the rifling marks. I know all that stuff. I watched *Law & Order*. But nobody explained how a guy, and I mean Gabe, winds up with his gun in his hand and naked, out on the beach."

Hayashida looked embarrassed. "There have been some ideas kicked around about him being naked there."

"Because he was waiting for me to show up and get naked with him. Do you want pictures, or will a simple Anglo-Saxon word do?"

"That's not important."

"Yes, it is. Who waits on a blanket in the bushes for his wife, his girlfriend, his lover, whoever, to come along, with a loaded gun in his hand—a gun that Gabe wouldn't even put together in the house? Gabe would take the damn thing apart in the car and carry it into the house like that, and put the ammunition clip back when he was in the car again. He hated carrying a loaded weapon, on duty or off. And he never carried one off duty."

"I know, I know." Hayashida nodded his head in sympathy. "But you heard Sadowsky back there—"

"Who?"

"Constable Sadowsky. Serge Sadowsky. We were sitting in his patrol car. You heard him say that people who are determined to do what Gabe did, they're unpredictable. They become obsessive, they change their patterns of behaviour." He glanced at his watch, took a long swallow of coffee, and stood up. "It's tough, I know," he said, looking at me. "I've never gone through it, having somebody close to me kill themselves. But I've been there when we told their wives or husbands or kids or whoever, 'Hey, your mom or your dad or your kid committed suicide,' and they usually don't believe it. How can they? You know what they say? They say the same things you're saying. 'He didn't do it, he couldn't do that, he seemed so happy.' That's what they say.

Eventually they come around, because they spot the pattern or see the clues they hadn't recognized before."

I stood up and followed him out of the kitchen toward the front door. "Thanks," I said. "For checking out the house for me. Did you look under the bed upstairs?"

Hayashida grew serious. "No." He began to climb the stairs, rather eagerly, it seemed to me. "You want me to?"

"Forget it," I said. "There's so much dust that anybody hiding there would've choked to death by now. And thanks for talking about Gabe. I'm the only person who doesn't believe he committed suicide, and it's taking me a while to accept it."

Hayashida took a step toward the front door, then looked back at me. "Actually, you're not the only one."

"Who else?"

He looked away, considering the question. Then, "You know Mel Holiday?"

"Of course I know Mel." Of course I screwed Mel, was how the words echoed in my head.

"He's starting to feel like you do. He's telling some of the guys at Central that maybe Gabe didn't kill himself, that maybe we're not looking hard enough to prove he didn't. He thinks Gabe was killed by somebody Gabe was investigating, or maybe somebody Gabe had put away or had charged. Keeps saying we've gotta keep digging. He says we're overlooking something, somebody, that Gabe had been investigating on his own. A drug dealer they found shot in an alley, a couple of guys running a car theft ring, maybe Mike what's his name, he's with the Mafia. He's telling Walter Freeman, you know Walter? He's telling Walter to start looking at that."

"And nobody believes him?" I leaned against the stair railing. "Mel's trying to get you guys to listen to him, and nobody believes him?"

"It's like . . ." Hayashida began. Then, "It's not impossible, I guess, but there has to be proof, and so far there's nothing. Just his opinion and yours. But I'll hand it to Mel, he keeps digging. He's following the forensics, asking for more tests, and pissing off Walter Freeman. You okay?"

I told him I was okay.

He pointed to the deadbolt. "Make sure that's in place."

"HELLO?"

It had taken six rings, but I was damned if I was going to sleep without talking to him. "Mel?"

He paused as though trying to decide if that was his name. "Josie?"

"Yeah." I wanted to hear his voice. "You know a detective named Hayashida?"

"What about him? Jesus, Josie, it's nearly three o'clock."

"He just left here. Hayashida, he just left my place—"

"What's going on?"

"He walked me back from the lift bridge. A guy died there tonight."

"On the bridge?"

"Under it. You'll hear about it when you go in today. I think he knew something about Gabe, this guy they found under the bridge. Nobody else believes me, but he wanted to talk to me when I went there with Gabe's ashes—"

"Gabe's *what?*"

I was tired. I was tired because it was almost sunrise, I was tired because I felt I had burned off every ounce of adrenaline in my body over the past few hours, and I was tired of trying to explain the world as I saw it to a bunch of men who called me "lady" and wanted to watch me from the garden shed and look under my bed. "Forget it," I said. "I'll explain later."

"So why did you call me?"

"Because Hayashida told me you don't believe Gabe committed suicide. He didn't, did he, Mel?"

"Maybe he didn't." His voice changed, and I could picture him lying back in his bed. I knew that bed. Once. I knew the apartment. A high-rise in the far end of the city. A balcony facing west at the sunsets. An Ansel Adams print on the wall in the living room. A brass bed. "I've got the same doubts you have. He was doing some stuff on his own, talking to some rough people. People who could do something like this."

"Thanks, Mel." I waited, listening to his breathing. Then I said goodbye, hung up, and climbed the stairs to bed.

13.

With planning that's not typical of me, especially when I've gone to bed after three a.m., I unplugged the telephone before falling asleep, and it was mid-morning when I woke to the sound of someone hammering on my front door.

I rolled out of bed and slipped on a green silk robe Gabe bought me last Christmas. Passing the mirror, I paused long enough to fluff my hair, wipe the sleep out of my eyes, and wish I had time to cover various wrinkles, but the thump-thump-thump on the front door resumed.

"Just a minute," I shouted down the stairs, and when I reached the door I opened it without checking to see if it was Mel or a newspaper reporter or a door-to-door religion salesman. It was none of them.

He was about thirty years old, with hair that looked as though it hadn't been washed since he'd shaved, which may or may not have been this year. He was wearing a denim shirt and grease-stained overalls cut off below the knee. Whatever part of me wasn't being offended by the sight of him was recoiling from the smell of him. I tried to close the door, but he was already attempting to push it open, his eyes as large as Ping-Pong balls and just as bouncy, looking over my shoulder, off to the side, down at my robe, and into the house. "Where's Grizz?" he started asking. "Grizz, you in there? Grizz, I gotta talk to you."

I screamed, "Get out! Get out!" He kept pushing against the door before stumbling once, regaining his feet, and stepping back, but he kept one strong arm on the door, preventing me from closing it.

"I gotta see Grizz," he almost whispered. "Please, okay? Please tell Grizz I gotta see him."

"I don't know any Grizz," I said, "and if you don't get the hell out of here I'll call the police!"

"Come on, lady . . ." Now he looked more hurt and confused than frightening, more panic-stricken than angry. He looked away and bit his lip, and when he removed his arm from the door I slammed it, slid the deadbolt in place, and walked to the living room window, where I watched as he turned and stumbled down the steps. He wandered off toward the canal, stopping once to look back at the house. If he comes back, I told myself, I'm calling the police.

I didn't need to. The telephone rang almost as soon as I plugged it back in, and I nearly jumped out of the damn robe. It was Mel. "I called twice this morning," he said. "I was about to ask a squad car to check and see if you were all right."

"Well, I was and now I'm not." I told him about the man in the denim shirt, demanding to see Grizz.

"Who?" Mel asked.

"He kept asking for Grizz," I said. "Who the hell's Grizz?"

"There's a guy . . ." Mel began. Then, "I'll tell you later today, maybe tonight."

"Tell me now, damn it."

"Not here. Not over the telephone. I'll meet you at Tuffy's at noon." His voice changed, became softer. "Jesus, Josie, what you must have gone through last night. I read Hayashida's report. Maybe you should think about staying with your sister for a while, go out to Vancouver."

I told him I wasn't going anywhere, but I wouldn't mind a few more patrol cars passing by at night.

MY FATHER SOMETIMES SANG AN OLD COWBOY SONG whose lyrics said something about a new world being born at dawn. You do not understand that idea until you encounter horror in the darkest moments of the night, the world that exists half-dead or temporarily so around three a.m., and a few hours later walk into a bright summer morning by a lake that's all sapphires and diamonds, with people and dogs playing on the sand and cotton-ball clouds sailing across the sky. Nothing as brutal as what I had witnessed beneath the lift bridge could have happened on a planet like the one I entered through my garden door that morning. It must have happened in another world, one that's in endless darkness. The world on the beach strip that day was born with the dawn, like the new world in the song my father sang.

I had dressed in red chinos, a white T-shirt, and sandals, and my first step into the garden gave me a floating sensation, a sense that life really did continue and was even worth living, despite the terrible things people did to each other. This feeling lasted about three steps, or until I saw the door of the garden shed still hanging open as it had last night when I returned from spreading Gabe's ashes on the water. I slammed it shut and twisted the metal closure, promising myself that I would buy a good padlock later that day. You won't need it now, I thought. Not since the bridge descended on that poor man's head last night, assuming he was the pervert. But I would buy one anyway.

On the boardwalk, among the children, the dogs, and the Frisbees and within sight of the boats far out on the lake, I began to regain that New World at Dawn sensation, and it grew stronger when I passed the picket fence separating the Blairs' garden from the beach. Jock Blair was bent over roses near the house, blue-grey smoke rising from his pipe. Maude sat in a chair with a kerchief around her head and her eyes hidden, as always, behind her sunglasses. Seeing me, she smiled and raised a hand in greeting. I called good morning to her, which brought a nod of her head and a wider smile.

Jock turned at the sound of my voice and smiled, although his eyes avoided mine. The complex crow's feet at the corners of his eyes deepened and his face, already the colour of ripe watermelon, grew more crimson. He had the whitest hair I have ever seen and wore plaid cotton shirts winter and summer. He was a shy man whose demeanour appeared threatened by the glance and voice of a younger woman. He loved roses. Once, I emerged from the back door to see him tending ours, the ones near the garden shed. "Rust, lass," he said, and he pointed to some black stems. "Best you stop it in its tracks." When I thanked him, he nodded and blushed and hurried away, back to the boardwalk and then to his garden, where I heard Maude scold him for being so forward, telling him I was more than capable of caring for my own roses, and ordering him inside to fix some tea and eat one of the warm scones she had baked just for him, the kind he liked, with currants inside.

I wondered what it must be like to spend fifty years of your life with the same man and still take pleasure in his company. Was it truly bliss, or was it like being one of conjoined twins, a relationship you accepted because no means existed of breaking it?

I used to talk like that with Gabe, saying I was obviously not a romantic, an idea that made Gabe laugh. "Your problem," he would say, "isn't that you're not a romantic. It's that you're *too* romantic, and it scares you so much you try to deny it."

I would reply that he sounded like one of those two-bit popular psychologists on television, and if he knew so much about me, maybe he should give me a full report, which would help explain a lot of things, including why I made so many stupid mistakes in my life.

His answer would be to stretch out an arm and squeeze me. "You'll work it out," he would say. "You'll work it out yourself, and then you'll understand better than if I told you." There are times, usually in the corner of my soul where it is always four a.m., that I wish Gabe hadn't been so trusting of my ability to work things out and had explained some things in detail for me. Because he had been right. When I worked things out and understood what he meant, they were harder to reject than if he had told me himself.

It was half a mile to Tuffy's. The beach and the boardwalk were crowded, as they are on every late-summer day. Walking among people and dogs, I felt safer from the creep who had appeared at my door looking for Grizz. What was behind his desperation to meet somebody named Grizz? Money? Protection? And why my house? Although I caught him sneaking a glance at other parts of my body besides my face, I didn't consider him a real threat to drag me inside and attack me. Nor did I find him pitiful. Whatever, whoever he was, I didn't want him back. He could find Grizz somewhere else, and I hoped he would. Somebody that desperate needed relief.

TUFFY'S ONCE HAD A SIGN mounted over the tavern door that said WE WERE HERE BEFORE YOU WERE BORN. The sign is long gone, lost among various renovations performed by its several owners. Nobody seems to lose money running Tuffy's, but there isn't much to be made from it either, based on the number of people who have owned the place over the years. Each new owner changed the layout, the staff, the menu, the paint on the wooden siding, and the faded sign dangling over Beach Boulevard. Heaven help them if they ever change the name.

Tuffy's opened in 1890 as Tiffany House, a dining spot for the wealthy summer people in their turreted cottages. When the summer residents wished to sample Tiffany's boneless pheasant, tournedos Rossini, or whole suckling pig in the privacy of their own summer digs, Tiffany's dispensed waiters in white tie and tails, driving an all-white carriage pulled by a team of white horses, to deliver the food and set the table for dinner or luncheon or picnic, complete with crystal stemware and British silverware. That's how rich the people who lived on the beach strip were back then. That's how well they lived in a place that was once a small paradise.

When the wealthy moved out and the blue-collar, sometimes-working class moved in, the immigrants and labourers melted Tiffany's down to Tuffy's, and it stuck. The imported claret was replaced with local beer, the British waiters with sullen students, and the white tie and tails with T-shirts and jeans. The closest the kitchen gets to pheasant these days is Buffalo-style chicken wings. Gabe told me he'd heard that an aging hooker had once worked out of an upstairs room in the back, which produced a bunch of jokes about suckling pigs, I'll bet. Still, most people appreciate Tuffy's for its honesty. It doesn't try to be something it isn't. Do not ask for a latte at Tuffy's or expect the furniture to match. The beer is cold, the chicken wings are hot, the cheese-burgers are greasy, the walls are green, and the clientele mind their own business. I love Tuffy's.

In Tuffy's, a woman can order a beer without stirring fantasies among the men shooting pool or watching the SportsChannel on television screens hanging from the ceiling. When I walked into Tuffy's, the pool players, the beer drinkers and the TV watchers looked up, then away. Guys who are basic and direct, like the men who favour Tuffy's, recognize body language when they see it. Mine said Leave Me Alone. And they did. I chose a table as far from the bar as possible and ordered coffee.

Mel came through the door about ten minutes later, wearing a light grey windbreaker over a blue T-shirt and jeans, the line of his shoulder holster visible beneath the jacket. Pausing near the bar, he removed his sunglasses and stood waiting for his eyes to

grow accustomed to the light. By the time Mel spotted me and
walked to my table in the far corner, near a window giving onto
the beach, every guy in the place had identified him as a cop.

"You look good," Mel said when he sat down.

"You look like a cop," I said. "They all made you as one. In
case you care."

"That's why I can't do undercover anymore." He swivelled in
his chair and signalled the guy behind the bar that he wanted a
Coke, then turned back to me. "You all right?"

"You always ask me that when you know I'm not," I said.

Mel sat silent for a moment. "What was it like there, last night?"

"It was horrible. What I saw was horrible."

"What the hell were you doing there, anyway?"

"Spreading Gabe's ashes. I wanted to spread them in the lake,
but there was an onshore breeze . . . never mind."

"But what made you go under the bridge? Hayashida said you
went down there with the bridge operator."

"He said something to me."

"Who? The bridge operator?"

"No. The man whose . . . the man who was killed. At least, I
think it was him. The bridge operator said he'd been living under
there for days. He told me he had seen something." No, that
wasn't right. I closed my eyes, remembering his words. "He said
that he knew what happened."

"What was he talking about?"

"Gabe's death."

"Did he say that?"

No, I realized. He hadn't. I shook my head. The waiter arrived
with Mel's Coke, and I waited for him to leave before asking, "Is
it in the papers today?" I hadn't seen a newspaper, hadn't turned
on the radio or television. "It must be all through the press."

"No details," Mel said. "Just that a man was found dead under
the bridge. That's all."

"Nothing about how he died?"

"Not if we can help it." He leaned toward me. "You don't want this kind of stuff out. Suicide stuff."

"Why not?"

"Copycats. It gives them ideas. Depressed people can walk around for weeks thinking about killing themselves and never do anything about it. Then somebody commits suicide in some spectacular way, and it's as though the other people get permission to do the same thing. So they don't give out that kind of information unless there's a reason for it."

"How about murder?"

"What're you talking about?"

"This guy . . . what's his name again? He knew me. I'm sure it was him. He called me Mrs. Marshall. They told me his name but I forget."

"I saw the report this morning. His name was Honeysett. Wayne Honeysett. He was a nutcase." He lowered his voice. "He was also a peeper."

He waited for that to sink in. A peeper? What, a little bird that shows up on your windowsill in winter? "A pervert?"

Mel nodded.

"*My* pervert?"

"Pretty sure of it. They're doing DNA testing now on what we scraped off the floor of the shed, comparing it to his."

"Are all perverts nutcases? I mean, I guess there's a connection, but some of the perverts I've met in my day seemed like pretty sane men on the surface."

"Honeysett was certifiable. He used to be a jeweller. Had a store on Barton Street—"

"Honeysett's," I said. "That's where I've heard the name before. That's him?" Radio stations in the city once carried commercials for Honeysett's Credit Jewellers. I remembered the white marble storefront, the big neon sign, the inane jingle—*Honeysett's has the diamond for your honey . . . for even less money . . . than you think.* I hadn't heard it for years. "Does he still have the store?"

Mel shook his head. "Couple of saleswomen said he assaulted them in the backroom. Nothing serious, just copping a feel. He tried to keep it quiet, but they started to press charges, took civil action, and he had to close the business. He moved . . ." He angled his head toward the front door of Tuffy's. "You know that old place up the way, next to the empty church? Big round turret, painted dark red?"

I pictured the house. The blinds were always lowered, the grass uncut, the roof sagging. "I thought it was abandoned."

"Honeysett moved there, alone. His wife died a couple of years before the thing with the saleswomen, and he bounced around in that old place, finally moved into the basement. We'd catch him now and then, outside houses on the beach strip at night, hiding in bushes near windows—"

"Or in garden sheds?"

Mel nodded. "He seemed harmless. He'd get a warning, his family would ask that we give him a break, let him stay with them, and the judge would agree. Then, a couple of months later he'd be up to his old tricks. Getting nuttier all the time. Last month, the city seized the old house for back taxes. He moved out. We didn't know to where, but apparently he was sleeping under the lift bridge. Which just proves how nuts he was."

"That doesn't mean he was suicidal."

Mel looked annoyed with me. "You an expert now?"

"I'm getting to be. Hayashida tells me you're becoming sceptical about Gabe shooting himself, right?"

Mel took a long swallow of Coke and set it down. "But not Honeysett. That's suicide, not murder."

"Why not?"

"You don't kill somebody by holding his head on a piece of concrete while a bridge comes down on it." He frowned and looked down at the table, as though blocking the picture from his imagination.

"Then how insane do you have to be to climb up there and do it yourself?"

"People can be that crazy, Josie. People can be that desperate."

Perhaps they can. But I could not believe anyone would be capable of either act. So I stopped trying, and said, "Who's Grizz?"

Mel breathed twice—I counted them—before answering. "You don't need to know."

"Yes, I do. You said you'd tell me. So tell me."

"We think he's a dealer."

"Drugs."

Mel nodded. "We just know his name. Gabe and I. We knew his name."

"You guys aren't even on the drug squad. How do you know about him?"

Mel looked back toward the bar and the pool tables, where everybody had resumed their games and conversations. "They found a body a month or so ago, in an alley off Barton Street. Gabe and I, we were called in on it. It looked like a hit, an execution." Mel raised his right hand, the index finger extended, and touched his head just above his ear. "One shot, here." He brought his hands together and stared out the window as he spoke. "We asked around, the usual people on the street, and they were scared. These guys, they're usually pretty tough, but this time they weren't acting that way for a change. Somebody told us a guy named Grizz did it. That's all we had, his supposed name, his street name. Plus that he's a dealer, and he scares the hell out of a lot of people who don't scare easily. Gabe was doing some stuff on his own, checking out the guy in the alley, looking for some connection we could use. I told you I can't do undercover anymore, but Gabe did. He made some contacts on the street, working on his own."

"So why was this creep at my door this morning asking about

Grizz? If this Grizz scares people so much, why is this guy looking for him?"

"What did he look like, the man asking for Grizz?"

"Asking? He was *demanding*. He was something else too."

"Desperate?" Mel said.

That wasn't the word I was looking for. I pictured him again,
unwashed, bearded, dressed like a street bum, pushing against
the door, more frantic than intimidating, more pleading than
threatening. I recalled his face, and how he didn't get angry when
I refused to let him in or when I told him I didn't know anybody
named Grizz. Did he know Gabe? Did Gabe call himself Grizz?
Boy, that hardly made any sense, but . . .

"Hey." It was Mel.

"What?"

"I asked you twice."

"Asked me what?"

"How old this guy was, the one looking for Grizz. Where were
you just now?"

"Thinking."

Mel's eyes softened and he lowered his voice. "About Gabe?"

I nodded. I was always thinking about Gabe.

Mel sat back. "We can talk about this some other time, okay?"
He looked around and leaned toward me again.

"Sure." Now I couldn't stop thinking about Gabe, and about
something Mel had just said. "This guy, Grizz."

"What about him?"

"Where was he shot?"

"Where was who shot?"

"The guy you think was killed by Grizz."

"I told you. In an alley."

"Not there. Where did the bullet go?"

Mel looked at me as though I had just asked what brand of
underwear he wore, before raising his finger and touching his
temple again. "Like I said. Here. Why?"

"That's the same place Gabe was shot, isn't it?"

"Well, sure, but—"

"That's what you said. Gabe was shot once the same way, wasn't he?"

"Josie, what the hell are you getting at?"

I didn't know. That's what I told Mel. I didn't know. I only knew, and I was more certain of this than ever, that my husband had not killed himself, that he had been executed while kneeling naked on a blanket, waiting for me to arrive and love him.

I finished the coffee, told Mel to take care of himself, and asked him to wait until I left. I didn't want anybody at Tuffy's to see me leave with a man. I especially didn't want them to see me leave with a cop.

14.

I had avoided reading newspapers since Gabe's death, but over the next three days I scanned them for news about Wayne Weaver Honeysett. The first day's coverage reported that a man's body had been found beneath the lift bridge and police were investigating it as either a suicide or homicide. What was the other option? Natural causes? The victim's identity would not be released until his next of kin had been notified, but he was believed to have been a resident of the beach strip.

The following day, the newspaper carried a much smaller story, saying only that the police were investigating the possibility of foul play in the death of the man found beneath the lift bridge on the beach strip. "Foul play"? It sounded like something an announcer might say when covering a baseball game on television. Crushing a man's head to the thickness of a sheet of paper was well beyond "foul," no matter how it happened.

That evening, it rained in the manner that told me summer was on its way back home to Florida. It wasn't the soft, warm rain of an August afternoon, but the hard, cold rain of a September night, arriving early and unwelcomed.

The rain and cool weather made me feel desperate enough to call Tina. Her husband, Andrew, answered. Most men named Andrew are called, at some point in their lives, Andy or perhaps Drew. Andrew is always called Andrew, except, I assume, when he is called Dr. Golden.

Andrew informed me that Tina was either shopping or visiting the anthropology museum, and he said it with a total absence of irony in his voice. These two activities, after all, bookended the values of Tina's life: either filling her head with things to talk about at bridge parties or filling her closet with Prada to wear to the bridge parties.

Andrew told me he was very sorry to hear about Gabe, whose company he said he had always liked, which struck me as an unnecessary and unusual thing to say, then promised to inform Tina of my call "the minute she returns." Dr. Andrew Golden, I suspected, had the bedside manner of a kitchen appliance.

Minutes after I hung up the telephone, the damn thing rang again, and I assumed that Appliance Andy had contacted Tina on her mobile phone and she was calling me back. On a silly impulse I picked up the telephone and said, "So what'd you buy me?"

Instead of hearing Tina's giggle, followed by a shopping list, I heard a male voice with a distinctive leer in it saying, "What would you like?" I know a leer is a facial expression and you're not supposed to be able to hear one, but the leer was definitely there.

Naturally I asked who it was.

"Who would you like it to be?" the voice asked.

Damn. Get rid of one pervert and another takes his place.

I hung up the telephone. It didn't ring again. Not even from Tina.

The following day, a story in the newspaper confirmed that the man whose body had been found beneath the lift bridge had been Wayne Weaver Honeysett, a former jeweller and prominent businessman who had suffered from depression since the collapse of his once-thriving business and the death of his wife. His two daughters were arriving from out of town to attend his funeral service. Police, the report said, were still trying to determine how he had died, which I found either chilling or amusing, depending on my mood and the time of day.

Tina called at noon, apologizing for not getting back to me sooner and asking what I wanted. I told her I wanted to know how she was doing. She said she was well. I said, "Good," and hung up. When the telephone rang less than a minute later, I assumed it was either Tina or Pervert Number Two. Talking to either was equally uninteresting to me, so I let it ring.

Later, Mel called a couple of times, "checking in," he explained. Harold Hayashida called as well, to ask if I had seen the newspaper reports and if I could recall anything else about the night that Honeysett, if that's who it was, spoke to me from beneath the bridge like the troll my father had teased me about when I was a child. I answered "Yes" and "No," in that order, then asked if the police still believed it had been suicide.

"That's the general consensus," Hayashida replied.

"Is that the same as a verdict?" I asked.

"The file's staying open."

"So you think there's a possibility that he might have been murdered."

Hayashida said something that grew first more sinister as time went on, and eventually more perceptive. "The question," the detective said, "is how."

The next morning, the newspaper carried Honeysett's death notice:

HONEYSETT, Wayne Weaver—Beloved father of Wendy of Calgary and Joyce of Halifax, and grandfather of Jacques, Michael, Lowell, and Christine. Predeceased by his wife, Jacqueline, who was the world to him. Mr. Honeysett was the founder and proprietor of Honeysett's Credit Jewellers for many years, and the family is grateful to all of his former customers and associates who have expressed their sadness at his sudden passing. Visitation at

> *McRae's Funeral Home, Wednesday from 2 to 4 p.m.*
> *Cremation to follow. In lieu of flowers, the family*
> *requests that you make a donation to your local*
> *mental health clinic.*

The next day was Wednesday. I decided to attend. I was, after all, perhaps the last person to whom Honeysett had spoken. And he had known me. Maybe going to his funeral would make up for not having one for Gabe. Or maybe I just needed a reason to wear a dress again.

IF FUNERAL HOMES HAVE NO RIGHT to look pleasant and inviting, McRae's was doing it correctly. Its original red brick exterior had acquired a patina of black soot, and the building had been designed to look like something between a small prison and a large animal shelter. Its front door opened directly from Barton Street with neither room nor intention for landscaping to soften the impact of its facade. Stepping inside from the late-morning sunlight, I wasn't surprised to encounter darkness. But when my eyes adjusted to the dim interior, I was amazed to encounter a familiar face. It was Harold Hayashida, who was more shocked to see me than I was to see him.

"I was unaware that you knew the deceased so well," he said, wearing that half-smile people display in a funeral home.

"And I didn't know police officers attended the funerals of suicide victims," I said.

We were in an alcove with plaster walls the colour and texture of oatmeal, and I looked down the corridor to see a small sign reading HONEYSETT above an open doorway. I turned back to Hayashida, who was scribbling something in his notebook, just as a middle-aged couple entered and stood blinking and looking around, waiting for their sight to be restored, as I had.

If Wayne Honeysett had been a groper, he had made friends in spite of his perversion. Or maybe they enjoyed it, because the room was crowded with sombre people speaking in low isn't-it-awful tones, and most were women. I saw this while standing at the entrance, waiting for two blue-haired women in dark textured suits to finish speaking to two younger women, whom I assumed were Honeysett's daughters, Wendy and Joyce.

When the first younger woman greeted me, I offered my hand and looked into attractive grey eyes set in a round face framed in thick golden hair. I had nothing to say, except, "I'm so sorry."

"How did you know my father?" the woman said.

"We were neighbours," was the best I could answer. "On the beach strip."

She smiled, nodded, and dropped her eyes, which would have been a cue for me to step forward and greet her sister, who was taller and heavier, with short dark hair, except that the first sister still gripped my right hand. When I tried pulling away, she tightened her grip, looked at her sister, and said, "Joyce." Joyce smiled at me, then she too dropped her eyes to my hand.

They were looking at the ring I had decided to wear, the ring Gabe had given me a few weeks earlier, the black opal that Tina had commented on. I managed to pull my hand away from Wendy's grip and fold it within my other hand. "Where did you get that ring?" Joyce asked.

"It was a gift," I said. "From my husband. Why do you ask?"

"Because," Wendy said, "it belonged to our mother."

"That's impossible," I said, and walked to a corner chair some distance from the door. I'm not good at improvising dialogue. I was remembering what Gabe had told me about the ring. *I got it from a jeweller*, he said. And it hadn't been stolen, he promised. *That ring cost thousands*, Tina said.

A carved wooden box sat at the front of the room among several long-stemmed roses. The box, I assumed, contained

Wayne Honeysett's ashes. Was everybody cremated these days? Were we that short of land that nobody was buried anymore? Flanking the flowers were two large sheets of plywood covered with snapshots and advertisements for Honeysett's Credit Jewellers. Behind the display a door led down the corridor to the left. Small knots of people moved past the photographs, bending to examine them closely, dredging up memories. I waited for the flow to ebb, then rose from the chair and walked across the room to the display, planning to check out a couple of pictures, put a face to the man who had died without a head, then leave through the door.

How did we remember people before photographs? And what will they be doing at funerals fifty years from now—watching 3-D videos of Uncle Farley riding his tricycle or cutting a birthday cake? I didn't know, but with cremation becoming as popular among old folk as sweatpants and athletic shoes, we need those pictures to remind us of who we are mourning, and why.

Wayne Honeysett may not have been a large man, but he had been something of a cutie. He also looked familiar, and I realized I had probably seen him on the boardwalk or somewhere on the beach. He had a warm smile, crinkly eyes, and, I noted in the family photographs, an attractive wife who wore her hair shoulder-length, as I did. They looked like a close family, the girls as small children and in their teenage years, smiling and laughing in a manner that said they truly loved being in the company of their parents. I mentally slapped down the cynic in me, who suggested that no one would display photographs of the family in any other mood but happy at a time like this.

I wondered, standing there admiring the father, mother, and two attractive daughters whose ripening with time had been recorded by the camera, if our lives traced an arc of happiness, if at the end of our allotted time on earth we could look back and recognize the summit, the day and the place where we had achieved the highest level of joy we would experience, and place our finger on it, touch it, and say, "I was never happier in my life than I was on that day."

I was actually reaching out to touch a snapshot of the Honeysetts, taken somewhere palm trees grow, when I felt a hand at my elbow and heard Hayashida speak in the special voice police officers use when they are being polite but would rather not. "Mrs. Marshall," he said when I turned to look at him, "do you suppose we could step into the hall for a moment?"

He moved aside and indicated the open door leading to the corridor, where the two sisters were standing, their arms folded across their chests, and their expressions no longer reflecting the pleased-you-could-come look they had applied to greet mourners. He herded us deeper into the funeral home, past the coat racks and into a small office area with one desk and two chairs. "May I see that ring?" Hayashida said, closing the door behind us.

I removed the ring and handed it to him. He took a small penlight from his pocket and shone it onto the inside of the ring, near the front where the stone was mounted. "Describe your father's mark, please," he said. He was not speaking to me.

Both sisters began to speak, but it was Wendy who raised her voice to drown out her sister. "It's a W over an H," she said. "The sides of the H, the upright parts, spread into the W above it. My father put that inside every ring he made."

I remembered seeing the tiny mark and thinking nothing of it. It was just as she said—a trademark, a maker's mark, whatever they call them.

Hayashida, squinting to see the mark, nodded and looked at me, his eyebrows raised.

"Okay, so your father made it," I said. "That doesn't mean it's stolen."

"Nobody said it was." This from Joyce, the bigger and now angrier sister. "Funny you should suggest it was stolen, isn't it?"

Hayashida held his hand up to silence her. "Where did you get it?" he asked.

"It was a gift from my husband," I said. "From Gabe."

Joyce hissed, "Bullshit!" and Hayashida waved his hand in her direction again.

"These ladies, Mr. Honeysett's daughters, say that the last time they saw this ring it was on their mother's finger."

"Right here," Wendy said. "In this funeral home. It was on my mother's hand while she lay in her coffin."

"I don't know what the hell they're talking about," I said to Hayashida. "So Honeysett made the ring. So what? Maybe he made more than one—"

"He did not!" Joyce spat at me.

"We have a picture of it," Wendy said. She was calmer now, and she rested a hand on her sister's arm, as though to restrain her. "My father had all of our jewellery appraised and insured. The photograph with the appraisal shows the markings on the black opal. Every opal is unique. The markings will match, for sure."

Hayashida looked at her. "How much was the ring appraised for?"

Joyce took a deep breath, as though she wanted to reply with all the power available in her impressive chest. And she did. "Six thousand dollars."

"Was Gabe in the habit of buying you gifts that expensive?" Hayashida asked.

I had been eyeing a particularly ugly wooden chair set against the wall, thinking that a chair so dark and elaborately carved could only have been made for a funeral home. I walked over to it and sat down. "Gabe was not in the habit of giving me gifts that expensive," I said. "Except for my wedding ring, that's the only jewellery he ever bought me."

"Did he say where he bought it?"

"No."

"Or how much he paid for it?"

"No."

"Was it a special occasion when he gave it to you?"

"No."

I would have answered Hayashida the same way if he had asked if the earth revolved around the sun. The truth is, I wasn't hearing him. I was hearing the voice calling to me from the shadows beneath the bridge, the voice that I knew had belonged to Wayne Weaver Honeysett. *I know what happened*, the voice had said. *Listen to me. I know what happened.*

Hayashida was speaking to the sisters, saying he would be dropping by after the service to retrieve the appraisal photo. The sisters left, reluctantly I sensed, for I was busy counting my fingers, and Hayashida closed the door behind them. "I don't suppose you have a sales receipt for that ring," he said. He had settled a corner of his butt on the desk.

"No," I said. "I never saw one." I looked up at Hayashida. "Are those women suggesting that Gabe took the damn ring off their mother's corpse?"

"Nothing like that at all. But somebody did."

"Her husband. Mrs. Honeysett's husband."

He nodded. "Probably. Before the coffin lid was closed. That's not unusual."

"So maybe, when he ran into money problems, he could have sold the ring to Gabe, right?"

"Sure. That makes a lot of sense. Except."

"Except what?"

"Did Walter Freeman ask you if Gabe had made any expensive purchases lately, or acted as though he had come into a large sum of money?"

"You know he did."

"And what did you say?"

"I said no. You probably know that too."

Hayashida nodded, a little sadly, I thought. "Do you remember when Gabe gave you that ring?" He withdrew his notepad from an inside jacket pocket as he spoke.

"Two, three weeks ago. Maybe a month."

"Why didn't you tell Walter about it?"

"Because Walter's a jerk. And I was upset, and I wanted to hold on to everything about Gabe that mattered to me. How's that?"

Hayashida nodded again, writing in his notepad.

I stood up. I wanted to leave as quickly as possible. "That man in there," and I raised my arm, pointing back into the room where Wayne Honeysett's ashes were, "he's the guy who talked to me. I know it. He told me that he knew what happened. He meant what happened to Gabe, I know that too. And now there's a connection between him and Gabe, isn't there?"

Hayashida finished making his notes, snapped the pad shut, put it back in his jacket pocket, and slipped off the desk. He opened the door and gestured for me to leave. "Just between you and me," he said as I passed, "I think Walter's a jerk too."

15.

Driving home from Wayne Honeysett's funeral service, without the ring Gabe had given me, I thought about cormorants and decided to start acting like one, which had nothing to do with swimming after fish and everything to do with taking charge of my life. At home I made a pot of tea, dumped a gurgle of brandy into it for flavour, and sat at my table, making a list.

On Saturday mornings, my father always made a list of things to do. The list would include all the chores he planned to finish by Sunday night. I do not know what was on the list or whether he did everything he promised to do. I only know that, while my father was not the brightest or the most successful man I ever knew, he was the most satisfied, and satisfaction sounded very appealing right now.

Here is the list I wrote:

Gabe is dead, and he did not kill himself.
Gabe was shot with his own gun, and the paraffin test showed whatever it is that says he fired a gun.
Gabe would never give his gun to somebody else.
Honeysett was a pervert.
Honeysett knew or saw what happened (with Gabe?).
Honeysett called to me from under the bridge.
Honeysett is dead, and he did not kill himself.
Gabe gave me the ring Honeysett made for his wife.

Walter Freeman thinks Gabe was involved in something crooked.
Walter Freeman is a creep.
Gabe was investigating a drug dealer named Grizz. Why can't
they find a guy named Grizz?
Some frantic guy was here looking for Grizz—why?
I have a part-time job and no husband.
Mel Holiday has the bluest eyes I have ever seen.

I added the last one because who wants to make a list with thirteen items? Then I used a magnet shaped like a daisy to fasten my list to the refrigerator door, where I could see it and remind myself about what I knew and what I needed to know, about where I was right and where I was wrong. I was wrong too often.

I sat reading the list over and over, and when I finished my tea and brandy I poured another drink, but this time I left out the tea. Which was when Dewey Maas called.

"Would you like to talk?" Dewey said. "I'd love to see you. Just for a few minutes. I'm not far away. Down by the lift bridge."

"What are you doing down there?"

"I heard about the man they found here the other night. It's not in the papers, but there are rumours that he put his head under the bridge when it came down. Can you imagine that?"

I told Dewey I would meet him, but not on or near that damned bridge. If he came to the gate behind our house, we could sit in the garden and have tea.

"THIS IS SO PRETTY."

Dewey and I were seated at the small, round metal table in the middle of the garden. He was wearing a golf shirt, a pair of chinos, and loafers with no socks. Dewey never wore socks.

If you wanted a specimen of a middle-aged man worth considering for a life partner or a weekend fling, Dewey would make the cut. He's tall, blond and muscular. His nose is hooked and his teeth are crooked, but his eyes crinkle when he smiles, which is often, and he has the kind of gentle disposition you get when you spend more time around dogs than around people.

"I'm a little confused," I said, pouring iced tea for both of us.

"About what?"

"About why you're here. It's been how long? Three, four years?"

"Nearly five." He sipped his tea, watching me over the rim of the glass. "Four years, eight months. Since we talked, since I saw you last."

"You're kidding me. Not that it's been that long, but that you remember so accurately."

"Josie." His hand reached across the table and rested on mine. "You know I'm a little, uh, confused about things, um . . ."

"Dewey—"

He pulled his hand away. "Do you know why I never made a serious pass at you?" He frowned and looked away. "I didn't, did I? Did I?"

I assured him that he hadn't, that he had been a perfect gentleman in my presence, warm and funny and sweet.

"The reason I didn't," he said, "was because, if I had and if you had turned me down or been insulted, we wouldn't, we *couldn't* be friends. Not the same way. And I loved you as a friend. I really did. But I also wanted to love you in other ways."

"Dewey—"

"But women . . ." He leaned back in his chair, frowned, and shook his head. "Women are so turned off when a man is less than totally masculine, they call it." He leaned forward again, speaking faster. "I mean, some men, I knew one guy especially, they get really turned on about the idea of having a relationship with a bisexual woman, thinking, I guess—"

"Dewey—"

"—they can fulfill some threesome fantasy about them and

two women together and there's no threat to them, the man, if the women start getting it on because—"

"*Dewey!*" A little sharper this time.

It worked. "What?"

"I don't care about fantasies, and I don't care who or what you sleep with, and I'm not even sure I understand deep friendships between men and women that don't have a sexual connection. But that's okay, to hell with it, let Dr. Phil or somebody else work that one out. I just want to know why, after four years and whatever—"

"Eight months." He smiled, embarrassed.

"Why, after all that time, you suddenly call me. I mean, after you called to say how sorry you were to hear about Gabe."

He seemed to consider that for a moment. Then, taking a deep breath, he said, "I always wanted to call you. Just to talk with you. But calling a married woman, especially one married to a police officer, a detective? It was just too . . . too risky, I guess. I was happy for you, Josie, really. I just haven't been so happy myself since you left the shop and got married."

I believed him. Dewey was that sweet. Who wouldn't believe him? "So," I said. "Who's minding the chihuahuas?"

"The dogs? It's Wednesday. I'm closed Wednesdays now. Give myself some time off." He looked around the garden. "This is so pleasant. I've never seen it from this angle before."

"This angle?"

"Well, I've seen it from, you know . . ." He was blushing. "The boardwalk back there. The beach, usually."

"You've been here?" I said. "Looking into my garden?"

"Only from the beach. A lot of people walk on the beach, Josie. It's a public beach, and sometimes I thought we might bump into one another, just to talk. I mean, I thought if we met here we could talk."

I was working this over in my mind when he added, "I saw

your husband. I saw Gabe a couple of times, him out in the garden here. I don't know where you were. I introduced myself once, and we kind of chatted about things—"

"You introduced yourself to my husband?" I said. "Did you explain how you knew me?"

"I said we'd been friends, Josie. That's all. I said we were friends, and Gabe wanted to know how we met, and I explained how I used to come into the veterinarian's now and then to help with the dogs."

"Gabe never told me he spoke to you."

"He seemed like a nice fellow. Really nice. He came over to the gate to talk to me. I was never in the garden, not like now. I told him I thought he was a lucky man to be married to you. That's what I said to him. 'You're a lucky man.'"

"And what did Gabe say?"

"He said he knew. Every day he knew just how lucky he was to be your husband." Dewey thought for a minute, then added, "I had a feeling he was preoccupied with something. I mean, he had been sitting right here, at this table, writing in a little notebook, and I think I interrupted him. He seemed to be doing more thinking than writing, so I didn't stay long."

"When was that?"

"The last time I saw him. He said you were out. He thought you were out shopping. That's the last time I was here, which was a week ago last Monday."

I sat back in my chair. "The day before he died."

"That's right." Dewey nodded. "That's why I wanted to talk to you. I mean, that's really weird, isn't it?"

I told Dewey I had errands to run, places to go, and gathered up the empty glasses. We shook hands, and I told him it was all right to call me again sometime, maybe in another week or so.

I didn't have places to go. I just had one place to go, and I should have gone there much earlier.

CENTRAL POLICE STATION HAS NO PARKING SPACE for visitors. I drove through the lot, passing spaces marked for judges, lawyers, cruisers, detectives, emergency vehicles, and maintenance workers. No one, I suppose, is expected to visit Central unless they're either official or arrested. I parked two blocks away and walked back, through the late-summer afternoon. It seemed everything had slowed to a crawl, including law enforcement investigations.

The uniformed cop behind the desk asked who I wanted to see. I told him I wanted to see Sergeant Hayashida. If he wasn't available, I would see Sergeant Mel Holiday. If he wasn't in, I'd settle for Walter Freeman, the asshole. I didn't say "the asshole" aloud, but I was thinking it, just to keep me in the mood.

The cop stayed cool, said he would call Hayashida, and asked me to sign in please.

THE FIRST THING I LEARNED ABOUT COPS after I married Gabe was that they are lousy housekeepers. Even the women cops I've encountered work among stacked files, dirty coffee cups, scribbled sticky notes, and general chaos. How can they find bad guys when they can't find a sharp pencil? Hayashida was no different, but he dressed better than other detectives—button-down shirt, knit tie, summer-weight jacket, pressed trousers, tasselled loafers. Not a *GQ* magazine cover, maybe, but he was the most fashionable thing in his work cubicle, except for me in my pink ruffled blouse and black pencil skirt, plus the alligator pumps I bought at Saks in New York on a holiday with Gabe. If you're going into a den of lions, it helps to look like a lioness.

"What's up?" Hayashida said when I'd settled into the only other chair in his cubicle.

I took my time crossing my legs, tugging my skirt over my knee, folding my hands primly, and taking a deep breath. "I want to see the report on my husband's death," I said. "The one that says he killed himself."

Hayashida seemed faintly amused. "Why?"

"Because I'm his wife," I said. "His widow, actually. And don't give me that stuff about it being confidential. It's a public document, and if I have to get a lawyer to demand a copy, I'll get a lawyer."

"I can't let you keep a copy."

"I don't want a copy to take with me. I just want to see it. Let me read it and I'll hand it right back to you." I smiled and tilted my head. "Okay?"

"What do you think you'll learn from it?"

"I have no fucking idea." I really did say "fucking." It was part of my attitude.

Hayashida handled it perfectly. "Well, in that case," he said, and swivelled to face the computer terminal on his desk, which he turned at an angle to prevent me from seeing the screen. With a two-fingered typing style, he entered whatever he needed to find the file on Gabe and slapped a few more keys. From the corridor beyond his cubicle, I heard the soft whir of a printer. Hayashida rose and left the cubicle, dropping three sheets of paper in my lap when he returned. "No pictures, okay?" he said. "If you want pictures, you'll need that lawyer."

"I don't want pictures," I said.

Hayashida sat at his desk and began scribbling something on a notepad. It might have been his grocery list. I didn't care.

The top sheet was headed "Non-Accidental Death Report" and listed everything I already knew—Gabe's name, address, birth date, all of that, plus the description of his body on the blanket, names of witnesses, with reference to the files containing their statements, and next of kin, which was me. Gabe's gun was identified as a standard-issue Glock G22 model, serial number HPD7836. Three Determination of Death choices were provided:

Homicide, Suicide, and Undetermined. Someone had checked the box next to Suicide. The form was signed by Walter Freeman, Chief Investigating Detective, and Melville Holiday, Assisting Investigator.

I turned to the second sheet, headed "Autopsy Report," which made me sit up straight, anticipating what I was about to read. It was easier than I expected.

The deceased, I read, had been a man in his early forties, 183 centimetres tall, 81.7 kilograms in weight, and in apparent good health. It listed his scars, eye colour, dental work, everything that I knew far better from the living Gabe than any coroner could expect to learn from the dead one.

Near the bottom of the sheet was a diagram of a body, one of those simplified genderless drawings with no hair and no genitals. A line had been drawn into the head, at a slight downward angle. Beneath the drawing, I read:

> *Projectile entered 2 centimetres above the right temporal line, 6.5 centimetres posterior to the aural canal, proceeding in a posterior angle of approximately 18 degrees from the lateral axis and 40 degrees from the vertical axis, penetrating the temporal lobe, medulla oblongata, lodging in the left temporal lobe as indicated. Powder burns noted, indicating close proximity to weapon muzzle. Brain matter emerging from entry wound weighed at 16.8 grams. Projectile is in good condition, confirmed as standard-issue Remington model 9-GM. Death attributed to massive destruction of brain, severe swelling resulting.*

I turned the sheet over to find more bureaucratic ways of saying someone's brains had been blown out. The coroner had been provided with a choice of four boxes beneath Determination of

Death—Accidental, Homicide, Suicide, and Unknown. He had checked Unknown. Now I had a buddy who disagreed with Walter Freeman. But then, most people did.

The third sheet was headed "Forensics Report," beneath an impressive stamp of the Attorney General's office. This one included four photographs embedded in the report, but they were of bullets not bodies. One bullet was pristine and pointed and, let's be honest here, penis-like. The other was crumpled at the front. Two other photographs showed dark angled lines on metal, as seen through a microscope, rifling marks they were called, made from the grooves inside guns to make the bullets spin when they leave the barrel, helping the little devils fly more directly to their destination in flesh and bone. God, I hate guns. I hate them so much I wish I didn't know so much about them.

Both bullets—"projectiles" in the language of the forensics lab—were identified as having been fired from Gabe's gun, the ugly-named Glock G22, serial number HPD7836. Somebody named Amanda at the forensics lab had confirmed that projectile A, provided by Sergeants Holiday and Hayashida, was from the same gun as projectile B, retrieved from the body as described in Non-Accidental Death Report HP-04-289, the one I held in my hand, the one describing Gabe's death. The lab also tested paraffin applied to Gabe's right hand by the coroner and, using GSR analysis by energy dispersive X-ray spectrometry, found particles containing lead, antimony, and barium.

"What's GSR?" I asked Hayashida.

"Gunshot residue. Stuff that's in the powder and leaks out when you fire a gun."

He probably knew what "energy dispersive X-ray spectrometry" was as well. I didn't care. The report said the bullet came from Gabe's gun and that Gabe had fired it. I kept staring at the words, looking for the line that said this was all crap, all a game. I didn't find it.

I looked up to see Hayashida watching me. "So?" he said, and reached to take the sheets of paper from me.

"Why does the coroner call the circumstances of Gabe's death unknown instead of suicide, like Walter Freeman says it is?" I asked.

Hayashida began crumpling the sheets and dumping them into his wastebasket, one by one. "Don't read too much into it. Walter needs evidence of criminal action. The coroner just needs to look for it, and when he doesn't find something obvious, he writes that it's unknown to him. If Walter finds evidence of homicide, he presents it to the coroner, who will confirm that it does not conflict with his findings." He rubbed his hands together, as though removing any evidence that he had ever handled the reports. "What else can I do for you?"

"Where's Mel Holiday?"

Hayashida stood and looked over the top of his cubicle. "Anybody seen Holiday?" he called. A disembodied male voice announced that he was out, gone for the day. Hayashida tilted his head at me. "Anything else I can do?"

"How about helping me prove that Gabe didn't shoot himself?" I said.

"Not my case anymore," Hayashida said, sitting down. He turned back to his computer, effectively dismissing me. "It's Walter Freeman's now. And Walter's not talking to anybody about it."

I STOPPED ON THE WAY HOME TO VISIT MOTHER. I was feeling more alone than ever, and secretly wished that I had been more sociable with our neighbours, or that Tina was still here haranguing me, whichever was easiest.

Marci, the girl on duty on Mother's floor, told me Mother was in her therapy session, so I asked if Helen Detwiler was available. I was feeling guilty about not doing my bookkeeping job, although I obviously needed the time to deal with Gabe's death. In truth, I was beginning to realize that I needed routine back in my life. I didn't know when I would be ready to return to work, but it would improve my sense of self-worth. It would also provide me with opportunities to visit Mother and talk with her, waiting for her response to my questions written with chalk in her lovely handwriting.

Helen greeted me by rising quickly from behind her desk and approaching me with outstretched arms. "You poor dear," she said, hugging me. "We've been so worried about you." She stood back, holding my arms. "Tell me you're all right. Tell me you're going to get over this somehow."

I assured her that I was handling it as well as I could, and asked about Mother.

"She's fine," Helen said, then added, "She's wonderful, actually. So emotionally strong." She glanced at her wristwatch. "Would you like me to bring her from therapy class?"

I told her no, just let her know I dropped by. "I'm hoping I can be back to work next week," I said. "Perhaps I could start Tuesday."

"Whenever you feel up to it," she replied. "Mind you, no one does the job as well as you. I wouldn't want you to think that we don't miss you. But I'll let the others know that we could see you here Tuesday. Perhaps you could let me know by the end of the week."

Her words were comforting, but I left feeling even more despondent and alone, which is a dangerous mood for me. I wanted to see Mother, but I didn't want to make a fuss about it. That was Mother's way. Don't make a fuss about things that concern you. Where Mother was concerned, I followed the rule diligently. At other times . . .

I stopped to buy groceries and a padlock for the garden shed, and arrived back on the beach strip just before four o'clock, wondering if I had enough energy to cook dinner and enough appetite to eat it.

Two men had been at my house while I was away. One was the mailman, who had brought me a notice from some police official informing me that the first of Gabe's pension cheques would be arriving soon, and I could expect to receive one each month for the next ten years. A quick calculation told me that the pension money plus my earnings from Trafalgar Towers would cover my expenses with a little extra for goodies, and that in ten years, when the payments would cease, I would be over fifty. Now I had two reasons to live it up over the next decade.

The other man had been in my garden shed, because the door that I knew had been tightly closed when I left barely an hour ago was now wide open. I walked out the back door and crossed the garden, unwrapping the new padlock and considering the best place to hide the keys. I had little intention of entering the shed in the future. I just wanted to ensure that the guy who went in while I was gone wouldn't be there again.

I was wondering just who this might be, since Wayne Honeysett was already dead, when I reached the open door and realized I was a little late in keeping somebody out. Because somebody was already there, glaring at me from inside the shed, holding an axe in his hand.

16.

I think I screamed. Not one of those screams that stop trains and break crystal, but the scream I might make if I saw a mouse run across the kitchen floor. I took a step backwards, unsure about what was more menacing—the axe, which Gabe had bought to break driftwood he collected on the beach for our fireplace, or the expression on Walter Freeman's face.

"What the hell are you doing here?" I asked. I kept walking backwards into the middle of the garden, where I knew people passing on the boardwalk behind the house would have an unobstructed view of me confronting a chief of detectives and potential axe murderer.

Walter slapped the face of the axe into his palm. "I wanted to ask you that down at Central," he said, in a voice that reminded me of wet gravel. "What the hell were you doing *there?*"

"It's a public building, Walter," I said. "This, on the other hand, is private property. That's a big difference, right? And why are you threatening me with an axe?"

Walter stared at me, wearing his Bad Cop face before looking at the axe and tossing it into a corner of the shed. "I wasn't threatening you," he said. "I was moving things, looking around. Threatening you? Me, threaten you with an axe?" He pointed a finger at me. I hate people who point fingers at me, but in this case I thought it was better than the alternative, which would have been the weapon inside Walter's jacket. "You really are nuts, aren't you?"

"Go to hell," I said. Then, "Better still, go back to Central and leave me alone."

"Why don't we just go inside and have a talk?" Walter said.

"Not bloody likely." Now that the axe was out of his hand, and assuming his finger wasn't loaded, I was getting my courage back. "You want to talk, we can talk here."

"Or down at Central. You seem to enjoy visiting there." He nodded in the direction of the war memorial. "My car's parked just down the beach. You want to come with me, or you want to ask me inside for a glass of water? Christ, it's hot in there."

WALTER SAT AT MY KITCHEN TABLE, looking around the room as though searching for something he might have left behind on a previous visit. I didn't want him there, but I knew he could find one reason or another for getting me into Central Police Station and, for all I knew, behind the bars of the lock-up cells if he really wanted to. You learn these things living with a cop. You learn what they can and can't get away with, and the higher you are in the pecking order, the more you get away with.

I dumped some ice from the refrigerator into a glass, filled it with water from the tap, plunked it in front of Walter, and stood back to watch him drink the whole damn thing. When he finished, he wiped the back of his hand across his mouth and examined the glass as though he wished it were full again. "Damn it's hot, ain't it?"

"You want to talk about the weather?" I asked. "Did you bring a warrant with you to talk about the weather?"

"No," Walter said, setting the glass on the table. "I want to talk about a really smart detective I knew who was married to a really stupid woman."

"Look, if you're upset because I insisted on looking at Gabe's investigation reports . . ." I began.

Walter twisted in his chair to look at me. It was one of those up and down looks that men give women when they're either undressing them in their mind or intimidating them with their power. I hoped it was the latter, in Walter's case. "Why did you lie to me?"

"About what?"

"About the ring you now say Gabe gave you."

"Why is it any of your business what Gabe gave me? I gave him gifts too. You want me to go upstairs and show you the cufflinks I gave him for Christmas? Or how about the plaid jockstrap I got him for his birthday last year?" This was true. I found it in a shop specializing in Scottish wear. A bright orange Buchanan plaid jockstrap. Gabe loved it.

"Did you buy the ring for yourself, maybe say Gabe bought it for you?"

"Why the hell would I say that?" Only later did I understand what Walter was getting at.

He ignored my question. "How do you explain that the man who gave the ring to you and the man who last had it in his possession are both now dead?"

I sat in the chair. I didn't want to argue with Walter, which would be a losing proposition for both of us, and I didn't want to talk about Gabe being dead either. "You forgot to mention that both of them supposedly committed suicide," I said.

"Supposedly?"

I shook my head and shrugged. I decided I would rather listen to Walter than talk to him.

"Any more gifts like that one that you and Gabe might have bought?"

"No." I began examining my fingers. I needed a manicure.

Walter seemed to think about that for a moment. Then, "If I find out you're not telling me the truth, I'll charge you with obstructing justice. I can always come back with a search warrant and tear the place apart, you know."

"Trust me, Walter," I said, still studying my fingers. "I don't want you here now, and if it kept you from ever coming back here again, with or without a warrant, I would swear the sky was orange, the world was flat, and that you have all the charm of George Clooney but you're better-looking."

Walter shook his head. "You don't seem to be the least bit interested in learning why I'm asking about Gabe or you having extra cash." He tipped the glass back and dumped most of the ice cubes into his mouth.

"You want to know why, Walter?" I said over the noise of him chewing the ice cubes. "Because the only reason you would ask is if you suspected Gabe of taking bribes or stealing evidence. Well, Gabe didn't do that. He would never do that. The idea is so ridiculous that I'm insulted you would even suggest it. You knew Gabe, and you know what he was like."

He sat chewing the ice cubes and, I assumed, turning my words over in his mind. "I liked Gabe," he said when he finished crunching the ice cubes with his teeth as though they were potato chips. "I don't like you. Never did. Gabe deserved a woman with more class than you've got."

"If this is an attempt to seduce me, it's not working," I said.

"See, that's what I mean. Try to have a conversation with you, talk about something important, and you make a joke about it. And you toss in sex, as well. That's the kind of woman you are. Gabe could've done better."

"Walter—" I began.

Walter interrupted. He had a way of interrupting that was impossible to ignore. "I know about you," he barked. "I did some investigating. Learned a hell of a lot about you. You could never keep a job for more than a year or so. Why is that?"

"Because I can't stand spending my days in the company of jerks. Which reminds me. Kindly get the hell out of my house now, or I'll call a cop and then I'll call a lawyer."

Walter smiled at that. He tilted his head back, dumped the remaining ice cube into his mouth, and chewed it like the others. When he finished, he stood up and ambled his way to the back door. "You should put that lock on your shed," he said over his shoulder. "Anybody can go in there."

"I know," I said. "Apparently it attracts perverts."

Walter paused halfway through the door into the garden and pointed his finger at me again. This time it appeared to be loaded. "I'm not finished with you," he said. "You keep poking your nose into things and getting in the way of our investigations, you'll hear from me again. And stay away from Mel Holiday."

I watched him walk through the garden, climb the stairs to the level of the laneway along the beach, and glance toward the caragana bushes where Gabe had died. Then he ambled off in the direction of the war memorial.

I closed the door and sat at the kitchen table, remembering, regretting, and trying to forgive.

BEFORE I MET GABE, I had a fling with a psychiatrist. I had gone to see him because I was feeling depressed over the kind of men I had been dating. When the psychiatrist convinced me after a couple of sessions that I was no crazier than the average divorcee, which did not make me feel as good as he intended, he suggested we have coffee sometime, since I was no longer his patient. He was a nice fellow, slightly British, with both the accent and the tweeds, and divorced like me. We had a few dinners and a couple of dirty weekends. We might still be dating if I hadn't acquired the sensation that he was always practising psychiatry, even when he was on top of me in a waterbed. It destroyed my fantasy life. No matter what I was thinking at the time, I always suspected that he either *knew* what I was thinking or was trying to *learn* what I was thinking. Either way, he would be evaluating me, and you can understand what that would do to my visions of sandy lagoons in the Caribbean—or whips and midgets, for that matter.

"Do you know what your trouble is?" he said during our last session in bed. We had been talking about my feelings and his sex drive, and vice versa. "Your trouble is that you're a very moral woman trying to live an immoral life."

Which may be the most profound thing any man has ever said to me. If I meet him again, I'll tell him that. But I probably won't thank him.

Sitting alone in the kitchen after Walter Freeman left, I thought about his words and I thought about what I had most recently done to prove they were true.

I LOVE TO DANCE. Waltz, jive, samba, quickstep, you name it and I'm out there shaking my hips with two right feet. I can dance anywhere with anybody. I am especially good at dancing around my own guilt.

A year ago, the idea of cheating on Gabe would have been as unthinkable to me as following the cormorants into deep water and chasing fish. Or maybe I was just fooling myself.

Something about Gabe had begun to bother me. He was quiet, he was wise, and he was thoughtful when he wasn't aloof. He was physically strong and comfortably predictable, and one day it began to dawn on me: he was my father. Not literally, of course, and not even emotionally. In all the characteristics that made him a man, however, he was my father or my father's son. Whenever the idea entered my mind, I gave myself a mental slap across the face. I would be fine for a day or two, then I would go back to playing mind games. Did young girls who love their fathers grow into women who look for the same kind of man to be their lover? It made sense. The way I see it, the odds are so high against finding a guy who is loyal, gentle, strong, and doesn't look as though he was a model for a gargoyle, that you might as well go for the tried and true, the comfortable and familiar. For most of us, those of us lucky enough to have good parents, this was their father. Or more accurately, a surrogate, a clone, a substitute. I think a lot of women do that. I worried that I was one of them. Maybe I was just bored.

In April, Gabe had to travel to Montreal to appear at the trial of a major gangster. The guy had been arrested here, and Gabe had interrogated him before releasing him to the Montreal cops. Gabe was needed to give evidence about the gangster's dirty work in Quebec, which would take him away from home for almost a week. I wanted to go with him, but he refused, saying it was business and he would take me some other time for a vacation, but not when he was travelling on public money. I threw a tantrum, a stupid spitting and hissing fit, when he left.

I had planned to keep busy working and visiting Mother, plus reading and painting the kitchen, but the night after Gabe left, Mel showed up in a V-neck sweater, tight jeans, and deck shoes, which I thought was just about the sexiest thing I had seen since Elvis died. Do I have to paint a picture? If I did, it would be with a bottle of Teacher's whisky before and tears after. In bed, Mel talked about leaving policing, about taking me to a B & B he knew in New England, about buying a place on a lake up north, where we could live together and listen to the loons at night, he and I in bed, naked under a duvet. "What would we live on?" I asked, and he said there would be enough money, but I didn't think much of loons and I didn't want to live anywhere except on the beach strip, and I had no plans to leave Gabe. I had just wanted—what? Maybe to prove I could love a man who did not remind me of my father. Maybe to help me get over becoming forty-one years old.

I said never again, and never lasted about a month, until I decided I might as well be hanged for being a whore as for being an adulteress, and I met Mel at his apartment in the middle of the afternoon, and once more at a motel down the highway to Toronto. And that was it.

I handled it the way most people handle things they are ashamed of doing. It's not them who did it, and it wasn't me who went to bed with Mel. It was some crazy person with totally different values. Okay, it *was* me, but I had become mentally unbalanced on three different occasions and was not totally responsible for my actions. The first time, I was drunk and lonely and angry and frightened, which sounded like enough excuses. The second time I figured, what the hell, the worst had already happened. The third time was closure. Two naked bodies humping on a swaybacked bed, thinking, We'll always have Paris, except it wasn't Paris, it was a Motel 6.

There is a line between knowing and suspecting, and Gabe straddled that line in the days before he died. Things were different in ways that I cannot identify or describe. Maybe it was how Gabe seemed to be watching me whenever Mel was around, or the way I would hand the telephone to Gabe when Mel called, without saying anything beyond hello. Maybe I talk in my sleep. It was the unknowing, the wondering if Gabe knew, that I couldn't stand. I would be selfish again. I would confess to Gabe. That's why I wanted to reveal everything to him the night he died.

The thing I couldn't figure out was, how could Mel and Gabe work together like they did? I wondered about that until I read a magazine article titled "Why Women Will Never Run the Boys' Club." The subject was the failure of women to become top business executives, and I expected the usual claptrap on female hormones and nest-building instincts. Instead, it talked about playing team sports, which interests me about as much as Bulgarian politics, but I read enough to understand the point of it. Boys tend to play team sports more than girls, and they are more intense and aggressive. The article explained that playing intense team sports teaches boys to co-operate with other boys they dislike. "He may be a jerk," the guy who wrote the article said, "but if he's a great linebacker," whatever that is, "and I need him to cover my flat, I can work with him." His flat what? I didn't know, but I understood the point: men can find a way of working together on something even when they're competitive with each other on something else.

Gabe enjoyed working with Mel, at the beginning at least. Cops, Gabe believed, needed a special way of thinking and acting. You couldn't think first and act later, because you could get shot or run over while pondering things. And you couldn't act first and do the thinking later—that's how innocent people get shot by cops who mistake a pocket comb for a gun when it's in some-body's hand and the light is poor. Gabe said Mel had the ability to think and act simultaneously. "Like an athlete," Gabe said. "Like a pro athlete. The only thing he's gotta control is his temper. Flies off the handle too fast."

Gabe said those things in the first few months of working with Mel. Lately, he had seemed to avoid talking about Mel at all. Which made me think he knew.

Mel had told me Gabe never gave a hint of suspicion about our affair. They continued working as a team, covering drug deals and homicides, which frequently overlapped. Perhaps Gabe could not believe that his friend and partner would sleep with his wife. Perhaps Gabe was better at hiding his emotions than I knew. Perhaps I was imagining Gabe's suspicion as a result of my own guilt. Perhaps Mel was shielding me from the truth.

I THOUGHT ABOUT ALL THIS AND MORE, sitting at the kitchen table after Walter left. When I grew bored with my known thoughts, I took another look at the list on the refrigerator door and realized that, when Walter Freeman was chewing the ice cubes, he had a perfect view of my list of fourteen things I knew for sure. Walter didn't have to be very bright to figure out that the list represented my attempt to unravel the mystery about Gabe's death and the role of poor Wayne Honeysett in it. And he didn't need the eyes of an owl to discover that I considered him a creep, although this wouldn't qualify as earth-shattering news to him.

It was the last item on the list that I kept reading over and over. Mel was the only one who was beginning to agree that Gabe might not have killed himself, so he was the only one I could trust. I would talk to Mel as soon as I answered the pounding on my back door, which I opened without checking to see who it was.

17.

This time he was almost calm, which made him threatening. He wore the same tattered clothes and his hair was just as matted, but he didn't rage like the first time, and although his eyes were red-rimmed and rheumy, they did not bounce like Ping-Pong balls dropping down a flight of stairs. They were fixed on me. The voice may have been calmer, but the script was unchanged. "Where's Grizz?" he said. I tried to push the door closed, but he pushed back against me. "I gotta see Grizz," he said. "Where's he at?"

I screamed, hoping somebody on the street or the beach would hear, but he was already inside the room and pushing the door closed behind him. I thought of the butcher knives on the rack near the stove, but when I tried to picture myself grabbing one and turning to thrust it into his chest, the picture changed to me losing a wrestling match and finding the knife in his hands instead. I kept backing toward the kitchen anyway, hoping that I would block his view of the knives until I found both my voice and the cordless phone.

"Get out of my house!" I shouted at him. "The police were just here. They're coming back—"

"Tell me where Grizz is," he said.

"I don't know who the hell you're talking about! Just get out, *get out!*" My hand found the cordless telephone, but my fingers were shaking too much to dial. My feet were as reliable as ever, and I turned and ran down the hall to the front door. I unlocked and opened the door before he could reach me and stumbled blessedly into the sunshine. Traffic was busy on Beach Boulevard and on the highway bridges, and a family was strolling past on the other side of the road. Instead of flagging down any of them, I dialed 911 and screamed at the operator, who answered with a maddeningly calm voice. I told her a strange man had burst into my house and I wanted the police here, damn it, to throw his ass into jail.

She took my address and kept me on the line, and as I spoke to her I walked to the side of the house where I could see him on the boardwalk, heading toward Tuffy's. He looked confident and relaxed, and the sight of him made me both angry and brave, roughly in that order. "He's on the boardwalk," I said, "heading south." Walking into the garden and up to the boardwalk level, I kept him in my sight and gave her a complete description of him—about five foot ten, maybe 175 pounds, around thirty years old, unshaven, straight sandy-coloured hair, greasy denim shirt, equally greasy overalls cut into shorts, worn grey Adidas sneakers, no socks.

He was perhaps a hundred feet ahead of me, strolling among the usual summer traffic on the strip—the in-line skaters, the skateboarders, the joggers, the boppers, the old folks, and two people in motorized wheelchairs. "Do not approach him," the 911 operator advised me, just as I heard sirens out on Beach Boulevard, first one, then another.

I told her the police had arrived and I ran back through the garden to meet the cruiser as it pulled into the driveway. "He's on the boardwalk," I said to the cop as he emerged from the car, "going that way. Did you get the description?"

"We got it," the officer said, and pulled at the microphone fastened to his shoulder belt. "Check the boardwalk from the first cross street south of here," he said. "I'm coming down from here. Frank, you there?" I saw a third cruiser arrive, and the first cop began trotting through our garden to the boardwalk. I watched three more officers, two from the second car that had stopped at the first cross street, and the third at the next street down, hustle toward the shoreline, heads up, their hands on their weapons, models of law enforcement efficiency. Each street extended up to the boardwalk. All four officers were in communication with each other, and all had their guns ready. There was no way the man who so desperately needed Grizz would escape.

"COULDN'T FIND HIM." It was almost an hour later. The first officer to arrive was standing at my garden door, writing something in his notepad. .

I thought he was kidding me. "You're kidding me," I said.

"I never kid," he said.

"He was no more than a hundred feet down the beach. I gave you everything but a DNA sample. How the hell could you miss him?"

The cop's pencil froze, but one eyebrow didn't. It climbed up his forehead when he looked at me, and he made sure I got the message before he spoke. "You're Gabe Marshall's wife."

"Widow."

He nodded. "Heard about you."

"You heard what about me? What the hell does that mean?"

He resumed writing, then tore the sheet from his notepad and handed it to me. "You have another problem, you call us." He pointed at the sheet of paper. "That's my name, my badge, and the report number." He turned to leave.

"Tell me what you've heard about me, damn it!" I shouted.

Over his shoulder he told me to have a nice day.

"THEY'RE NOT BLOODHOUNDS, JOSIE."

We were parked under the highway bridges, near the canal and facing the bay. Traffic roared above us on the bridges at sixty, seventy miles an hour. It was after dinner. Autumn was being held back by the sun. The breeze was no longer off the lake. It had matured into a wind from the north, drier and cooler. A chill wind. A September wind.

Two men were pulling a boat from the water and onto a trailer. In the distance, steam blossomed white above the steel company. The cormorants were returning in silent squadrons. I sat with my hands in my lap, wanting to be wrapped up by someone, anyone.

I shook my head. "I could have found that guy walking backwards and wearing a blindfold."

"He might have ducked into one of the houses down the way."

"Wouldn't they check that?" I said. "Isn't that what you do, knock on doors and say, 'Excuse me, but is there a deranged man around here, aside from your husband, of course, or did one arrive recently asking to borrow a cup of sugar?' I had the feeling these guys spent their time discussing donuts and the Blue Jays."

"They'll be watching for him—"

"I really can't take this, Mel." My little girl voice arrived, unbidden. "I'm still missing Gabe, I'm trying to get over that poor Honeysett man, his daughters think Gabe was a thief, I come home to find Walter Freeman in my garden shed, I answer—"

"What was Walter doing there?"

"He wanted to know about Gabe, and about that ring. He was upset with me because I hadn't told him—"

"Josie, stay away from Walter."

"That's funny. He said the same thing about you."

"Josie—"

"Mel, if you don't tell me what the hell is going on—"

"I tried to—"

"Well, try harder. Walter Freeman's questioning me. He thinks I know more than I'm telling him, and I don't, but everybody else knows more than they're telling me, and I want to know what it is."

Mel took a while to ponder my words. I was doing the same thing—what the hell did I just say?

"I think we should get together."

"You want another night at some Open Arms Motel? Forget it."

Mel looked away. "I have to be able to trust you," he said.

"To do what?"

"To be quiet about things you shouldn't know about."

"Do they have anything to do with Gabe?"

This time he looked at me and nodded.

"You don't think Gabe killed himself either, do you?"

He shrugged. "It's difficult to counter. All the evidence, Josie, the forensic tests . . ."

"What tests? Tell me."

"His gun was used—"

"I know that."

"The paraffin tests on Gabe's hand—"

"Big deal."

"They prove he recently fired a weapon. The gun was in his hand and he pulled the trigger."

"You know all this?"

"Josie, I worked with the lab, I filed the reports, I work with the lab people all the time—"

"So why don't you agree with everybody else? Why are you and I the only ones who don't believe Gabe would kill himself?"

Mel leaned toward me. I could smell his aftershave. I knew that aroma. I had wanted to buy some for Gabe to wear, and in a rare minute of wisdom decided not to. "Because we knew him better than anyone else."

I closed my eyes. "We also know he had a motive, if discovering that your buddy at work has slept with your wife is enough motive for a guy to kill himself."

When I opened my eyes, Mel was staring at me. "There's something going on down at Central," Mel said. He had lowered his voice as though there were someone in the car, eavesdropping. "Gabe did an audit of our evidence locker last month. We rotate the duty so there's no way to hide what's going on. Gabe found we were short on some cocaine being held for a trial."

"Somebody stole drugs from a police evidence locker?"

"That's what was happening."

"And sold them?"

"Or used them." Mel sat back. "But yeah, probably sold them. For sure."

"Gabe reported it, right? He would report something like that."

Mel nodded. "To Walter."

"Okay." I shrugged. "But it doesn't concern me, and it doesn't prove that Gabe killed himself. Because he wouldn't. Damn it, he wouldn't, especially not when he knew I would find him."

Mel leaned toward me, and his hand gripped my wrist. "There are things you don't know, all right? I'm trusting you here. If you don't want to hear about them, fine." He released his grip on me and sat back again, raising his hands, showing his palms. "I'm sorry," he said. "I didn't mean to frighten you."

I rubbed my wrist where his hand had gripped it so tightly. "You've come this far. Tell me the whole story."

And he did.

The man found dead in an alleyway, shot behind the ear, had been facing drug charges, his trial scheduled for two weeks later. Drugs taken from him were in the locker that Gabe had checked and found a kilo short, and Gabe had been using him as a means of tracking some murders over recent years, small-time dealers shot to death, their bodies dumped in back alleys with nothing to connect them beyond the drugs they dealt. This particular dealer's name was Dougal Dalgetty, and he lived on the beach strip, over the upholstery shop down near the bikers' clubhouse.

"The crazy woman," I said, and Mel said, "What?" I shook

my head, too busy absorbing everything Mel was telling me to go into details. I could see the woman standing on the boardwalk glaring toward our house, madness in her eyes, and her mouth moving as though forming silent curses, before turning and walking away, head down. Long hair combed into a bird's nest. Weary dresses. Worn shoes. When I passed her on the boardwalk, she never appeared to notice me. Something about our house closed a switch in her brain. Or opened one. Just another casualty of a hard life, I thought. Just another mad soul.

Dalgetty, Mel explained, had been a connection, a link between Grizz and Pasquale Pilato, whom everybody, for a reason I've never understood, called Mike.

"Mike Pilato?" I said. This was serious stuff.

Everyone in the city—and maybe in the Western world—knew that no one except Pilato's mother ever called him Pasquale. He was always Mike Pilato, especially to the news reporters and the cops who identified him as the head of the most powerful organized crime family in the area. Mike Pilato claimed he was a small businessman running a hardware distribution company in the old North End of the city, in the neighbourhood where I grew up. Near the shadows of the blast furnaces. Pilato's neighbours said the police were pursuing a continuing vendetta against Mike, who lived in the same house he had been born in and who contributed thousands of dollars every year to the neighbourhood. He had purchased a couple of vacant lots and donated them to the city, then paid to have them neatly landscaped. The vacant lots became Pilato Park, with slides and swings for children and benches for pensioners. Was this a bad guy? Was this the kind of gangster who could have people disappear by doing little more than nodding his head? That's what the neighbours asked.

Mike Pilato was a people's hero, so it didn't matter to his neighbours if he was rough around the edges. The people loved him. There were rumours that Mike had beaten men to death with a baseball bat in his younger days. Heroes tend not to do these things, so it was easier for Pilato's neighbours not to believe the stories. They hadn't seen it happen, so they didn't have to accept it. This kind of thinking makes life easier for a lot of people.

Whenever Mike Pilato's picture appeared in the press, rarely in recent years, he wore oversized dark sunglasses and a battered hat pulled low on his head. Months would pass when Mike Pilato was unseen in town, leading some people to claim he no longer even lived in the area. He was in Florida, in Sicily, in prison, or in a grave somewhere. On other occasions, the media would catch him strolling in the company of men you would not want to meet anywhere except in heaven—an unlikely location for them—on the street in front of White Star Hardware Distributors, his business on Cathcart Street.

"This can't get out," Mel was saying.

"What can't get out?"

"What I just told you."

"About Mike Pilato?"

Mel looked angry. He leaned forward. "About the internal investigation."

I had been lost in the Mike Pilato legend and hadn't been listening. "Tell me again," I said, and Mel began, speaking each word as though he were counting to four. "Walter. Is. Being. Investigated. By internal affairs."

My throat felt like I had been eating cotton. "Walter signed Gabe's death report. He said it was suicide." I looked across at Mel, who was nodding his head slowly. "Walter wants me to believe that Gabe killed himself."

"He almost talked me into it," Mel said. "And we signed the lab report submission, Harold Hayashida and I."

"Walter was the first detective to arrive. When they found Gabe." Another nod.

"Walter doesn't want me to have anything to do with you."

"Because I'm co-operating with the investigation."

"Walter was in my garden shed. Where the pervert was. Looking around, he said."

"You told me that."

"What about the guy asking for Grizz?"

Mel closed his eyes and sat silently for a moment. "Walter is a senior officer."

"I know that."

"With a lot of influence." Mel looked away, then down at his watch and frowned. "They said they couldn't find him, this guy who showed up at your door? That's what they said?"

"You're saying they did."

"Figure it out for yourself. I have to go." He started his car.

"I'll walk back," I said, opening the car door. "I think better when I'm walking."

He drove away and I headed for the beach strip, trying to put everything together in my mind, especially the idea that Walter Freeman might have killed Gabe and made it look like a suicide because Gabe learned something that the internal affairs crew suspected. Kill a man and make it look like a suicide? That was something a guy like Walter Freeman could do. But was he capable of it? How damned corrupt could the police be?

I worked out all the pieces and tried putting them together. I couldn't. All the king's horses and all the king's men . . .

The only thing that could work, that might work, would be for Mel and I to keep working things out together. Perhaps I could find things that Mel didn't know. And Mel, I knew, would work with me because . . . well, because, damn it, we shared the same memories from the last few weeks, and his weren't weakened by guilt.

18.

What do men dream about? An endless supply of insatiable women? An endless supply of money and liquor to attract insatiable women?

Did my father have those dreams? Maybe, once. Maybe he fantasized about women or money or a cabin on a quiet lake somewhere, but those weren't his dreams. The difference between dreams and fantasies is that dreams attract us and fantasies disturb us. Everyone wants their dreams to come true. Most of us are not so sure about realizing our fantasies.

My father had only one dream I knew about, and he died trying to make it true. I had a fantasy, and maybe Gabe died in part because I made it a reality.

My father's dream was simple and attainable: he wanted to pay the mortgage on our house before he turned fifty and live the rest of his life working for pleasure instead of working for the bank. He was a victim of limited ambition. Instead of wanting to own his home free and clear, he should have aimed higher. Not president of the steel company. Too high. Maybe something in the executive suite. Plant manager. Head of blast furnaces and washrooms. Or flying to the moon. That's a reasonable dream, isn't it? Why not dream of flying to the moon? You could die in bed knowing you had tried to be an astronaut or an executive or a song and dance man, like Gabe wanted to be. You could swing back and forth between dream and fantasy, imagining how you might achieve your dream and fantasizing about what it would be like.

My father's dream was to burn the mortgage on our house while he was still young enough to enjoy the freedom from payments. Then he would quit working at the steel company and do other things. Perhaps make furniture for disabled people. He liked that idea. He had drawn plans for chairs that were easy for disabled people to rise from, and tables with adjustable sides to accommodate people with wheelchairs. Or maybe he would buy a fishing camp on some remote lake up north. He liked that best of all. He described it to me once, how it would feel to wake up every morning to the sound of wind through pines and fall asleep every night while loons sang across calm water. My father was a dreamer. Some days I honestly believe the world needs more dreamers and fewer doers.

To realize his dream, my father worked double shifts whenever they were offered, or filled in for other men whose jobs were below his abilities. Like directing trains that carried steel and coal and whatever else was needed within the sprawling steel company. Just so he could make his simple dream come true for him and for us.

My father died before he could realize his dream or any of his fantasies. He did not die in bed imagining them. He died watching the back end of a train move toward him while he screamed for it to stop because he couldn't move out of the way. He had been walking backwards, leading the locomotive to a string of railway cars loaded with steel coils, and he walked back into an automatic railroad switch just as it closed on his boot and held him like a mouse in a trap, on the side of the tracks where the engineer couldn't see him unless he looked into his rear-view mirror or turned around, but he didn't, and oh god, *Oh God!*, it has always been too horrible for me to imagine, and yet I do from time to time.

Some men who worked with my father ran toward the locomotive, waving their arms and screaming for the engineer to stop, while my father waved his arms and tried to pull his foot away from the rails that held him, but the engineer was looking the other way or down at the floor or up his own ass, I don't know. He stopped the locomotive six feet too late, with my father's body, or what was left of it, jammed under the wheels of a railroad car. My father suffered a lifetime of horror in the ten seconds between the moment the steel rails clamped on to his boot and the instant that the rear of the locomotive sent him backwards and cleaved his body. That's how the coroner described it. "It cleaved his body." Cleaver. Noun. A steel chopping instrument used to break apart carcasses.

The doctors said Mother's stroke had nothing to do with imagining my father's terror through the last seconds of his life when he knew what was going to happen and how, because my father's death had occurred so many years earlier. I say my mother held back for years that knife-edge hemorrhage that prevents her from speaking, purely with the force of her will, and when she grew too old and too weary to keep holding it back, it sliced an artery in her brain like a microscopic cleaver.

Do we need a new definition of irony? Here's one: my father screamed until his throat bled, and my mother cannot make a sound louder than a sigh. God needs a new comedy writer.

THE BEACH STRIP IS UNIQUE IN MANY WAYS, and one is the strange way the weather unfurls here. The silly weather boy on the local TV evening news called it a microclimate. A beach strip microclimate. Temperatures, wind, sky, all of it can be the same for miles around, and utterly different along the beach strip. The climate here is like one of those tulips you plant in the fall that are all supposed to be red, and a stupid white one shows up in the middle of the flower bed when spring arrives. Weather on the beach strip is the tulip nobody expects.

It had been cool and blustery beneath the highway bridges over the canal, but on the beach strip it was warm and benign. Walkers, skaters, and joggers herded themselves along the boardwalk like shoppers in search of bargains, which is what they were. This late in the year, every warm day is a clear-out, an end-of-season event. Get it while it's hot and cheap.

While walking back to my house, I thought about my father and how horribly he had died nearly thirty years earlier. I entered the garden from the boardwalk on the beach strip. The garden shed door looked secure, the impatiens blooms were orgiastic, the grasses in the sand along the fenceline were harvest brown and no longer reaching for the sun. Everything had that melancholy feeling you recognize as a schoolkid when you realize summer vacation is over, and the feeling remains with us as adults.

At the wire fence separating the Blairs' house from the laneway, Jock Blair stood puffing on his pipe, his head a mobile jack-o'-lantern, round and pink above a plaid shirt and dung-coloured trousers held up by red suspenders. His face bloomed into extra creases with his smile, and when he saw me he ducked his head and said, "Good day, good day," repeating it like a shorebird's call.

I smiled back, raising his blush level higher, just as Maude Blair rose from behind a large plastic garbage pail into which she had been dropping cuttings from a dogwood bush. She waved and began tottering toward me on hockey stick legs that ended in canvas sneakers, holding one arm up and calling, "Josephine! Josephine!" in a burr that always brought me visions of wool tartans.

Brushing her husband aside, she reached to grip my sleeve and pull me away from the boardwalk, looking around as though searching for something lost. "There's a man been in your garden," she hissed. "Jock saw him, didn't he?"

"What did he look like?" I asked.

"He'd a bushy beard, dressed like a poor soul come outta the gutter, Jock tells me. And wild-eyed. Frightened the jeepers out of Jock, he did. He's gone now. Jock said he watched him leave, tottering like a Glasgow drunk toward the canal. You didn't see him, did you?"

I told her no, I had not seen anyone like that. I knew who she meant, of course.

She leaned closer to my ear. "Jock, he's worried about you, lass. I can tell. All the tragedy you've been through, and Jock and me, we don't want anything bad happening to you now."

I wanted to wrap her in a hug for her concern, but I didn't. I simply thanked her and smiled over her shoulder at Jock, who remained at the fence, his face glowing in deeper shades of crimson like a setting sun.

"Will you be needing more marmalade?" Maude called out as I began walking along the boardwalk again. "I'll send some over with Jock."

I didn't need the marmalade, and I didn't want to enter the house yet. I thanked her and joined the other people in the sun, hearing Maude's voice, her nagging softened by the highland burr, telling Jock he should put the cover back on the rose spray, asking, "An' were ye born in a barn? Because ye never close anythin', never." I smiled at the things that both bond and destroy marriages, the imperfectness that challenges romantic illusions. It reminded me of Gabe and me. It reminded me that neither of us achieved the perfection in reality that dominated our image of each other. If I was imperfect enough to cheat on Gabe, could he be imperfect enough to kill me for it? And himself as well? Did the alcohol in his blood confuse him so much that he decided to do himself first when I was late arriving?

I had been having these thoughts, and variations on them, since Gabe's death. They invaded my mind like musical earworms, those old songs you don't even like that keep playing in an endless loop within your mind. Thoughts about what might

have happened that night had become my own personal earworm.
I would have preferred something by Captain & Tennille.

THE BOARDWALK WAS FILLED WITH JUST ENOUGH PEOPLE to
make me feel secure, and the sun's last rays actually appeared
to grow warmer as the day began dying. I walked toward Tuffy's,
past the house with the helicopter on the front porch and past
Hans and Trudy's castle.

The bodies moving ahead of me were a chaos of speed and
rhythm, earthbound gliders on in-line skates and stuttering
strollers with canes, and amid them I saw the bird's-nest hair of
the silently screaming woman. She crossed the boardwalk on a
path leading from the lake back to Beach Boulevard, vanishing
between stands of high grass on the shore. I stepped toward the
beach through the nearest break in the grass onto a section of the
shoreline that had rocky outcroppings, a thin strand unattractive
to bathers. A man ahead of me was tossing a stick into the water
for his Labrador to retrieve, over and over. Three stubborn pines,
their limbs twisted like the arms of spastic dancers, marked the
edge of the grass line. I stood among them, waiting for her.

She emerged from the grass, head down, arms folded within
a pink cotton cardigan over straight and bony shoulders that
appeared like the last rung of a short ladder, legs clad in plaid
slacks. She walked with her eyes fastened three steps ahead of
her, measuring her world that way, and approached the pines.
When she was a step away, I spoke aloud to her. "Hello."

She stopped in front of me, startled but not prepared to flee, as
I had expected she might. Instead, she stood frowning as though I
had delivered a mild insult, and I realized she was trying to place
me, trying to identify me.

"Are you Mrs. Dalgetty?" I asked.

She nodded dumbly. I saw ancient beauty amid the lines of

her face and around a mouth shaped like an inverted crescent. She could not have been more than a few years older than me, but the currency of those years had been spent differently. In that moment, I thought of my own concerns about aging, of how reluctant I was to let go of those parts of myself that I had treasured when I was young, to leave them for the passage of time to raze and finally level. First we ripen, then we rot. Mrs. Dalgetty was outpacing me in the rotting stage.

"You live over the upholstery shop."

She nodded again, and her mouth actually formed a semblance of a smile. Someone knew who she was. Someone could confirm she existed. "That's me," she said.

I offered a hand. "My name is Josie Marshall," I said.

She pulled away as though ducking a blow, and I reached to grab her arm.

"Why do you stand behind my house and stare at it?" I asked.

She shook her head, and I realized she was unafraid of me, but she continued to look around, confirming that no one was eavesdropping.

"Talk to me, please. My husband is dead, and . . ." My mouth tasted like sand and I had to start over. "I'm sure someone killed him. I just wondered if you could help me. Can you help me? Because the police say he committed suicide, and I don't believe that. I can't believe that."

Her head kept moving as she spoke, twisting from side to side, looking up and across the strand in a motion that I thought at first was spastic, then realized was driven by fear. "He killed Dougal," she said. "He killed him, Dougal, my husband."

"No," I said. "Gabe did not kill anyone. Not your husband, not himself. Gabe would never do that."

"That's what I heard," she said. "That's what they told me."

"Who? Who told you that?"

She pulled away, dismissing me with a wave of her hand.

"Tell me about this man they call Grizz."

She looked back at me, then at the sand near her feet. "Who?"

"Grizz. Your husband worked for him. Is he one of Mike Pilato's men? Where is he? Where can I find him?"

She looked directly at me for the first time. "I never heard of no Grizz," she said. "Don't go sayin' that I know anybody named Grizz, 'cause I don't, you hear me?"

"Someone keeps looking for him, at my house," I said. "The police can't find him. Have they asked you? Have they talked to you about this person?"

She shook her head, turned, and walked quickly away, with her arms folded across her chest and her head down.

19.

The lane along the beach extends five miles beyond the canal. I have walked its length. I walked it after Dougal Dalgetty's widow left with her arms folded and her head down. I had walked it with Gabe on autumn days very much like this one when we talked about books and music and people we passed on the way. And I had walked it when Gabe was away for a few days testifying in Montreal and something happened.

Gabe and I had argued before he left. I love Montreal and wanted to go with him. He would be gone almost a week. I could go shopping or just stroll through Côte-des-Neiges while he waited to testify. Gabe said no. He was being paid to be there and it was work. He would take me at our expense some other time. I accused him of wanting to chase women while he was there. Wasn't that what men did, alone in Montreal? Wasn't it that kind of city?

The accusation made him angry, as angry as I have ever seen him, and he left in that mood, calming down a little when he called from the airport, but I was still furious and screamed at him before hanging up.

The next night, he called from Montreal and we had another argument. I drank some Teacher's, sitting alone, and Mel arrived, and that's when I said fuck it, or fuck him, who cares? I used the Scotch as an excuse, as a crutch, as whatever name you care to hang on it.

This is how it started. Mel and I sat staring at each other and talking about nothing until every phrase sounded like a double entendre. When Mel got up to leave, I asked if he would like a kiss goodbye, flirting really, having fun, and he smiled and I walked to him and took his face in my hands and kissed him, open-mouthed. I thought he would say what I did was stupid and stop it, but he didn't. We were on the sofa, and then we were on the floor and his head was between my breasts with his mouth searching for my nipple and when he found it, when his tongue began circling it, I know I said, "Lick it! Lick it!" aloud, and Jesus . . .

I loved it because it was bad and it was wrong, and I hated myself because it was bad and it was wrong, but not as much as I loved it.

I had not had an orgasm with Gabe for months, but it happened with Mel and then it happened again and again, like a string of damp firecrackers. When it was over, Mel kissed the back of my neck and I told him to get the hell out of my house, and he did.

And I dreamed about it the following day, walking the length of the boardwalk and sleeping alone in my bed. Dreamed about Mel and me, and I made up with Gabe over the telephone that night, and when he returned I resumed my life of working two days a week at the retirement home and visiting a mother who could offer me wisdom but no spoken words and painting the kitchen and telling myself I was happy with a great guy. But a month later I was at Mel's apartment in the middle of the day, and we didn't even get undressed this time because I wore this wide denim skirt . . .

The third time was all my idea. Gabe was attending a police course in New York. The subject was interrogation techniques. I called Mel and said, "One more time," and he said, "Where?" and I said, "Not here and not at your place. Pick a motel somewhere."

Fantasies. That's what I wanted. A savings account of fantasies I could draw from after my next birthday, when I turned forty-one. Turning forty hadn't upset me. It was a cosmic joke. Everybody made jokes about turning forty. Turning forty-one was scary, serious.

In the shower, with the water running. That's the fulfilled fantasy. Mel and me, standing in the shower, warm water flowing over our bodies, and moving, moving until he moaned. Then we dried each other off, I dressed and left. It happened and it was over. Three strikes. I was out. Two months later Gabe was dead.

Did Gabe know about Mel and me? I was afraid he did.

Yes, he could, I began to think. Yes, he could have been angry enough to shoot me and then perhaps to shoot himself. Yes, he could have grown so despondent when I didn't arrive that he could commit suicide just to stop the pain he was feeling. Yes, I might have killed him in that manner that lovers kill each other by turning away a head, withdrawing a hand, ignoring a word.

If I could believe that, and I felt the idea begin to embed itself within me while I walked the beach strip on that late summer's afternoon, perhaps I could relax somewhat. The universe, as a great man once said, was unfolding as it should. Gabe was dead, Honeysett was dead, Dad was dead. Mother, Tina, and I were alive.

That was all I knew. I sat on a bench alongside the boardwalk and stared out at the lake while tears coursed down my cheeks and people glanced at me as they passed, a sad woman staring at the water, waiting for the cormorants to return.

He killed my husband. That's what Dougal Dalgetty's widow said. She believed Gabe had killed her husband. Impossible.

I wiped the tears from my eyes, rose off the bench, and found the nearest pathway from the shore to Beach Boulevard. Across the boulevard and two blocks away, I saw the upholstery shop in the small two-storey frame building and walked toward it. How dare this woman, in her mourning and sadness, claim Gabe was a murderer. Had she been telling other people the same thing, walking up and down the beach strip, telling lies about my husband?

I know nothing about upholstering. I'm a slipcover kind of person, I guess. If it's stained, wash it. If it's torn, mend it. If it's ugly, cover it. So I have no idea if the upholstery business is profitable or not. Based on what I could see of Beach Upholstery, it was not. The display windows were crammed with dead and dying plants, although given the amount of grime on the window, the state of each plant's health, not to mention its species, was difficult to determine. Lights shone from inside the shop, but I saw nothing moving, nor did I hear the tapping of a hammer or the whir of a sewing machine. I had never seen anyone enter or leave the upholstery shop either. But a cardboard sign on the front door, its upper left-hand corner dirty and worn from, I assumed, decades of being turned over at the beginning and end of each day, declared it open.

I had no need for upholstery. It was the door beside the shop I wanted, the one with a mailbox on one side, a doorbell on the other, and 212A above it. I pushed the doorbell button, heard a satisfying ring inside and shoes descending the stairs. A latch clattered, a bolt slid aside, and the door opened on Dougal Dalgetty's widow's worn face, remaining that way just long enough for me to place a hand against it and prevent her from closing it.

"I need to talk to you," I said.

She moved behind the door and began pushing it, but I was already through the opening and inside the small foyer at the foot of the stairs.

"Please talk to me," I said.

She closed her eyes, then turned and began walking slowly up the stairs, and I followed her into the three rooms that appeared to be her world.

I had expected antimacassars, splintery furniture, and worn carpets. Instead, I stepped on thick broadloom beneath several pieces of good-quality oak furniture. There were interesting prints on the walls, and lovely ceramic lamps cast a warm light in the room. An oak-mantled fireplace filled one corner. In another corner a Persian cat stood up, stretched and yawned, blinked in my direction, and walked off toward the kitchen in a manner that was clearly a rebuke.

"You want some tea?" Mrs. Dalgetty asked, avoiding my eyes. She was wearing the same pink cardigan and tartan slacks.

I told her no and thanked her. She appeared relieved. I asked if I could sit down. She said, "Sure," and I chose a tweed loveseat. "Didn't Wayne Honeysett live around here?" I asked.

I had meant it as a conversation starter. Mrs. Dalgetty took it as a threat. She stepped back, looked out the window toward the steel mills on the bay, and shook her head. "I don't know nothin' about what happened to him," she said.

"But he did live near here, didn't he? On one of the side streets?"

"What do you want?" She was biting her bottom lip, looking at the floor, at her worn nails, everywhere but at me.

"I wanted to ask about something you said when we met this afternoon. About my husband, and your husband."

Her head remained in constant motion, even after she settled herself in a leather armchair. When she said nothing, I went on.

"You said my husband killed your husband. Why did you say that?"

"Because he did."

"How do you know?"

"I just know, that's all."

"But who told you that?"

She shook her head from side to side.

"You know my husband is dead," I said.

A change of direction. She nodded her head once.

"They think he committed suicide. The police do. I don't think he did, but I don't know. I don't think my husband was capable of killing anyone, including himself."

She looked directly at me for the first time and, as I had seen when we met on the boardwalk, the remnants of her beauty were visible. She had pretty eyes.

"Mrs. Dalgetty," I said, "we have both lost our husbands recently, and I'm sure your husband's death was as devastating to you as mine was to me—"

"Glynnis," she said. "My name is Glynnis."

"That's a lovely name," I said. "Thank you. And I'm Josie. Josephine, actually, but—"

"Wayne Honeysett was murdered," she interrupted. "Somebody crushed his head under the bridge. Didn't they? That's what everybody around here says."

I told her yes, that's what I thought. It was horrifying to imagine it, but I believed that's what happened.

"And if your husband didn't commit suicide and somebody killed him," she said, "were they all murdered by the same person? Your husband and my Dougal and Wayne?"

"Then you knew him. You knew Wayne Honeysett."

She nodded and stared out the window. "We grew up together. We were kids here on the beach strip. Wayne had his problems. He wasn't perfect." She smiled, looked down, and straightened the front of her cardigan. "He was kinda nice-looking, and he liked me. He knew me when I was young, and he liked me because he thought I was pretty. And I was. Not beautiful, maybe. Just pretty." She opened her cardigan, revealing a small silver brooch in the shape of a peacock, with a green stone for its eye, pinned to her blouse. "He gave me this because he liked me. It's white gold. The stone is an emerald. A real emerald."

"It's lovely. When did he give you that?"

"Two, three months ago." She was fingering the brooch. "I never told Dougal that he gave it to me. I said I bought it for a couple of dollars at a garage sale and that it was just a cheap piece of junk. Dougal never knew nothin' about jewellery. He bought my wedding ring when we got married and that's all, so he didn't know this is real gold and has a real emerald." She looked up. "It is. I went into the city and had a jeweller look at it, and he said it's a real emerald and real white gold. Said it's worth a lot of money."

"Mr. Honeysett must have liked you very much."

"He liked women. He always did. He liked women to like him. It wasn't even about sex, I think. I mean, I don't know for sure. But he would give you gifts if you were a girl, a pretty girl. I knew him when we were kids, and he was always like that. I think Wayne became a jeweller so he could make things for women. Men, too. But he loved making things for women, brooches and earrings and stuff."

She looked out the window, remembering. "We both grew up here on the strip. He was kind of sweet on me when we were fourteen, fifteen years old. I married Dougal and he married Florie, whose family had the money to get him started in business. The jewellery business." She looked away from the window and, with her head down, said, "I should have gone to his funeral, Wayne's, I guess. I thought about it, but I don't like going too far from home nowadays. People talk."

"Mr. Honeysett had his problems, I understand."

She looked up and nodded. "Only after Florie died. Poor Wayne. People said terrible things about him, or said he was doing terrible things. Bad things. I don't know if any were true. We've all done bad things in our lives, I guess. Most of us, anyway. I just know he was nice to me and some other people, I hear."

"When did you see him last?"

"Two, three weeks ago. He stopped me when I was walking on the beach strip. He wanted to know how much I liked the peacock pin. He was always asking me that. Whenever we met after he gave me the brooch, he wanted to know if I still liked it, and if I still liked him, I guess. I told him it was just about the most beautiful thing I'd ever owned, which was the truth. That seemed to make him happy." She shook her head and smiled. "Some men are strange that way. They like to make women happy because that's what makes them happy. The men, I mean."

"Some women are like that," I said. "About men."

She nodded and stared out the window again, across the strip and toward the lake.

We sat in silence as the cat returned, passing within reach of me without looking in my direction. Out of respect, I waited until it was settled in the same corner of the room it had occupied when I arrived. Then I said, "I need to know why you think my husband was involved in your husband's death."

"Mike Pilato told me."

"When did he tell you that?"

"At Dougal's funeral." She closed her cardigan, hiding the peacock from view. "He paid for it, Mike did. The funeral."

"Why?"

She shrugged. "Dougal did some work for Mike. Mike's a nice guy, no matter what a lot of people say. I mean, he's, you know, he does a lot of stuff, but listen, Mike didn't do nothin' bad to us, Dougal and me. He did some good things for us. We helped each other out, Mike and Dougal and me." She looked at a picture on the wall. "We helped each other out."

"What kind of work did your husband do for him? For Mike Pilato?"

"None of your business. None of anybody's business." Her eyes were still on the picture.

"Do you think Mike Pilato would talk to me?"

She looked across and smiled. "Sure," she said. "You're pretty. Mike always talks to pretty women."

"Thanks." I stood up. "What do you know about this man called Grizz? Have you really never heard of him?"

"No." Her smile was gone. "You in cahoots with him or something?"

"With Grizz?"

"With that son of a bitch who keeps coming here asking for him. He's crazy." She pulled back into herself, hugging her chest with her arms and pulling her legs onto the chair, avoiding my eyes again, withdrawing into her madness. "He comes here again, I'll kill him. You tell him that. He comes here again, I'll get a knife and I'll kill the son of a bitch."

She was shaking with fear or anger, or perhaps both.

"Is this man about thirty, bearded, dresses like a bum?"

"You tell him," she said, pressing her face into the back of the chair. "You tell him I don't know nothin'. I just want people to leave me alone."

"Mrs. Dalgetty," I began. "Glynnis. He's been to my place as well. I have no idea who he is, honest."

She remained enveloped within the chair, seeming to will it to embrace and hide her.

I thanked her and walked down the stairs and out into the sunshine, where I stood thinking about all she had said and listening to a tap-tap from within the upholstery shop. It was open, after all. Someone was inside, driving tacks into wood.

20.

Power is different depending on who has it and uses it. You talk power to a man and he thinks about a football team or a truck engine, the kind of power that's dynamic, in motion, like a railway locomotive. Or maybe political power to get other people to do what you want or not do what you don't want. Or the power of money, which is nearly the same thing.

Talk power with a woman, especially a woman who knows her way among men or even around just one man, and her idea is different. It's not dynamic. It's subtle. All right, it's sexual.

I remember my first husband, the good years with him, the early years when we were both working and struggling. We had an old car that wouldn't start in the rain or if it was too cold, and we lived in a small apartment where we were trying to save money for a down payment on a suburban split-level.

Anyway, we had a fight about something. It must have been substantial, and I know it was at the dining-room table, because my clearest memory of the fight is tossing my dinner plate at him, and it missed and splattered against the wall. The point of the fight is long forgotten, but I recall the broken china and mashed potatoes and canned peas all over the floor and my husband fleeing the house because he was either frightened that my aim might improve or concerned that he might kill me.

I knew he would be back. So I cleaned up the broken china, did the dishes, and told myself I needed to do something in my power to get past this, and I did. I fixed my face, slipped into a pair of lace stockings, and put on a black negligee I hadn't worn since our honeymoon. Then I sat in a chair in the corner, with all the lights out and waited for him to return.

He said nothing when he came home, turned on the lights, and saw me there. Just looked away, trying to keep from smiling, I'll bet. Kept that grim face on while I rose from the chair and tippy-toed across the room, put my arms around his neck, and said that I was sorry and that the things he wanted me to do and I didn't, well, I would do them all night if he wanted, just to prove how sorry I was.

You can't pull freight trains across the country or win a Super Bowl with that kind of power. But it works for other things. Especially when you're female and young. At this point in my life, I could forget young. Younger would have to do. Younger than Mike Pilato, anyway. I chose the black pencil skirt, this time with a black sweater that was just a little too small and the pumps from Saks.

It was mid-afternoon by the time I located Mike Pilato's offices. He was in the hardware business, officially anyway, in an old residential area of the city that ended at Pilato Park on the shore of the bay, west of the mills and factories. The two-storey brick building across the street from the park was neat but otherwise unimpressive, surrounded by a high wire fence. A worn sign on the roof announced it was the site of White Star Hardware Distributors. Business did not appear to be very good at White Star. In fact, it was non-existent. Two large doors at one side of the building, one marked SHIPPING and the other RECEIVING, were closed. Dusty blinds covered the windows on both levels. No vehicles sat in the parking lot, and the only truck I saw was a plumber's van parked across the street in front of a crumbling brick cottage where, I assumed, someone's toilet was backing up.

A man wearing coveralls and a battered fedora was sweeping the wide sidewalk leading from the door marked OFFICE, moving a broom back and forth with little enthusiasm.

I drove past the building, parked the Honda, and walked back to White Star, reputedly the headquarters of the most powerful crime boss in the city. The man stopped sweeping and leaned on the broom, watching as I approached. I asked him if Mr. Pilato was inside.

"He's a-busy," the man said. He was sixty, perhaps seventy years old.

"I'd like to talk to him," I said, wondering if he could be carrying a weapon under those coveralls.

"What about, eh?" He was studying me. "You wanta buy hardware? I don't think you wanta buy da hardware."

"I need to talk to him about my husband."

"Mr. Pilato, he knows you husband?"

I was becoming tired of this routine. What was I doing, talking to a guy sweeping the sidewalk who could barely speak English? I turned to walk toward the door again, but his broom swung up to block my way.

"What's you name?" the old man asked.

"Josie Marshall. My husband's name was Gabe Marshall. He was a policeman, and he died about two weeks ago. He was shot to death."

"You tink Mr. Pilato have something to do with it, eh?"

"I don't know." I should go back to my car, I began telling myself. Get in it, sit down, and drive away. "I don't believe what everybody is telling me about my husband and why he died. How he died. That's all. Somebody said Mr. Pilato may know what happened. That's why I'm here. In case he knows."

The man's face softened. As did mine. Every time I talked about Gabe something within me began to melt. There is a limit to power of any kind.

"Wait a-here," the man said, and he walked through the office door, which was metal with a small, barred window, closing it behind him. After about thirty seconds, the door opened again and he emerged and stood to one side, beckoning me in, and I entered a small, empty foyer leading to a heavy oak door that swung open as I approached and closed after I passed through it.

From the outside, White Star Hardware Distributors may have appeared to be struggling, but Mike Pilato's office looked like a Wall Street success. The room was large and substantial, with oak-panelled walls, silk carpets on a polished slate floor, draperies that had never come within shipping distance of a Walmart, and nicely framed oil paintings on the wall.

At one end of the room, an oak desk resembling one I had seen in pictures of the Oval Office sat on a riser. Behind it was a large leather chair that held . . . nobody. I sat facing the empty desk, the empty chair, and the bookshelves covering the wall behind them, the shelves overflowing with hardcover books whose perfect spines indicated they had probably never been read.

The door behind me opened and closed, and footsteps approached. A man stepped onto the riser with some agility, considering that his stomach was prominent and his white hair flowed down to his shirt collar. He wore heavy black-framed glasses, a black and gold silk shirt stretched over his paunch, and black pleated trousers. I noticed the details of his clothing because I preferred them to his face, which was round and scowling. His eyes never left me while he found his chair and settled into it. For a moment I flattered myself that he liked what he saw, but then I realized he was watching to see if I might pull a gun or a hatchet out of my purse.

"What can I do for you?" he asked. His eyes shifted away from me for short instants, glancing around the room as though confirming that everything was in place, then returning to me. His voice was deep, the words delivered with neither warmth nor threat.

What the heck am I doing here? I thought. Then, He's a man, older than you. Maybe he's killed a guy or two, but he's still a man, and you know about men. "First of all, thanks for seeing me—" I began.

He waved my words away. "What do you want?" he said in the same flat delivery.

"I'm a little nervous," I started to explain.

"You think I might hurt you?"

"Well—"

"Relax. The plumbers know you're here."

"Plumbers?"

"In the truck. Outside. Three, four guys from downtown. They took your picture. They take everybody's picture. So you're safe." He actually permitted himself to smile briefly. "Pretty safe."

"My name is Josie Marshall," I said in my best headmistress voice, "and I came here, Mr. Pilato, on a serious matter. My husband is dead. I believe someone killed him. I was told perhaps you would know something about it."

He acted as though I had insulted him. Perhaps I had. His head jerked back and his chin rose so he was looking down the length of his nose at me. "Do you think," he said, and I felt an edge to his words like the feeling you get when you press a thumb against the sharp side of a carving knife, "that every time somebody gets killed in this city, it's because of me? Is that what people like you think?"

"No, of course not," I said. It was the beginning of a lie. Maybe not everybody.

"What do you need to know that's so important you think I know it and other people don't?" He spoke precisely, each consonant bitten off. "You tell me that, okay? Tell me now."

A picture appeared in my mind. It was a picture of a terribly foolish woman wearing a skirt that was a little too tight and a little too short, under a cotton sweater as form-fitting as she would ever want to wear in public, and she was sitting alone in an office with a man who had a reputation for reassembling other peoples' brains with a baseball bat.

I'm usually good at being cool under pressure. Okay, I wasn't cool when Gabe's body was found. This was different. I folded my hands in my lap and looked directly at Mike Pilato. "I am not making accusations," I said, trying to match Pilato's precise enunciation. "I would never do such a thing. I'm not a police officer, I'm not a lawyer, I'm nobody except a woman who loved her husband and wants the truth of his death to come out, whatever it might be."

Pilato leaned back in his chair. "Nice speech," he said.

What the hell. "It was no damn speech," I said, tossing aside any concern about consonants or my safety. "It's what I need to do. Somebody said you knew my husband. If you say you didn't know Gabe, fine, I'm gone. If you knew him, please help me. That's all I ask."

He nodded. "Better speech." Before I could tell him to go to hell, which I figured would either make him kiss me or shoot me, he said, "Ask anything you want. I'll answer it, if it doesn't incriminate me."

I asked if he had ever met Gabe.

He placed his hands on the desk in front of him. "Yes," he said. "I have met most detectives in this city. Sometimes we're in the same business. Different sides, same business."

"When did you speak to him last?"

"Maybe two weeks ago."

"Where?"

"In a bar down the street. Place called Mahady's." A glance at me, so he could watch my reaction. "I own it."

"What did you talk about?"

"Not what. Who. We were talking about someone. Your husband wanted to know what I knew about this person."

"What was the name of this person, the one my husband asked about?"

Some successful people are actors when it comes to getting others to do things, or to hear things in a certain way. It's timing, it's the delivery, it's the expression, it's the voice. It's acting. Pilato was an actor. He paused and watched me, building suspense. Then he said, "Eugene Griswold."

"Who is he?"

"Was," Pilato said, his eyebrows back in place. "Who *was* he."

My god. Another murder victim. "What happened to him?"

A shrug. "He died."

"From what?"

"Probably old age." He leaned forward, his eyes on mine. "Some *manichino* named Eugene Griswold, the only guy with that name I found, or had people find for me, opened a place in Connecticut, I don't know, somewhere around 1776. An inn, a hotel, whatever you want to call it. Opened it with his brothers. They ran it, the three of them. Partners. It's still there, the inn. You can look it up. The Griswold Inn, someplace in Connecticut. Might go there someday and look at it." One more smile, quick and cold. "Maybe you come with me, eh? Have a dirty weekend together?" Instead of fading this time, the smile widened into a grin. His teeth were too porcelain-perfect to be real.

When I didn't respond, he leaned back in his chair. "That's the only Eugene Griswold I know about. It's the only Eugene Griswold anybody knows about. I had never heard that name before your husband met me at Mahady's and asked if I knew him. 'Who's Eugene Griswold?' your husband says, and I say, 'I don't know, should I?' and your husband tells me Griswold is some big shot, some new *capo* in town, and maybe I should look him up. So I do. I have somebody look him up, this Griswold. Nobody knows him. Somebody, you don't have to know who, it's none of your business, gets on a computer and finds out about this guy in Connecticut, started a bar two hundred years ago. That's all I know about a Eugene Griswold. That's all anybody knows about him. Probably more than your husband knew. Your husband thought he was local, some new local guy. Your husband was wrong."

"I was told," I began. I swallowed, closed my eyes, and began again. "I was told that this man, this person worked for you—"

"Do I look that old?" He grinned.

"—and his street name was Grizz."

"I was told that too."

"And you never heard of anyone by that name?"

"Never."

"How about Dougal Dalgetty?"

He stared at me as though considering whether to answer or not. Finally, "What do you want to know about him?"

"Did he work for you?"

"He worked for my company." Pilato was finding something interesting on his thumbnail. It gave him a reason to avoid my eyes.

"Doing what?"

"That's no business of yours. It's no business of anybody's."

"Do you know who shot him?"

His eyes jumped from his thumb to me. "No," he said in a voice that reminded me this was not a man to cross or insult. Or even, for that matter, to question. "And if I did, I wouldn't tell you."

"You told his widow, Glynnis, that my husband killed him."

"I said possibly. Your husband possibly killed him."

"Why? Why would you say my husband might have shot Dougal Dalgetty?"

"Dougal and I talked. He told me things. About dealing with police officers."

"Were you sorry to hear Dougal was killed?"

"I'm sorry to hear anybody is killed. Always I'm sorry. But what can I do?"

"If you knew who did it, who shot Dougal Dalgetty, would you do something about it?"

"What, you mean get revenge?" I wasn't sure if he was amused or angry. "You think I get revenge? You think I'm playing in a schoolyard, you take my bicycle, I take yours?"

"I'm just—"

"You hit my friend, I hit your friend? You think that's how my world works?"

"It's what most people would think."

"Most people are stupid, right? I believe in punishment, not revenge. Punishment is not revenge. Punishment is better than revenge. Punishment is to reduce crime and reform the criminal. Those are a woman's words. Her name was Elizabeth Fry. Reduce crime and reform the criminal. That's what she said. I punish people who need it. I don't take revenge."

I twisted in the chair to look behind me. We were still alone. The room was quiet. Everything was quiet. No noise entered from outside. Not the rumble of trucks on the road or trains on the nearby railroad track. Nothing. The room also appeared to be darker than when I had entered.

I looked back at Pilato, who had been watching me with amusement. "Do you have other people working for you?" I asked.

"Sure."

"Why aren't they here? In this building?"

"How do you know they aren't?"

He was toying with me. To my surprise, the realization made me relax a little. Maybe we could find something in common. "What do you think of Walter Freeman?" I asked.

"Big shot cop."

"Not a nice guy."

He shrugged.

"Maybe even crooked?"

"Crooked? Do you mean dishonest? Shady?"

"Any of them."

Another shrug. "Who knows?"

"You would."

Slowly shaking his head, he said, "No, I wouldn't. I never know who's trying to steal from me or steal from somebody else until it's too late. I keep getting surprised by people I think are bastards and sometimes it turns out they aren't. And other people, the ones who act like they're models that the rest of the world, people who would spit on me if they could or see me locked up for the rest of my life, the rest of the world thinks they're *grandi uomini* and they're . . ." He shrugged and looked away, searching for the words he wanted. He looked back and studied me for a moment, and I had the impression that this might be one of the longest conversations Mike Pilato had had with a woman in some time without being in bed with her. "Is that what you think of me? That I steal money and kill people?"

"I think—" I began, not sure what I would say next. I didn't have to say anything. He cut me off with a wave of his hand.

"It doesn't matter what you think. I'm not interested. But let me tell you something. Do you know St. Patrick's, the church over on Murray Street?"

I told him I knew of it. I had never visited it.

"Go. Go sometime, go look at the old marble baptismal font in the vestibule. Everybody loves it. Me," and he made the classic gesture—shoulders hunched, palms up, eyes closed, bottom lip thrust out—"what do I know? I'm just a dumb Luigi, a pasta eater, a garlic lover. All I know is, it's four, maybe five hundred years old. That's what they tell me. Penteli marble, sat for hundreds of years in an old church in Agerola, near the Amalfi Coast, before an earthquake knocked it over, the church. Do you know it? The Amalfi Coast, south of Naples?"

I said I didn't.

"You should go sometime. Nice, sexy woman like you. You go with a man who can show you the sights, somebody who knows where to find good food, good wine, nice scenery. Anyway, I go there last year, somebody offers to sell me the font, I pay money, a shitload of money, and I get it sent here at my expense, pay every dime, you wouldn't believe how many dimes I paid. The bishop takes it, puts it up front in the church, holds a Mass, blesses it, says it's a gift from God, doesn't mention me. That's okay. He wants people in the church to think it came from God instead of Mike Pilato, what can I do? Then a week, two weeks later, he's talking about all the low-lifes in this town, how the police've gotta clear out all this criminal element, and if they don't, God and his angels will do it for them, lightning bolts and eternal damnation, all that *merda*. It was in the newspaper, the stuff he said. He's pounding on the pulpit, the same guy who wet his pants over the marble font he got from me, saying just because people try to do good things, make parks and stuff, this doesn't make up for the bad things they do, how they offend God. So who's he talking about when he says that, eh? Everybody knows."

He stopped talking to wave his hand, indicating the outside world. "Everybody knows. The next day I go into the church, and there's the font, all polished and shiny. The one I gave him, the one he thanked me for, and nobody knows. Nobody knows I gave it to him—to the church, but to him too."

"That was very nice of you," I said. "Very generous."

"Not my point. You got any idea what it takes to bring something like that, four hundred, five hundred years old, out of a country, out of Italy?"

"I don't do that kind of thing very often."

"You better not. The cops'll be all over you." His voice rose and the edge hardened. "You only do it with people you know, people you trust, people like yourself, and then you gotta grease their palms, put enough money in the right hands, and maybe they give you the papers to export it, and maybe the guys at this end, over here, maybe the assholes in customs here think the papers are real, so they let you bring it in. That's how you do this kind of stuff, all right? Everybody knows that. Including the bishop."

I was getting his point. "And he didn't care."

"He didn't care. He didn't ask, he didn't want to know. He just wanted his marble font for his *brutto* little church. And he got it. Then he treats me like *immondizia*. He treats me like garbage."

"Why did you do that?"

"Do what?"

"Go to the trouble and expense of bringing the font into the country."

He actually thought about this for a moment. Maybe no one had asked him before. "The people around here, they like it," he said. "I thought maybe the bishop, he'd put one of them little brass signs on it, the font, just to say it was a gift from Mike Pilato in memory of his mother or his dog, I didn't care. Or maybe he recognizes me at a party, a reception I go to and I write cheques for this and that, feed the children, save the whales. But he doesn't. Just turns away, finds somebody else to talk to. When I gave it to him, the baptismal font, I said, 'Maybe you can put something on it, says I gave it, okay?' and he says it wouldn't be appropriate. 'It wouldn't be appropriate.' It was appropriate for me to pay some dago son of a bitch in Naples enough money to buy himself a used car so I can get the font out of Italy, but not appropriate for the bishop to thank me. Doesn't matter." He looked to one side, with an expression that said he was lying. "The people here on my street, the people who like me, protect me, they know who brought that font over." He glanced at his watch. "That's all I got to say."

"What did you think of my husband, Gabe Marshall? You said you met him. What did you think of him?"

"Nice guy. For a cop."

"What about Wayne Weaver Honeysett?"

Again, his expression floated between amusement and anger. "What, maybe I should get a lawyer in here? You think I got time to sit here and have you talk to me like I'm in court? You're some broad." And he actually smiled.

"Please," I said. "I appreciate your time and everything."

"Honeysett? The jeweller they found under the bridge, his head crushed? Never met him."

"How do you know his head was crushed? There was nothing in the newspapers about it."

"You think I'm the kind of guy needs to read newspapers to know what's happening?" He began sucking on a back tooth.

For an instant, I considered asking Pilato what else he knew about Honeysett's death. Then sanity returned, and I had another question. "Why is some guy, who looks like he's lived on a desert island for a couple of years, knocking on my door and demanding to see somebody named Grizz?"

"I don't know what you're talking about."

I was out of questions. "Thank you," I said, standing up. "I'll go now."

He followed me to the door, where, I realized, we had been locked in with a complicated system that operated from an electronic keypad. He entered a combination on the keypad, and we both stood in silence while the mechanism whirred and a green light on the wall began flashing. The door swung open, and I walked ahead of Pilato through the dull, dusty foyer to the outer door. As I approached it, it swung inward, opened by the man with the broom and the old fedora.

"Thanks for your time," I said, turning back to Mike Pilato, who remained inside the building, out of sight of the plumber's van.

"Sure." He stood watching me, in no hurry to return to his office.

"I'm sorry if I asked too many questions," I added.

"It's not the questions you asked you should think about," he said. "It's the question you didn't ask."

I closed my eyes. What the hell. "Did you kill my husband?"

"No."

I opened my eyes and saw him looking at me. How could I believe him? "Thank you," I said. I walked through the open area, still vacant, to the outer door.

"That's not the question I meant."

I turned to see Mike Pilato turning to enter his office, saw the door close behind him, and heard the mechanism lock him inside.

The man with the broom and the fedora resumed sweeping the immaculate walkway, stepping aside to permit me to pass.

The plumber's van remained where it had been parked when I arrived. I smiled and waved in its direction.

21.

The telephone was ringing as I arrived home. I usually play the game of speculating who might be calling before I answer. Two weeks earlier I would have believed it was Gabe. I was almost assuming that as I picked up the receiver and said hello.

"What would you like me to buy you?" a male voice said. I recognized it from the call a few days earlier. I also recognized it from somewhere else. I knew that voice. At last, a pervert I could identify, over the telephone, at least.

"I don't want you to buy me anything," I said. "But I want you to tell me how you got this number."

The voice lost its threatening edge and actually stuttered over the next few words. "I . . . I, uh, I did . . . didn't want to upset you, Mrs. Marshall. You're in the telephone book, and I just wondered if you would like to talk, maybe over a coffee or something, you know?"

"No, I don't know. And why are you calling me, anyway?"

"Maybe I'd better call back some other time." He hung up before I could hit him with a decent Oscar Wilde put-down.

I was left standing with the receiver in my hand, telling myself over and over, I know that voice, I know that voice . . .

THE YEAR AFTER MY FIRST HUSBAND LEFT ME for Little Miss Lemon Hair, I lived with a man who called himself a nihilist, a word I looked up in the dictionary after our second date. He made it sound like a career choice, like being a philosopher or a dentist. I figured it was just another way of explaining why he couldn't keep a job.

He was a bright guy with a quirky sense of humour, and the parts of his brain that had avoided being hollowed out by too much LSD remained brilliant. His intelligence attracted me, along with the fact that he was a lost soul whom I figured I could rescue. I had no plans for anything permanent with him. I thought I would clean him up, dress him well, put him on display, and move on to the next lost soul. Tina called it ugly puppy syndrome. "Women like you," she lectured me, "choose the ugliest runt in the litter and think you can turn him into best of show, but you know what? He'll still be a mutt." Her husband, I assumed, came with a pedigree.

Anyway, the nihilist wasn't much to look at and was even less appealing to live with. In fact, the only clear memory I retain of him and his two-room hovel over a butcher shop was a poster he had pinned on the wall beside his bed. The poster showed two buzzards sitting on a dead tree in the middle of the desert. One buzzard is saying to the other, "Patience, hell. I'm gonna kill something."

I was running out of patience. I didn't need to kill something, however. Somebody else had done that work. There's always someone else. Or something else . . .

Gabe had said that when he called me the night he died, when I was with Mother. *There's something else,* he said, and I said, *I know,* and Gabe replied, *How could you know?*

How could I know that I had slept with Mel? That's not what he meant. Gabe meant there was something else he had to tell me, something I could not possibly know.

Patience, hell.

I DON'T KNOW WHY anybody would want to be a cop. Really. All that stuff about wanting to grab bad guys (what do they do about bad women?) comes from people who sit around writing scripts for movies and TV shows. Every male cop I've ever known, and this includes Gabe, wants three things from the job: a chance to meet and screw women under various circumstances; an opportunity to hang out with people who complain about the same things; and a fat pension.

Cops will say they do it because they want to solve crimes and rid the world of bad people, but that's not entirely true. And they don't do it for the excitement, either. Not detectives.

Most detective work doesn't involve car chases, handcuffing suspects, or driving above the speed limit with red lights flashing and sirens screaming. It involves reading dull reports and interviewing even duller people who either don't know what the hell you're talking about or don't want to talk to you in the first place. A lot of it's done at battered desks in cluttered offices with dusty computer screens and wastebaskets filled with empty coffee cups. So I expected to find both Harold Hayashida and Mel in the detective squad area at Central Police Station. I was only half right.

Waiting for the duty cop at the reception desk to finish talking on the telephone, I saw Hayashida in his cubicle, bent over his desk with his palms flat on the surface and an expression on his face that looked as though he was working on a difficult crossword puzzle. Watching him gave me something to do while the duty cop muttered into the telephone receiver, making comments that convinced me he was talking to his mistress, his wife, or someone's lawyer.

"Yeah . . . No . . . Uh-huh . . . Never . . . Impossible . . . Not likely . . . Got it . . . Will do . . ." His last words before hanging up sounded like a sermon. "When it all comes down the pike and everything starts going off the rails, remember who stirred the pot and got the ball rolling, all right?"

He slammed the receiver down and looked up at me. "What would you like, lady?" he asked in his best civil servant welcome.

I resisted the urge to ask if I could borrow a metaphor and requested to speak to either Sergeant Hayashida or Sergeant Holiday.

He asked what about.

I replied, "A murder."

He reacted as though I had said a parking ticket. "Whose?"

"My husband's."

His eyes narrowed and he actually smiled. "Gabe Marshall's?"

By this time Harold had noticed me standing behind the counter, and he called across to the duty cop, saying it was all right, I could come in.

"YOU'RE HERE TO HELP THE INVESTIGATION, RIGHT?"

We were in his cubicle, although Hayashida clearly wished I was somewhere else. He avoided my eyes, keeping his on a handful of papers I couldn't read.

"If I can." It was all the justification I had for being there.

"You can help if you have any information to pass on to us." He tossed the papers aside and looked directly at me for the first time. Something I had done or said, or something someone else had done or said, had upset him. More to the point, it had pissed him off. "Have you?"

"I have a name," I said. "Eugene Griswold."

Hayashida's face was a blank. Clearly, I had told him something he didn't know. "Who?" he asked.

"Griswold. On the street, he's apparently known as Grizz."

He sat back in his chair and stared at me. "How do you know this? That the guy's name, the guy called Grizz, is really Eugene Griswold?"

"Don't you guys know?" Dumb question. Hayashida didn't. "Mike Pilato told me."

"What the hell are you doing talking to Mike Pilato?"

"Why can't I talk to anybody I want? In fact, Mike Pilato was a lot more willing to talk to me than you guys are. And why do you keep parking a plumber's truck in front of Pilato's place? He knows who you are, what you're doing."

"I don't know anything about a plumber's van, okay?"

"You just can't talk about it. Pilato's right. You're both playing games. Meanwhile, people get killed. Like my husband."

Hayashida absorbed this, then reached for a pencil and pad of paper. He began writing, I assumed, Eugene Griswold's name on the paper. I confirmed it by leaning forward to watch, and began spelling Griswold's name aloud. "G-R-I-S—"

Hayashida muttered that he could figure it out for himself, damn it. "This Griswold guy," he said, tossing the pad aside. "He work for Pilato?"

"Doesn't work for anybody. He died about two hundred years ago. In Connecticut."

He tilted his head. "Why are you wasting my time?"

"Mel Holiday knows the name," I said. "And so does Mike Pilato. And you know this guy named Grizz. But nobody can put the pieces together. What is this, a police investigation or a game of charades? And why were you upset with me for wearing the ring Gabe gave me? You think he stole it?"

Hayashida was calm enough to ignore my questions. "Who else have you been talking to? About Gabe's death?"

"Glynnis Dalgetty, Dougal's wife. Dougal Dalgetty was supposedly killed by the guy called Grizz, although she thinks Gabe was—"

"Just so you know," Hayashida interrupted, "Glynnis Dalgetty was convicted of manslaughter about ten years ago."

My turn to sit back in the chair. "She was? Manslaughter?"

"Shot a guy in a hotel room. Said he was trying to rape her. Which, back then, might have been a possibility. Except she couldn't explain what she was doing in the hotel room with a guy who used to work for Mike Pilato, one of Pilato's guys who maybe tried running his own show or was caught skimming from Pilato's take, we don't know for sure. We don't know where Glynnis Dalgetty got the gun, either. Or why the guy was naked. Or why she shot him six times, including twice in the head."

"Glynnis?" I tried picturing her with a gun in her hand, pulling the trigger six times.

"It was enough to get her maybe fifteen years for second-degree murder, based on the facts. I mean, it was such an obvious set-up to us. The court didn't see it that way, as a set-up, I mean. The court considered it practically justifiable homicide. All she got was a two-year suspended sentence on the lesser charge. Nobody here went for a murder conviction. Man with criminal record tries to rape helpless woman, woman defends herself, man loses his life, who cares? That's what the court decided, based on her defence."

"Sounds like she had a good lawyer."

Hayashida nodded. "Took a week for him to talk her into a plea deal and accepting probation, and even less time for the prosecution to accept it. She wanted the charges dropped. She acted like that's what she expected to happen, she'd just walk away scot-free. A month after she walks out of here, she and Dougal are driving around in a shiny new Mercedes-Benz, drinking good liquor until Dougal filled himself with too much Jameson one night and made a wrong turn off a dock into the bay. Somebody saw them and got them out, Dougal and Glynnis. I understand the Benz is still down there."

"Who paid for the lawyer?"

"You want to guess?"

"You're saying Mike Pilato got Dougal and Glynnis to kill somebody for him."

Hayashida turned back to his computer. "No, I'm saying that you should be careful where you go or you could wind up next to Dougal's Mercedes."

"He was pretty talkative today. Almost charming."

"Because he wasn't talking business. He never talks business in his office. He's afraid we've bugged it."

"Have you?"

Hayashida smiled. "He takes lots of walks. With people he wants to talk business with. And he doesn't want anybody listening in."

"I don't give a damn about his business, whatever it is, and it's sure not hardware. What's wrong with asking about Gabe? What's wrong with flattering him a little, letting him think he's charming me?"

He looked across at me. "I'm serious, Josie. If Mike Pilato snaps his fingers because he wants you dead, you'll be gone before he can put his hand back in his pocket."

I had come in like Nancy Drew and been reduced to Anne of Green Gables. "Glynnis Dalgetty thinks Gabe shot her husband."

Hayashida said, "Maybe he did."

He was staring at me, waiting for my reaction, which was to tell him that it was total crap, Gabe never shot anybody. Including himself.

Hayashida thought about this while I watched him watching me. Then he stood up, looked around to make sure no one was eavesdropping, sat down again, and leaned toward me, his hands on his knees. "I think you should go get a coffee."

I thought he wanted me to play cop station waitress. "Where's the machine?" I asked, looking around.

"Not here." He kept his voice low. Anyone beyond the cubicle wouldn't hear a thing. "There's a Tim Hortons down the street, about four blocks down on your right. Go have yourself a coffee. In the last cubicle near the rear exit, if it's available. Okay?"

When I stood up to leave, Hayashida whispered, "Ten minutes," but it didn't register immediately because I was looking beyond the cubicle to the open corridor leading to Walter Freeman's office. I knew it was his office because the sign on the door said CHIEF OF DETECTIVES WALTER FREEMAN and because the oversized son of a bitch was waiting for a man to enter the office ahead of him, a guy with sandy hair and a good physique wearing a neat blue jacket over a white shirt and brown chinos, a guy who was calm and smiling slightly and not foaming at the mouth and screaming for me to tell him where Grizz was, which is what he had been doing the last time I saw him. Just as he entered Walter's office, Walter scanned the squad area to see who was watching, and I enjoyed a brief thrill of Up Yours when his eyes locked on mine.

"That's—" I began, leaning toward Hayashida, who had been busy adding something to his notepad.

Hayashida looked up at me, frowning. I wanted to say more, but Walter had closed the door behind the guy in the windbreaker and was walking toward me, gesturing for the cop on the reception desk to join him as he approached.

I expected Walter to ask what the hell I was doing in a place where he didn't want me, but he didn't speak to me at all. Instead, he spoke to the duty cop, who was hustling across the floor at Walter's command. "Evict this woman," he said in his best supreme commander's voice. "Tell her she's been witnessed consorting with a convicted felon by law enforcement officers and inform her that if she sets foot in this building again without a direct request from someone in this department, she will be charged with trespassing."

"This is a goddamn public building," I said to Walter, who was already heading back to his office. "I just might charge you with police harassment, Walter. Consorting? What the hell does that mean? And what are you doing with a junkie in your office?"

The last few words were aimed at the door to Walter's office, which did not answer back because it was closed.

The obedient duty cop appeared to be deciding whether to use kind words or pepper spray to encourage me to leave, but I gave him time to use neither.

"YOU'RE LATE," I said to Hayashida when he slid into the booth opposite me. It was half an hour later.

"Walter," Hayashida said, "would have me downtown patrolling washrooms if he knew I was here."

"So why are you?" I asked. "Here, I mean."

"You said something back there that's important."

"I said something important? You're sure it was me?"

He looked across at the donut display. Cops are around donuts like squirrels are around peanuts. What is it, the fat? The sugar? The shape? "You said Glynnis Dalgetty believed your husband shot her husband."

"She's wrong."

"I agree." Hayashida tore his eyes away from the chocolate-iced lovelies to look at me. "Except, today the lab confirmed that the bullet that killed Dalgetty came from Gabe's gun."

"Then they're wrong too. Gabe did not shoot that woman's husband." Before Hayashida could speak, I added, "And Dalgetty was killed, what? A month ago? Six weeks ago? And you've just learned he was shot by Gabe's gun? Hey, when're you going to hear that Princess Diana died?"

Hayashida opened his hands and stared at his palms. "We got a tip from somebody to say we should compare the slug from Dalgetty's head with the one . . . the one we removed from Gabe. We knew they were both the same calibre, and probably came from the same kind of gun. But it never occurred to us to put both under the scope and check."

"Dalgetty was executed."

"That's right."

"Then so was Gabe."

"Or, having killed Dalgetty, Gabe might have been remorseful or threatened with being identified as the killer . . ."

"Which would drive him to suicide."

"It's a possibility."

I needed time to absorb this. "The guy who went into Walter's office today," I said, "wearing a blue windbreaker. He's a nutcase, a junkie, looking all over for Grizz because he needs a fix, I guess, or whatever they call it now—"

"He's a narc." Hayashida was watching me as though daring me to react, which was enough to shut my mouth. "Undercover. Sent over from Toronto. Trying to flush out the guy named Grizz. That's how you do it. Get somebody putting out the word and hoping for a reaction. By the way, I hear the guys in the plumber's truck got some good shots of you entering and leaving Mike Pilato's place. I hear they're pretty flattering."

I said, "I need more coffee."

"You say a word about this, about the narc or about Gabe's gun being identified as the weapon that was used on Dougal Dalgetty, and Walter will find a reason to turn your house upside down and arrest you for having your lipstick smeared."

"I don't tell stories I don't believe."

"Doesn't matter what you believe. I've been here nearly fifteen years. Biggest lesson I learned? Don't screw around with Walter Freeman."

I held my head in my hands. Nothing was what it had seemed a couple of weeks ago. So I thought about the Buddhist.

I dated a Buddhist just before meeting Gabe. I had been looking for somebody gentle, trustworthy, spiritual. He was all of that. He was also a strict vegetarian. I never got tired of the sex, but I sure got tired of tofu and being told that the world does not exist as we see it but as we imagine it. Or something like that. He was drifting from Buddhism into a mild addiction to hashish, which seemed to strengthen his spiritual side. It made me think that drugs are for people who can't handle religion. Didn't Karl Marx say something like that?

I was staring into my coffee cup, thinking about Buddhists and Karl Marx and remembering what it was like to live with a guy who ate one meal a day and how I never wanted to do anything with my life except live with Gabe on the beach strip and how that dream was gone forever and maybe I was the one who had destroyed it by sleeping with Mel Holiday, when Hayashida mentioned his name. "What?" I said, looking up.

"Mel Holiday." Hayashida drained his coffee cup. "Talk to him. He's been working hard on Gabe's case. You need somebody to lean on. Maybe protect you."

"Protect me? From what? From who?"

"We're dealing with a murder and two suicides. Or maybe two murders and one suicide. Anyway, somebody was involved, somewhere."

"Which suicide are you questioning?"

Hayashida stood up and looked around at everything except the donuts. "I don't know."

22.

That Buddhist I mentioned? He was a photographer. He did weddings, parties, bar mitzvahs, portraits, anything people would pay him to aim a camera at. On sunny days, he would make a point of going outside just before sunset. He was waiting for the magic hour. That's what he called the time when the sun was about to go down. In summer, the magic hour lasted, he explained, a full sixty minutes. In the winter, you were lucky to catch ten minutes of it.

The magic hour, he said, was when more light reflected on you from the sky than from the sun. It was indirect light, and it was flattering to everything. It was the best light in which to take photographs, and also the best light to study and appreciate the world around us. "It's soft light, full light. Rich light. Look at trees during the magic hour," he would say. "They are more majestic, more alive than in the hard light of noon. And look at people in the magic hour. They are more beautiful, more open, more accessible."

At first, I was impressed with his artist's eye. I saw what he meant. I understood his meaning. But his raving about the way the world is lit just before sunset became something of a rant by the tenth time he repeated it. Which is when I told him I agreed entirely, and what I really wanted to see in the light of the magic hour or the light of a candle wasn't another bowl of tofu and bean sprouts, but a greasy cheeseburger I could call my own, and that this particular romance was over.

After Hayashida went back to Central, I left Tim Hortons in the magic hour. The world didn't look any more attractive or accessible than it had an hour earlier.

I HAD LEARNED that Glynnis Dalgetty had killed a man, probably on Mike Pilato's orders. I wanted to ask her about it. I wanted to know what it was like to watch bullets enter a man's body and see him writhe on the floor until, I guess, she shot him in the head. Twice. What did the gun feel like in her hand? What was she thinking while she killed him? The colour of the Mercedes-Benz she'd get? Leftovers in the refrigerator? But I couldn't believe it had anything to do with Gabe's death.

I had also learned a little about Mike Pilato. I wanted to learn more.

The street where White Star Hardware Distributors was located had been deserted barely an hour earlier. Now the plumbing van was gone, and in the early moments of the magic hour it had become a combination playground, village square, and movie set. Teenage boys raced their skateboards along the pavement and up over the curbs. Girls their age in halter tops and shorts exchanged earbuds for their iPods or other music devices, closing their eyes, raising their clenched fists, and dancing on the spot to music only they heard and, I suspected, only they could tolerate. Two older women, their heads wrapped in bandanas, stood speaking and gesturing to each other while two men their age, who I assumed were their husbands, watched the procession on the other side of the street, the side where White Star Hardware Distributors was located and where Mike Pilato was.

Pilato still wore the black and gold shirt and black trousers. He walked with two men, Pilato doing the talking while the men kept pace with him and listened, nodding and sometimes gesturing with their hands to communicate expressions I interpreted as agreement, surprise, or anger. They were accompanied by four younger men, two about twenty feet ahead and two a similar distance behind. All four appeared to have purchased their clothes from the same tailor: open-necked shirts with wide collars, dark trousers, and black pointed-toe shoes. They also appeared to buy their sunglasses from the same place: dark Ray-Bans that hid their eyes completely. The three with hair seemed to patronize the same barber, a man who appreciated thick, dark hair and did his best to enhance it. The fourth man's head was shaved, the better to reveal a tattoo on his skull. The tattoo was an arrow pointing forward to a word above his forehead that I couldn't read.

The seven men—Mike and his two partners, plus the four men who reminded me of outriders in old movies about cattle drives—were performing some kind of choreography. Whenever Mike and his friends stopped while Mike said something obviously important, the outriders halted as well. When Mike began walking again, the younger men matched their pace, their heads swivelling constantly from side to side.

When I slowed the car, lowered the window and called out to Mike, all seven men stopped walking and glared at me. I felt as though I had been asked to identify myself at a border crossing and had used the name Mrs. Osama bin Laden.

Instead of speaking to me, Mike looked at the two outriders ahead of him and nodded.

The man with the arrow on his head walked quickly into the street ahead of my car. His partner, I sensed, was behind me. I suppose, if I had pressed the accelerator to the floor, I could have run down Arrowhead, but I assumed this would be a suicidal act. Arrowhead walked to the open window on my side of the car and spoke without looking at me. "Keep moving," he said.

I said I wanted to speak to Mike Pilato for a moment.

"You can't," he said. "Just get the hell out of here."

"Why won't he talk to me? He's right over—"

"Drive away."

"Okay, he's busy, I can see that—"

"Drive away. Now."

"Will you give him a message?"

"No."

"Well, I don't see why—" I began. This time it wasn't Arrowhead who prevented me from finishing my sentence. This time I stopped talking because something struck the back of the Honda with the force of a gunshot. I twisted in my seat to look behind me. Arrowhead's partner had hair on his head, a misaligned nose on his face, and a small sledgehammer in his hand. Where the heck had he gotten a sledgehammer? It hardly mattered, because he swung it again, and the Honda lurched forward from the blow.

Before pressing the accelerator to the floor, I looked across at Mike Pilato, who raised one hand, palm out, and someone barked a short flurry of Italian words as the Honda, like a horse who had just been slapped in the ass, sped away from White Star Hardware Distributors.

"I HAVE TWO DENTS IN MY CAR that you could hide grapefruit in."

The hand holding the last of my brandy in a glass from the kitchen was shaking. The hand holding the telephone was not, so Mel's voice remained loud, clear, and comforting in my ear.

"I'll talk to him. I'll talk to Pilato, tell him he's gone over the line."

"How can those guys do that? How can they just walk out on the street and start smashing somebody's car with a sledgehammer?"

"They went too far. So did you."

"Mel, it's a public street, damn it!"

"Not when Mike Pilato is having a meeting on it."

"Meeting? He's walking with two greaseballs—"

"And talking business. Makes it harder for us to bug him."

"So you let him get away with this?"

"Pilato will probably pay for the damage."

"I don't care about that. I'd like somebody to go after *him* with a sledgehammer and leave a couple of dents in *his* rusting old body." When he said nothing, I added, "You're smirking, aren't you?"

"No," he said. "I'm serious, and I'm concerned about you."

"Mel, I don't have any idea what's going on, except that everything is linked. Gabe's death, what happened to Wayne Honeysett, Glynnis Dalgetty . . . did you know she was convicted of manslaughter and would have gone to prison if Mike Pilato hadn't hired a lawyer for her, and when she got a suspended sentence . . . you know all this, don't you?"

Mel said yes, he knew. He knew more that he couldn't tell me.

"Why not?"

"Because there are things going on, Josie, that you don't want to be involved in."

I told him he was wrong. I told him I wanted to know everything that involved Gabe's death.

"Then I'll tell you. Soon." He promised to call me the next day.

When the telephone rang five minutes later, I assumed he couldn't wait.

It wasn't Mel. It was Pilato. "First you're not home, or not answering, then you're talking to somebody so's you can't answer. All the time, I'm calling, calling, getting nothing but ringing or a busy signal. Good thing I'm a more patient man than people think, eh?"

"Why did your thugs smash my car?" I said. I am very brave when separated from a gangster by a telephone cord.

"Why did you go to Central Police Station when you left here?"

"How do you know that?"

"You ask me that? I ask you this. What's it look like, some woman I never met comes into my office, talks about somebody murdering her husband, then goes to the police? You think I like that? You think I don't wonder what you're saying, why you see me? Huh?"

"So that gives you the right to have two of your hired hoods smash in my car?"

"Get it fixed and send me the bill."

"No, I won't. I'll drive that poor little car into the ground, and every time somebody comments on the dents in my trunk lid, I'll tell them that's what I got for driving down a public street in front of your office. How's that?"

"You think that's a big deal to me? You think I haven't been accused of bigger things than putting a couple of dents in that piece of crap you drive?"

"Like murder?" Nobody was going to swing a sledgehammer at me through a telephone receiver.

"You accusing me of that? Because you better be careful, Mrs. Marshall. You be careful with stuff like that. You come to see me, I'm nice to you, try to help you out, tell you a couple of stories. You start saying people get killed because of me, you forget about us being friends—"

"*I am not your goddamn friend!*" I shouted through the telephone. "The only thing . . ." I began. My throat had gone dry. I began again. "The only thing I ever want to discuss with you is the death of my husband, and if you had anything to do with it, I'll see your Italian ass in prison." I really said "Italian ass."

"You watch yourself, okay?" Pilato replied. "You watch yourself. You're pissed, you're upset because you think somebody killed your husband. Okay, okay. You loved your husband, that makes you a good wife, a good woman. I like that, it's good. But you watch who you yell at like that, you hear me?"

"Did you have my husband killed?"

"I already told you, no."

"No, you said you didn't kill him. I just asked if you had him killed. Do you think he committed suicide?"

"Again, no."

"Then who killed him? I mean, the police are saying he killed himself and that he shot Dougal Dalgetty."

"They're saying that? How come they're saying that?"

"They say Gabe must have shot Dougal Dalgetty because the forensics lab matched the bullets, the bullets came from the same gun that killed Gabe, and I don't think I was supposed to tell you that."

"Too late."

"So there's something going on here that I can't figure out and maybe you can. Or maybe I shouldn't say anything more, so whatever you do, you didn't hear it from me, right? About the bullets matching, okay? Hello?"

Mike Pilato had hung up on me.

"WHENEVER YOU SEE A BEAUTIFUL SUNSET," my Buddhist photographer boyfriend of a few months told me, "turn around and look 180 degrees in the other direction, to the east. All sunsets are pretty much alike. But the light they cast is always somehow different."

Facing east across the lake, I was reminded of his words. This was an evening like the one he meant, soft and glowing, with the immediate world acquiring a tangerine radiance that I always find both uplifting and melancholy. Why did Mike Pilato appear to find it so interesting that the lab report identified Gabe's gun as the one that killed Dougal Dalgetty? Obviously, I had told him all he needed to know, because he hung up on me without asking or waiting for more details. As if I had them.

I walked through my garden, noted with some comfort that the door to the garden shed remained closed and locked, and stepped up to the laneway to look across the expanse of water that lay ahead of me, flat and smooth and glassy. Buildings on the shore to my left and right shone like jewels in the gold rays. I could make myself believe, with a little effort and a larger dose of imagination, that I was looking at an artist's rendering of an idyllic scene.

The image, like all of my fantasies, lasted only for an instant. I became aware of people around me. An elderly couple walking hand in hand on the water's edge, both wearing white trousers, the cuffs rolled up over their calves, each carrying their shoes so they could feel the coolness of the water on their bare feet. The woman, her hair silver-grey, leaned her head against the man's shoulder and laughed at something he said to her. Three guys in their twenties were walking in the other direction, across the sand, passing a bottle of beer between them, laughing and looking constantly around to make sure everyone saw how cool they were, and keeping an eye out for cops who could make things very uncool. Here came Hans and Trudy, walking their schnauzer and maybe discussing recipes for sauerkraut. They waved and were about to greet me when I noticed the slim, balding man about twenty feet to my right, leaning against a tree next to the boardwalk, watching me.

"Who's minding the bridge?" I called to him, and Tom Grychuk smiled and pushed himself away from the tree to walk toward me.

"Wondered when you might notice me," he said. He wore a striped golf shirt, cotton trousers, and sneakers. Mister Suburbia with a civil service salary. Hans and Trudy passed, watching us carefully. I smiled to reassure them and turned back to Grychuk. "Okay," I said, "I caught you. You're it. Now what?"

"I just wondered if, I don't know . . ." He looked at his shoes, then, as though he had read something on them, looked up with a grin that made him look as shy as he no doubt felt. "I was wondering if maybe we could have a coffee together, or maybe a drink at Tuffy's."

I wasn't listening as closely to the words as I was to the voice. "You're the guy," I said.

"The guy?"

"The one who called me. On the telephone. Saying you would buy me something."

"Oh, yeah." He looked away, then down at his shoes again. "Well, you answered the telephone the first time I called and asked what I had bought you, remember?"

Of course I remembered. I thought it was Tina calling back. It was Grychuk.

"You're asking me for a date?"

He shrugged. "Maybe just a talk."

"About what?"

He shrugged again. "Things."

I felt like I was back in grade eleven, talking to some nerd from algebra class. "Some other time," I said, and turned toward my gate. "And don't hang around my house anymore, please. You perverts are liable to trip over each other and wreck the roses."

"I'm not a pervert, Mrs. Marshall."

I walked through the gate, closed it, and looked back at him. He was caught in the same setting sunlight as the rest of the scene and, like the rest of the scene, it made him look nostalgic. Not Grychuk himself, who was hurt. Just the whole picture, the sunlight, the lake, the sky.

Grychuk put his hands in his pockets and walked toward me, lowering his voice. "I just thought you were a nice woman and might need some company. Seeing as how you lost your husband and I lost my wife last year, we could talk about things. That's all. Not really a date. You gotta talk about things sometime, right?"

"Sure," I said. "Maybe sometime. Not now."

I left him standing in the lane, watching me walk through the garden and through the back door of my house, which I secured with the double locks.

23.

I woke the next morning resigned and determined. Resigned to the fact that I was not likely to learn the truth about Gabe and Wayne Honeysett and the whole damn thing until Mel or someone else let me in on the secrets they were keeping from me. And determined to get on with my life. I would not stop searching for the truth about my husband's death, but I would find things to do that gave me as much sense of normalcy as I could expect.

One thing I could do was return to work at Trafalgar Towers. I would need the income more than ever, it would provide a reason to get out of bed, and the job would enable me to see more of Mother.

It was another mild and sunny day, so I decided to walk to the retirement home, crossing the lift bridge on foot for the first time since Wayne Weaver Honeysett had spoken to me from beneath it. I stared straight ahead to avoid seeing the bridge operator's window, although I knew Grychuk wouldn't be there so early in the day. Crossing the bridge, I followed the road leading back to Lakeshore Boulevard, turned right at the second street, and climbed the steps to Trafalgar Towers, surprised by how comforting it felt to return to a familiar routine.

Intuition is never turned off. Not mine, anyway. When I entered the reception area, Candace, the day receptionist, glanced at me with a smile that faded almost immediately, and looked back at her computer screen. Candace and I were hardly sorority sisters, but I could usually make her smile with some snappy observation. She once took my advice about ditching an abusive boyfriend and thanked me for weeks, so her response at the sight of me entering the reception area was confusing.

"I'm back," I said when I reached her counter. "I need the work, I need the money, and I need to see your smiling face. How're you doing?"

Candace said she was fine, never taking her eyes from the computer while reaching for the telephone receiver. "I'll tell Helen you're here," she said. After one quick glance at me, then away again, she added, "She wants to see you."

This was strange, but so had my life been for the past couple of weeks, and when Candace said, "You can go up now," I took the elevator to the third floor and Helen's office.

The elevator faced Helen's door, and both opened simultaneously. I stepped out to see Helen standing at the entrance to her office, waiting for me to arrive. "Come in," she said, and when I passed her, she said, "Please sit down," and closed the door behind her.

"What's going on?" I asked when she settled herself in her chair, facing me across her polished and empty desk.

"I'm not sure what you mean." Her hands were clasped in front of her.

"First Candace treats me like I'm some broom peddler off the street, and now you're acting as though you'd prefer not to see me."

"Actually, I wanted to see you," she said. "Are you here to discuss your job?"

"And to see my mother."

"I'm certain she will be pleased to see you. She is concerned about you." She frowned at a spot on her desk, pressed her index finger on what I assumed was a speck of dust, and wiped it on her dress.

"Why are you acting like this?" I asked. "Last week you were hugging me and now you're behaving as though . . . I don't know, as though I'm a threat or carrying some kind of disease . . ."

"We had a visit yesterday from a senior police official." When I said nothing, she added, "He was making inquiries about you."

"About me? What kind of inquiries?"

"So far . . ." She was uncomfortable. Good. So was I. She began again. "So far they have been only empty charges, only suspicions, nothing definite—"

"Helen," I interrupted, "I don't have any idea what the hell you're talking about. For god's sake, get to the point. What is going on?"

"This officer, this detective, wanted to know if anything, uh, untoward has occurred in our finances lately. If there is any money missing or improper cheques issued, that kind of thing."

"You mean they're wondering if I'm crooked? They're suggesting I'm stealing from the place, skimming money, submitting false invoices, getting kickbacks, that kind of thing?"

This seemed to give her confidence. She arched her eyebrows and sat up straighter. "You certainly appear familiar with those activities," she said.

"Did you believe him, whoever it was who came here?"

"The allegations were made, as I said, by an individual in an office of some authority with the police department, and I would be foolish to ignore them."

"Well, you were an ass to believe them," I snapped. "Who told you these things? Who's accusing me of stealing from you?"

She raised her chin, and with a voice and attitude that would have done Queen Victoria proud, she said, "I prefer not to identify the individual."

She didn't have to. "Walter Freeman, right? Big guy, nose like a walnut, head like a melon?"

She twisted her mouth and looked away.

"He's upset with me because I refuse to believe his crap about my husband committing suicide. My husband was murdered, Helen, and Walter and his incompetent creeps are pissed at me because I insist on them getting off their asses to find who did it. That's why he came in here to spread rumours about me. I haven't taken a damn penny from this place that wasn't mine."

"We are making other arrangements," Helen said. "For your job. Of course, if our audit reveals that the allegations are false, you may be invited back to reclaim your position."

"I don't plan to reclaim anything," I said, standing up. "Except my mother."

"Your mother is a wonderful woman," Helen said to my back as I headed for the door. "She will always be welcome here."

I'LL GET OUT OF HERE AS SOON AS I CAN, Mother wrote on her blackboard. I had finished describing my encounter with Helen Detwiler.

"Don't," I said. "I'm not moving, and there's nowhere else this nice for you that's close to the beach strip."

Mother erased the words on her blackboard and wrote, *You have been difficult, but you have always been honest.*

"Not always," I said. "Mother, I have not done anything wrong here. You believe me, don't you?"

And she wrote, *You are my sweetheart. You always have been. Of course I believe you.*

I was damned if I would shed tears in front of Helen, but at the sight and the meaning of Mother's words, I sank to my knees and lowered my face to her lap while she stroked my head and wiped away my tears.

WALTER FREEMAN WOULDN'T SPEAK TO ME. "He said you could leave a message," the duty cop at Central told me over the telephone. "If you have a complaint about his conduct, you can write the commissioner."

I promised I would, after the audit at Trafalgar Towers cleared my name.

But before I did that, I would go to Vancouver.

It wasn't Tina I wanted to see. It wasn't even Vancouver, which I have always considered a city that's like somebody else's attractive spouse. You visit because it gives you a thrill, you have a good time, and after the thrills have ended you get the hell out of there. Later, you feel silly about being seduced by mountains and ocean and mild weather and tofu, and you forget about them until the next time you realize your own spouse is boring. So where do Vancouver people go for that kind of sensual fix?

It didn't matter. I had so many things in my head, none of them good, that I just wanted a few days away. Let someone else worry about the meals and the dishes and the dusting and Walter Freeman and perverts. Tina and Andrew had a house you could park a jetliner inside, and a full-time maid. It would do.

I found a noon-hour flight the next day at a price that wouldn't convert my credit card into an improvised explosive device, then called Tina, who became appropriately hysterical.

"I love it! I love it!" she said, and I pictured her almost jumping up and down. "We'll go shopping, we'll do lunches, we'll gossip." Tina is as predictable as a perpetual calendar. "We'll cruise Robson Street. There's this sweet little café where the waiters are athletes, two of them from the Winter Olympics—and I think a couple of them are gay, but who cares—and Andrew would love to talk to you, he always loves talking to you, and the only problem is my bridge club."

I asked why her bridge club would be a problem.

"Because this week it's my turn to host it, but if you don't mind . . . you play bridge, don't you?"

I asked with whom I might play bridge, here on the beach strip.

"But you know how? I mean, I know Daddy taught you. He taught both of us. Anyway, sometimes we need a fourth hand for one of the tables, and maybe you can fill in. I promise not to ignore you." She took a deep breath, long overdue, and a new Tina was speaking, the quiet, solicitous one. "Oh, sweetie, I'm so glad you're coming, really. I can only imagine what you've been through, and I'm sorry I wasn't more help when I was there with you."

"You were all the help I needed, Tina," I assured her. "Don't worry about it. You've been the perfect sister." And she had been. From time to time.

I could almost feel her tears through the receiver. "That's lovely, Josie. Really. Thank you. What time does your plane arrive?"

The officious Tina returned. She told me not to bring too many clothes because we would buy a whole wardrobe, and besides, I shouldn't have a bag big enough to check, carry-on was always better, and she was going to tell Goldie to put new sheets on the guest bed, Andrew's brother had slept there last, he was a carpenter in Moose Jaw, and those sheets just wouldn't do, she had some flowered 600-thread-count Egyptian cotton sheets in the prettiest pattern with lilacs at the edge—

I cut her off before I changed my mind and cancelled the trip in the interest of self-preservation. And who the heck was Goldie?

I RETURNED TO TRAFALGAR TOWERS, driving this time, and avoiding eye contact with staff members when I got there. Mother was alone in her room, reading an Elmore Leonard novel. For her birthday two years earlier, I'd bought her a leather-bound set of *The Collected Works of Jane Austen,* which she kept displayed on a side table like a family heirloom. *Good writer, but a prude,* Mother wrote to me on her blackboard. She preferred tough talk over sense and sensibility.

Good! Mother wrote when I told her I was going to spend a few days with Tina. *When you come back, they'll have done their audit and will know the truth!*

She was pleased to hear I was visiting Tina because it was preferable, I suspected, to having Tina visit her.

Mother loved Tina, because Mother was a good woman who loved her children, which is what mothers are supposed to do. But there had been too many clashes between them over too many years, and I honestly believe that when Tina announced she and Andrew would be living in Vancouver and would keep in touch one way or another, Mother was relieved. Her daughter was married to a successful doctor. They would be living two thousand miles away. And they would not be having any children, meaning no grandchildren for her. Well, two out of three . . .

We didn't discuss this, Mother and I. "I'll be back within a week," I explained. "I just need a break, somebody to do the things for me that you always did," and I began to cry.

Mother reached her arms to me and I bent into them, her sitting silent in the wheelchair and me, for the second time that day, becoming ten years old again, just for a minute, to enjoy the feeling.

MY DECISION TO VISIT TINA may not have been profound, but it was popular.

"Josie, you don't know how good this makes me feel," Mel told me. We were in a café down the lake toward Toronto, the remains of our dinner in front of us, the lake shining beyond the window. I had suggested we have dinner together. I didn't want to meet Mel in my home or his apartment. I just needed a bit of normalcy, or as much as you can have with an ex-lover.

He wasn't surprised to hear about Walter Freeman's visit to Helen Detwiler or his suggestions that I might have been stealing from the retirement home. "He's fixated on that expensive ring and where Gabe got the money for it," Mel said. "But more than that, he's really upset with you. Walter's not used to people standing up to him, not treating him with the respect he wants. He's getting back at you in the best way he knows how. Maybe the only way." He reached across the table and took my hands in his. "This will all blow over, and when it does . . ." He searched for words. "I've been worried about you, and confused about what happened between us."

"Confused?" I had expected guilt.

He looked out at the lake, gathering more words. Plastic surgeons could use his profile as a template for every male patient who wanted his face corrected—the perfect squared chin, the full mouth, the straight, ideally proportioned nose, the narrow eyes, the uncreased forehead . . .

"I'm sorry about the pain it caused Gabe." He turned from the window to face me again. "But you know what? I don't regret it completely, because of what you came to mean to me. That's why, sometimes, I might appear tongue-tied or say the wrong things or not say the right things." He lowered his head and leaned toward me. "Do you understand?"

I told him I did. I told him we both shared whatever amount of guilt needed to be passed around. I told him I would love to talk about what we had done, and how, when enough time had passed, when all the mystery and questions surrounding Gabe's death had been resolved. At that point, we might renew our relationship, if we were both comfortable. "Do you know what I would like?" I added. "I would like you to play some of that music you played for me once, that nice bluesy stuff, and tell me who it is and what became of the musicians."

He smiled and said, "Sometime soon," then looked at his watch and told me he had to check on a stakeout team down on Barton Street. "Things are coming together," he said.

I drove home pleased that I was going to Vancouver and even more pleased about what I would be returning to.

24.

The warm Tina and the cool Andrew awaited me at the airport in Vancouver, Tina running toward me with arms outstretched and Andrew hanging back, clutching a bouquet of flowers. I felt like a bride arriving at her honeymoon resort.

I survived the hugs and took the flowers and Tina's arm, and we all walked out of the airport and into Andrew's Lexus, Tina boasting about the Vancouver weather and the dinner that she and her new maid, Goldie, were planning for us, while Andrew drove us past glass walls and greenery. Everything in Vancouver is green from rain, and maybe from misplaced envy.

An hour later I was sitting in the den on Point Grey Road, the den's picture window framing a view that the local tourist bureau no doubt approved and had perhaps even created. We looked across English Bay to the downtown core, its office towers and condominiums shining in the sun. Beyond them, marking the horizon, mountains shone, capped with enamel-white snow. I have been jealous of few things or people in my life, but the view through that window made my dream of living on the beach strip seem about as ambitious as putting on socks in the morning.

Andrew made me a drink, a vodka and tonic with a perfect slice of lemon and a sprig of mint, served in a Waterford crystal glass. He refilled both our drinks within five minutes while he and I nibbled on buttery Camembert served with crackers shaped like flowers. Dorothy Parker was damn straight: living well really is the best revenge. Tina was in the kitchen, supervising Goldie, based on the clatter of pots and dishes that drifted up the hallway toward us.

"I must tell you," Andrew said after I assured him that I was more than pleased with the drink, "how excited Tina has been about your coming here." Andrew is lean and tall and speaks with a mild English accent. He looked around and lowered his voice as though assuring himself that my sister was not hiding around the corner, eavesdropping. "Tina can be a little, uh, wrapped up in herself at times," he said.

"You mean narcissistic?" I suggested.

He smiled and nodded. At heart, Andrew is a nice man. I often felt that he shared some genes with certain jazz musicians who, I remember reading, become truly at ease with themselves and the world only when they are making music. Andrew, I suspected, was truly at ease only when in an operating room, an anaesthetized patient in front of him, a surgical team around him, and a scalpel in his hand. A little ghoulish, maybe, but wouldn't it be comforting to know that the man who is about to slice open your body and expose its innards to the world didn't want to be doing anything else with his life?

"Mind you," Andrew said, "the word 'narcissistic' has a pejorative sense to it, and I'm not sure that I would want to apply it in a cavalier manner to Tina, who, as you know, has many admirable qualities."

Two of the most admirable qualities in a man are his easy use of phrases like "cavalier manner" and his quick defence of his wife, whether she deserves it or not. I assured Andrew that I meant no disrespect to my sister by using the term "narcissistic." Andrew was so pleased with my comment that he didn't notice when I checked to confirm that my nose hadn't grown.

"She is so fond and so envious of you," he said, sampling his own drink.

"What would I have that would ever make Tina envious?" The vodka was warming. I decided I would drink less brandy and more Smirnoff.

"Your outlook. Your sense of self. Your . . ." He smiled over his glass at me. "Joie de vivre."

Thank goodness. I thought he was going to say my boobs.

He was still talking. The vodka was loosening him as much as me. "Tina wraps herself up in material things because she lacks your ability to take life as it comes. Those are her words, by the way. Not mine. 'Josie would be happy living in sneakers and jeans every day,' she has said to me a couple of times. 'She just knows how to take life as it comes and not give a damn about anything else.' She meant that as a compliment. I mean, Josie, she really adores you. In her own way."

"We're different," I agreed. "But we're close. In our own way."

He looked toward the open door again and began sliding his chair closer to me. "I know she spends too much time and effort on incidentals in life." He paused and actually smothered a giggle before speaking again, which suggested that his drink was stronger than mine. "Sometimes I tell people I think I'm married to a centipede when I see all the shoes she keeps in her closet. Did I mention we converted the guest bedroom, the one next to ours, into a closet for Tina's clothes?" He drained his drink. "Another?" he said, holding his empty glass for me to inspect.

Like a dutiful sister-in-law, I passed the empty glass to him, and he turned to the small bar next to the window just as Tina leaned in through the open doorway. "How are you two getting along?" she asked. She had changed from the sweater and skirt she wore earlier into a satiny green dress under a flowered apron. She had even changed her lipstick from coral red to a deep crimson, a better match for deep green. At least her hair colour was the same.

"We're having a fine old time," I said, "talking about you."

"I love it when people talk about me," she said. "The nastier the better." She held up five fingers. I thought she was showing off her manicure. "Five minutes," she said. "Ten at the most." She disappeared down the hall.

"We may have to do more drinking and less talking," Andrew said, handing me my third drink.

"The key to sociability," I said, and we touched the rims of our glasses together. I was beginning to like Andrew. "Your work is so interesting," I said. "Can you tell me about it?"

He gave it some thought. "After a while . . ." he said, and began again. "After all the years I've been doing surgery, more than twenty now, there are few surprises, and the surprises I encounter are never good news, only bad. I regret that a little. I think our lives are better when we are surprised from time to time, don't you? I don't mean big surprises like your spouse announcing that she's leaving you or . . ."

He looked away. I knew what he had been about to say. He had been about to say we don't need surprises like finding your spouse dead.

We both began speaking at once. I started to tell him that he needn't be embarrassed, it was a normal thing to say, but when I heard him speaking, looking out the window at the mountaintops, I stopped. "I have come to believe that a truly happy life is poised on the edge between routine and normalcy and risk and surprises," Andrew said. "Maybe that's why people do things like skydiving or riding roller coasters."

Or having affairs with their husband's partner, I thought.

"Anyway, I'm sharing office space at the clinic now with a urologist," Andrew said before taking a long pull from his drink. "We have a lot of fun together. I call him the plumber and he calls me the butcher." He laughed at his own joke.

The sounds drifting up the hall from the kitchen were growing louder, along with Tina's voice barking instructions to the silent Goldie.

"Tina is very lucky to be married to you, Andrew," I said.

He blushed. What makes a celebrated surgeon blush? A compliment.

"Thank you," Andrew said, and set his glass aside. "Thank you, Josie, that's very kind. You know," and he pulled his chair a few inches closer, "I know Tina has her faults and all of that, and we have our little disagreements over things, but I could do worse. Than be married to her, I mean. Some of her friends . . . are you playing bridge with them Thursday?"

"Actually, I hope not."

"Avoid it if you can. A couple of her friends, Charlene and what's the other one? Davida. Charlene and Davida, they are really over the top. Kiss you on the cheek and stab you in the back. Simultaneously." He stumbled through that word, adding an extra syllable or two. "I came home . . ." He glanced at the doorway, confirmed that Tina wasn't lurking there with a shotgun, and dropped his voice so low it was my turn to pull my chair closer. "I came home one afternoon just as the bridge club meeting was breaking up. Davida had already left with a couple of other girls—that's what they call themselves, and that's all right, I guess—and three or four of them were getting ready to leave. I got some kisses from them, and then Charlene discovered that someone had walked off with her handbag. She knew it was Davida because they both have the same Louis Vuitton purse, so it was an easy mistake to make. But what happened next was that Charlene and the other women—except Tina, I'm proud to say—when they knew it was Davida's purse, they opened it and practically ransacked it, looking at all her receipts, her pictures, her address book, everything. I mean, that's just—"

"Dinner is finally served," Tina said.

"Wonderful." Andrew smiled, then stood up and took my arm. "Josie and I are starved, aren't we?"

I agreed I was, which meant I avoided commenting on Charlene and Davida and their purses and friends.

25.

Dinner began with a cold potato soup that Tina kept insisting was not vichyssoise, which I said was fine because I was never sure if I was pronouncing the damn word correctly anyway, which caused Andrew to snort in laughter and me to giggle.

"It sounds like you two did more drinking than talking in the den," Tina said, visibly annoyed.

Through the rest of the soup course, while Tina discussed her problem with damask drapes and grumbled about the terrible job her garden maintenance people were doing, Andrew and I avoided looking at each other lest we both break into giggles. Three glasses of vodka had reduced us to eight-year-olds at summer camp. It was delightful.

The main course was grilled lamb chops and thinly sliced baked potatoes served on a sauce that I must admit was as gourmet as I ever expect to eat. My compliments were sincere enough for Tina to call Goldie in from the kitchen to take some sort of culinary bow. "Goldie is from Guatemala," Tina announced in a tone that suggested a Guatemalan maid was a notch or two higher in the Vancouver social strata than one from Mexico or, for all I knew, Kurdistan. Anyway, she was a shy, petite woman with coal black hair and eyes, and Andrew and I toasted her with the Châteauneuf-du-Pape that Tina had made a point of informing us cost eighty-five dollars a bottle, but it was worth it, wasn't it? I agreed, and said if she cared to break the empty bottle I would be pleased to lick the pieces.

Dessert was a mango sorbet. It went well with the coffee and not so well with my head, which was bouncing between the appetite satisfaction of the meal and the rapid fading of the alcohol.

Something was bothering me, had been bothering me since before I sat down at the dinner table. It was a voice in my mind, and if voices can have colour, this one was as dark as Goldie's hair but not nearly as attractive. I kept trying to listen to this voice, absorb what it was saying to me, but all I could hear was Tina discussing boxwood hedges and cracked flagstone.

"Josie." It was Tina, reaching to grab my arm. "Where are you, anyway?"

I turned to stare at her, my eyes unfocused.

"You have forgotten," Andrew said, "that the poor girl is still on Eastern Time, which means," and he looked at his watch, "it's well past eleven at night to her inner clock. She must be very tired."

I looked at Tina and told her Andrew was right. I was very tired.

Within minutes I was in the guest room at the far wing of the house, a second-floor suite with the same view across the water to downtown Vancouver that I had enjoyed in the den. A quick tour of Tina's toiletries, a turndown of the bed, and a kiss on the cheek were followed by blessed darkness and silence and the even more welcome blessing of the soft bed and the duvet and the gentle slowing down of the spinning room.

I WOKE UP AND I KNEW.

I knew what happened that night, the night Gabe waited for me on the blanket and died. I knew how and why he had died, and I knew what I had done and what I had not done to cause his death, the story like a picture, and the picture developing like the one the horny Buddhist photographer had shown me in his darkroom once, an image on paper beginning to form. I had been dreaming that I was in the darkroom alone, watching the image appear on the paper in the tray, an image of Gabe on the blanket. In my dream I began to cry, and I was crying when I awoke.

It was the purses. The identical Louis Vuitton look-what-I've-got-you-bitch purses.

The face of the clock next to the bed glowed 2:15.

Going back to sleep was out of the question. I needed to walk. I needed to think things through, to decide what to do and how to do it. I dressed, went downstairs, and opened the side door into the garden.

Tina had told me almost everything about her house, about the custom cabinetry made of Philippine mahogany, the special floor tiles imported from Mexico, and the solid brass door fixtures from a small foundry in England. She had never mentioned the security system.

Opening the door triggered a speaker somewhere in the house, pulsing a high-pitched tone. Lights in the garden and under the eaves of the house lit up, and while I stood waiting for my addled mind to explain what the hell was happening, the telephone rang.

I closed my eyes and the door, and waited for Tina to find me, deciding what I would say to her.

"JOSIE, YOU'RE NOT WELL." Tina was following me through the house while I asked her to tell me where the goddamn computer was. "Maybe you have that post-traumatic stress thingy or something."

"Thingy?" I stopped and looked at my sister, wrapped in her silk robe, her arms folded across her chest. Andrew had spoken to the security people, assured them that the house had not been invaded by cannibalistic Vikings or anything nearly as threatening, and cleverly gone back to bed. "I've solved my husband's murder and you think I have a *thingy?*"

"Josie—"

"*Show me your fucking computer!*" I believe I have never shouted louder. I may have awakened Andrew. I probably woke up Seattle.

Tina threw her hands up and turned into a room off the hall that I had assumed was a washroom. It was a small office. The computer on the desk stared back at me blankly. "Thanks," I said, sitting at the desk. "Now go back to bed, Tina. Because I'm not. I can't. And give me your password. I have to look up a lot of things before dawn."

IT WAS FIVE IN THE MORNING and the sky was as dark as it had been at midnight. My flight left at seven, putting me in Toronto at three-thirty and home on the beach strip in time for dinner. I did not plan on having dinner.

I had spent two hours on Tina's computer, making my flight reservations and searching the Internet for information on many things and many people. Some details confirmed what I already knew. Some were dead ends. None contradicted what I believed had happened. Everything confirmed it. Now I was standing near Tina and Andrew's front door, waiting for the lights of the cab I had called to take me to the airport.

Andrew was silent, sipping a coffee. Tina was agitated.

"For god's sake, Josie," she said, "tell me why you have to go now. Talk to me, talk to Andrew, we'll listen. How can you be so sure?"

"Because I am." It was all I could say, the only way I could respond.

"What are you going to do when you get back?"

"Make some telephone calls. A lot of telephone calls." This was only half right.

"To whom?"

"To the people who helped kill Gabe. All of them."

"Damn it, you can't go making accusations . . ." We had been having this one-sided conversation since I emerged from her office and began packing my bag, which is when Andrew awoke again and made coffee, wearing a silk robe in a blue and purple paisley pattern. I knew Tina had bought him that robe. She didn't have to tell me that. No man would choose a robe like that for himself. Now she turned to him. "Talk to her, Andrew," she said. "Talk some sense into her."

Andrew studied his coffee cup for a moment, then said, "Josie has always made a lot of sense to me," which released a low squeal of exasperation from Tina. I was saved from witnessing Tina's revenge by the sight of slowly approaching headlights.

"My cab's here," I said, and hugged first Tina, who refused to uncross her arms from her chest, then Andrew, who squeezed me tightly and advised me to take care of myself.

"Josie." Tina reassumed the role of a caring older sister. "Promise me you'll at least rely on Mel what's-his-name."

"Holiday. Blue eyes."

"For god's sake, don't go playing games with some of the other people you've told me about, the Mafia guy, the woman who shot somebody in her hotel room, that dope dealer . . ."

I assured Tina I wouldn't. I planned to count on Mel more than I ever had. More than I ever expected I would.

The cab was in front of the house, the driver getting out of the car.

PEOPLE WASTE TIME AT AIRPORTS, thanks to all the security. I wasted no time at all. I spent an hour on the pay telephones, calling ahead to Walter Freeman, to Harold Hayashida, to Mike Pilato, to Glynnis Dalgetty, to Maude Blair, to Tom Grychuk, and, of course, to Mel.

"I'll meet you at the airport," Mel said when I told him I was returning, and I insisted no, I needed to follow up on something else, and I asked him, almost begged him, to see me that evening, because without him nothing could be done.

Mel told me I wasn't making sense. "Josie, nothing's happened since you left yesterday. There's nothing new to talk about, just a lot of investigations going on. At least give me an idea what we'll be looking for, who we'll be looking at, who'll be involved."

So I told him. "Grychuk."

"Who?"

"Tom Grychuk. He operates the lift bridge. Over the canal."

"How does he fit in? He's not even on our radar."

"They're calling my flight. I have to go. Tell me you can see me tonight."

"I can see you any night," he said, which was just what I didn't want to hear at the moment.

"I'll call," I began to say around the lump in my throat, then began again. "I'll call you at seven. On your cell. All right?"

They hadn't called my flight yet. I just couldn't bear to keep speaking to him with so much distance separating us.

I FELL ASLEEP SOMEWHERE OVER ALBERTA and woke when the pilot dropped the aircraft heavily in Toronto, landing the plane as though knocking a bookcase to the floor.

I headed for the arrivals area with my carry-on bag, running through all the things to be done when I arrived home and pushing aside a few small niggling doubts. I knew enough to be sure about what happened to Gabe and why, but the few details I lacked kept gnawing at my confidence like mice on a pantry door.

Walking through the sliding doors and into the concourse where the taxis and limos waited, I saw the friends and relatives of passengers watching the doors like spectators at a dull baseball game. The only person who stood out was a tall, gap-toothed man in a blue chauffeur uniform smiling back at me and holding a white cardboard sign with MRS. MARSHALL scrawled across it in black crayon.

"Hello, Alex," I said. Alex reached for my carry-on bag, which I snatched away from him. "How's Tina?"

From behind the wheel, Alex informed me that Tina had reserved the limousine and insisted on paying the fare. From the back seat, I informed Alex that it was very nice of Tina and I was going to enjoy her generosity and his careful manoeuvring of the limousine, but I was not going to take part in any damn conversation on the way.

Alex nodded and looked hurt.

It took forty-five minutes to reach the beach strip. It felt like forty-five hours.

When Alex opened the door, I stepped out, thanked him, walked directly to my front door, unlocked it, and collapsed on the living-room sofa. I needed five minutes alone to gather my thoughts and my courage again. When I had done so, I made a few more phone calls.

26.

Mother looked up in surprise when I entered her room. Her expression suggested that she thought something was wrong, perhaps with her memory. Hadn't I left the day before, saying I would be gone for a week? Had a week passed? Had she missed five days of her dwindling life, lost somewhere in the routine of eating, sleeping, and waiting?

"I'm all right," I said, hugging her. "I came back early because I have something important to do."

I brought us tea from the commissary, ignoring glances from staff members. Back in her room, Mother waved at the television set, indicating that I should turn it off, then reached for the black-board and wrote on it, *Talk to me. What is wrong?*

I wanted to cry, so I did. Just a little, enough to dampen my eyes and wet my cheeks. I realized for the first time that we had both lost the men we loved, lost them in terrible ways. Not slowly, to disease or decline, but violently and agonizingly. When you lose someone in that manner, you lose something else as well. You lose the sense that the world is a good place, and at times a beautiful place. It's more than losing your innocence; we all lose our innocence earlier than we know. When someone we love is taken from us in a brutal manner, we lose our sense of home, our notion that we can withdraw to a place where we are loved unconditionally.

When Mother saw me crying, she reached to wipe my cheeks and brought her lips to them and kissed me. Had she been able to

243

speak, I know she would have repeated words to me that she had spoken when we lived in the house near the steel mills, when my father carried a lunch box to work each morning, and the lunch box contained a sandwich made with more mustard than meat, wrapped in waxed paper, along with a Thermos of hot tea and perhaps a piece of cheese or an apple, and sometimes a note from Mother. Tina found one of the notes when she was ten and I was seven. The note said, *Always remember.*

"Always remember what?" I asked.

"Always remember that she loves him, you ignorant twerp," Tina said.

I began apologizing for the pain I knew I had caused Mother, especially in the years before I married Gabe, when I had met men in bars and discos and once while hitchhiking home, and the harsh words I used when she tried to caution me.

She lifted my face when I began telling her how sorry I was for all the ways I had let her down, for all the times I had not been here with her, for all the nasty things I had said to her, and all the sweet things I should have done and failed to do. She held up her finger and shook her head, silencing me. Reaching for the blackboard, she began writing on it, glancing up at me from time to time before handing it to me, her eyes waiting for my reaction.

She had written: *Accept the things to which fate binds you, and love the people with whom fate brings you together, but do so with all your heart.* It was a Hallmark moment.

"That's lovely, Mother," I said.

She beamed with pride, took the blackboard from me, erased the words, and wrote, *Because a thing seems difficult for you, do not think it impossible for anyone to accomplish.*

Like many women of her generation, Mother had qualities that the world refused to acknowledge because it refused to grant her the opportunity to reveal them. I had known this about her, but never expected she was capable of spouting such wisdom. "This is wonderful," I said. "Any more? I can use a little backbone right now."

Another smile, another swipe of her arm over the blackboard, and she added, in her lovely cursive writing, *You have power over your mind, not over outside events. Realize this, and you will find strength.*

This wasn't Mother speaking. She was a wonderful, wise woman, but . . .

"Where are you getting this?" I asked. I believe I raised one eyebrow.

She laughed, silently of course, reached into the wheelchair cushion beside her, and withdrew a paperback edition of *The Meditations of Marcus Aurelius* that had been Gabe's, and that I had brought to her a few weeks ago.

"That's quite a leap you made," I said. "From Elmore Leonard to Aurelius. You almost had me fooled, quoting a Roman who's been dead two thousand years or so." I reached to give her another hug. "Thanks for this," I said. "I'll see you tomorrow, and I think I'll have good news."

When I released her, she was looking at me, her mouth shaping an O and her eyes sparkling at the idea that her daughter would finally bring her good news. Then she reached for her pad again and wrote, *Mel Holiday?*

"Yes," I said, and she frowned and shook her head no. "I have to," I said, and leaned to kiss her goodbye, not aware at the time of something that should have been obvious.

Leaving the rest home, I tried to maintain the self-confidence that Mother and Marcus Aurelius had planted in me. I remembered a few lines from a book Gabe had been reading some months ago: *If something offends or distresses you, it is not the thing that causes you pain but your emotional reaction to it, and it is in your power to control and use all of your emotions.*

I think it was also Marcus Aurelius. Or maybe Dr. Phil.

I LIKE CLEAN BREAKS. From friends, from lovers, from clothes I don't want to wear anymore, from everything. Even seasons. Leaving Mother that night, I felt a clean break from summer to fall. The air was cooler and dryer, the breeze more insistent, the lake more choppy. The sun was already behind the steel mills, slouching toward Kitsilano. A month ago it would still have been high in the sky and warming. It was the end of August and the beginning of autumn—and the beginning of something else, as well.

"I'VE BEEN WAITING FOR YOUR CALL." I knew he had been by the way he answered the telephone before the first ring ended. "Josie, what's going on?"

"Tell me you love me." I had been wanting to say this all day.

"Josie, you know how I feel about you . . ."

"Tell me."

I could picture him closing his eyes, the way men do when something is going to pain them. "I love you, Josie."

"Thank you. Now tell me you'll meet me down near the canal lift bridge in an hour, in the parking lot on the bay side. Near the sandbank at the back of the lot. Closest to the bridge."

"What's this about?"

"Just meet me, Mel. Park the car facing the bay. Right up against the sandbank so you can't see it from the parking lot."

"Not until you tell me why."

"Damn it, Mel!" I breathed deeply and began again. "There's a window in the office where Grychuk works. The lift bridge operator. The guy—"

"I know who he is," Mel almost snapped.

"Sorry. I promise I'll explain. Just meet me there. Park your car where I said."

"Why can't I pick you up? At your house?"

"Mel, it's only a couple of hundred yards."

"I can still meet you there. You can tell me what's going on."

"Because we'll be watched."

"By whom?"

"That's what I want to explain to you. In an hour. Okay?"

I counted two breaths.

"Josie, please don't do anything silly."

"I promise you, Mel. This is the least silly thing I'll ever do."

It always feels good to tell the truth. Or at least not to tell lies. Which is not necessarily the same thing.

I had an hour to kill while the sun went down, and I thought it would never set. See what I mean about time passing at different speeds?

I FILLED THE TIME BY APPLYING MAKEUP and choosing a woollen sweater that Gabe had always liked. I believe he liked it, sweet man that he had been, because other men liked it, or at least liked the way I looked when I wore it. And a loose skirt, in case I had to run quickly. And rubber-soled shoes for the same reason. And gathering as much courage as I could from myself and not from a bottle.

At five minutes to eight, I made a final telephone call. Then, together with my nervous knees, I left the house, crossed Beach Boulevard, and began walking toward the canal bridge. To my left the horizon was the colour of roses, the sky the colour of gravel. The wind was east, off the lake, and gusty.

Ahead of me, the lift bridge control room shone with lights from within, where Tom Grychuk sat. On the bridge itself hung green lights for the traffic. Yellow lights marked the bridge outline, and red lights flashed from the top, for low-flying aircraft, I assumed. I had never thought about the bridge lights before. I was seeing them now because it was easier than thinking about what I expected to happen in the next few minutes.

I stopped and looked out at the lake. I tried to look all the way to the Thousand Islands.

Gabe had visited the Thousand Islands with his first wife. They took a boat tour and stayed for a week in Gananoque. When he told me about the vacation I asked him to repeat the name of the town. He did. He pronounced it "Gan-an-ock-wee," and I commented that the prettiest place names in all of North America were First Nations names like Gananoque. Allegheny. Mississauga. Manitoba. Musical names. Rhythmic names. He agreed, and named some of his own. Nipissing. Kapuskasing. Saskatoon. Muskoka. We played a game of musical names together, each of us thinking of one in turn, because Gabe wanted to cheer me up. Gabe always understood what I was thinking when I became melancholy, and picturing a young Gabe with his still young and faithful wife on a long-ago summer's day in a town called Gananoque overlooking a thousand granite islands dotted with pine trees and wildflowers made me melancholy.

I stood remembering Gabe and the Thousand Islands because I needed strength. I was about to do something I had never imagined myself capable of doing, and I needed to remind myself why it was necessary. And what could happen to me if something went wrong. I told myself I was doing it for Gabe. But I wasn't. I was doing it for myself, and if life was to unfold for Mel and for me in the way that I believed it must, I needed to be strong. More than that, I needed to be wise.

I've never doubted my inner strength. It was my habit of acting like a hysterical chicken in a hot kitchen that was worrying me. If I had made one error in logic, I was about to look terribly foolish in the next few minutes. I drew some comfort from reminding myself that looking foolish was infinitely preferable than looking dead. Which was also a possibility.

I took a final glance in the direction of the Thousand Islands and resumed walking, turning left before crossing the bridge and following the road that fishermen and boaters took to get to the shoreline of the bay. The road crossed a sandbank before dipping down to the water's edge, and when I reached the bottom of the low grade I looked to my right to see Mel's car parked as I had asked. Mel was watching me through the windshield, his face lit by the setting sun, red like molten slag. Behind and above him, I saw a man in the window of the lift bridge control room, silhouetted against the light. I raised my arm. He raised his.

Mel leaned to open the passenger door. I slid in, closed the door behind me and sat back, closing my eyes.

"You all right?"

I opened my eyes to see Mel studying me with that special expression of his, his brow furrowed and his smile wide and warm. He was wearing his blue jacket, with jeans as tight as a second skin. "No," I said. "I need something from you."

The smile faded. "What?" he asked.

"A hug, for a beginning. A really warm, solid squeeze."

I reached toward him and half pulled him close, then leaned away. "Take your gun off. Do you know how uncomfortable it is to hug somebody who's wearing a shoulder holster?"

"Okay," he said, withdrawing the Glock from the holster and setting it on the dashboard, then reaching for me. I remained within his arms, feeling his breathing and hearing his heart, long enough for him to tilt my chin up and look at me, perhaps preparing to kiss me.

"I can't, Mel," I said.

"Can't what? It's too soon?" Meaning, I guess, too soon after Gabe's death for us to become lovers again.

"Just let me sit up for a minute."

He released me and I sat with my back against the passenger door, watching him in the dying light. Then I leaned forward. Instead of reaching for another embrace, I took the gun from the dashboard, held it in both hands and pressed my back against the passenger door again, aiming the Glock at Mel's blue eyes, those beautiful blue eyes, which were already squinting in surprise.

"I swear," I said in a voice that surprised me with its strength. "I swear, Mel, if you try to take this from me, I'll blow your head off."

"You're crazy." I understood why Mel said that. I didn't feel entirely sane at the moment. Just very calm and determined.

"Probably. But it doesn't matter. Because I'm going to sit here with your gun pointed at your head, and we're going to talk about how you killed Gabe, you son of a bitch."

27.

I had imagined all the things that Mel might say in this situation, and how I would respond. So his first reaction didn't surprise me.

"You can't fire it," he said. "The safety lock's on."

"These guns don't have safety locks, Mel. That's why you cops like them. You don't have to grope for the safety lock while the bad guy puts a bullet in you. When you pull the trigger, you release the safeties and the gun fires. No fumbling around. I pull this trigger and the bullet comes out. Simple as that. Right, Mel?"

"Gabe teach you that?" I hated the way he said it.

"No. Gabe hated guns. A little time on the Internet. That's all it took."

"Is that where you got this crazy story about me shooting Gabe?" He sat back as though trying to move out of range. He looked calm, except for a small twitch at the corner of one eye.

"It's not a crazy story," I said. "And it didn't come from the Internet. It came from you and Hayashida and Walter Freeman and Mike Pilato—"

He forced himself to laugh. "Mike Pilato? You're believing the biggest gangster in the city?"

"—and Glynnis Dalgetty—"

"Who?"

"—and Andrew Golden and two snooty women who got their Louis Vuitton purses mixed up. You killed him, Mel. You shot Gabe while he was waiting for me, naked on the blanket inside the bushes, and before that you shot Dougal Dalgetty, and later you killed Wayne Weaver Honeysett, trying to cover up everything with your story about drugs missing from the police locker and Gabe suspecting Walter, which was when I really started wondering about you. Gabe wouldn't take home a two-dollar notepad, and you tell me he might have been taking drugs from a police locker? Walter knew it too, in the depths of his stupid soul. He knew Gabe was no thief, so he started believing I was. You killed Gabe, Mel. I know how you did it, and I have a good idea why you did it, and if I don't put a bullet first in your balls and then in your brains before the cops get here, we're going to go over all the details. Right here. Right now."

"You've got officers coming?" Mel twisted to look around. "That's good. Because when they see you with my weapon, they will either shoot you or arrest you, and probably both. And whatever story you come up with will be the product of a delusional woman who can't believe her husband killed himself because his wife didn't want to fuck him."

He looked directly at me, and I saw the flash of anger that Gabe had told me about, so long ago, the one I had seen in small doses. *Mel has the ability to think and act simultaneously.* Gabe had said that. And: *The only thing he's gotta control is his temper.*

He was speaking to me again.

"Right, Josie? Isn't that right? A drunken man finds out his wife's been screwing his partner, and when she doesn't show up as promised, he loses it and turns the gun on himself. That's what happened, right?"

I wanted to scream and shoot, not necessarily in that order. I spoke instead, in a calm voice that continued to surprise me, while Mel listened, too interested or perhaps too frightened to interrupt me. "No," I said. "You shot Dougal Dalgetty because he started to squeeze you. He was turning the tables on you after you'd been squeezing him and Mike Pilato, threatening to arrest

Dougal for drug dealing unless he and Pilato paid you off. How much did they pay you, Mel? Enough to buy that place by a lake and do what, Mel? Just lie around and spend the money you took from Pilato and Dalgetty and maybe some others? Or maybe take me or some other woman to that inn in New England? The Griswold Inn, right? Eugene Griswold, innkeeper. Two hundred years after Eugene died, he gives you a name for a drug dealer that never existed. You make him up as a big dealer, telling Gabe this Eugene Griswold is new in town and throwing his weight around, going up against Mike Pilato and killing one of Pilato's dealers, Dougal Dalgetty. And when Gabe starts checking on his own, talking to people like Mike Pilato, trying to find Griswold, he realizes there is no Griswold or Grizz, and since you were the only person saying there was, you must be lying, which meant you were hiding something."

Mel opened his mouth to speak, but I knew what he was going to say and interrupted him before he could say it.

"How much did Dalgetty and Pilato pay you before they decided they'd paid you enough, and if you didn't knock it off they'd drop the word about you to Walter Freeman? Especially when you didn't lift a finger to get the charges against Dalgetty dropped? How scared were you about that, Mel? Did you think Dalgetty would turn on you in court, saying he'd been paying you off? Or maybe they paid you in more than cash. Were they slipping you bags of dope, Mel? Cocaine? Heroin? What was it?"

Mel wouldn't look at me as he spoke. "It was Gabe," he said. "Check it out, Josie. It was Gabe's gun that killed Dalgetty. Gabe. Not me."

"It was you, Mel. And it was you who was under the lift bridge when Wayne Honeysett told me he had seen everything."

He turned to face me. "That's crazy."

"Your cell phone records say so. The date, the time, the location . . ."

The sun had set, and the light inside the car and all around us was weighing down with the greyness of dusk, but I could still make out Mel's expression and pallor. His expression was concern. His pallor was as grey as the dying light. "You don't have my cell phone records," he said in a voice that sounded like high noon in Death Valley.

"No," I agreed. "Hayashida has them. Got them this morning. I called from Vancouver, asked him to check them out. He did, and confirmed what I suspected. The night Wayne Honeysett died, you were within a hundred yards of right here. You saw him, Mel. You saw him because you were trailing him, right? You were trailing him because you started checking the interviews with all the local perverts, like the good cop you pretended to be, because you realized he might have been in the garden shed the night you shot Gabe. You figured Honeysett was the peeper who hid in the garden shed, the poor sap who fell all over himself when he became infatuated with women like Glynnis Dalgetty, and me, I guess, and a bunch of other women he gave gifts to. He was too shy, too totally screwed up to give me the ring he made for his wife, so he gave it to Gabe and asked him to give it to me, and Gabe did, probably because he felt sorry for Honeysett and wanted me to wear it. What happened, Mel? Did Honeysett start talking about what he knew, what he saw, the night Gabe died? Is that why you had to kill him?"

Mel, still thinking about his cell phone records while staring through the windshield, muttered that I didn't know what the hell I was talking about.

The silence made me uncomfortable, so I kept talking, waiting for what I knew I had to do, and it all spilled out of me in a torrent.

"Honeysett didn't go to the police because he was afraid they would charge him with being a pervert again, and he probably would have gotten a jail term. What happened, Mel? Did you see him run from the shed after you shot Gabe? Or maybe as you were coming into our house, through the garden? Did you decide you had to kill him before he figured out what you had done, before somebody like Walter Freeman took the miserable little guy seriously? You must have been under the bridge when I scattered Gabe's ashes. Is that where you were, Mel? Hiding under the bridge, waiting to talk to Honeysett? Did he know you'd be there? Were you going to shoot him like you shot Dalgetty and . . ." I had to swallow the lump in my throat. "Like you shot Gabe?"

He turned to look at me. For the first time, he appeared truly frightened, because he understood how much I knew.

I had more to say, not to impress Mel as much as to finally speak aloud all the things I had been telling myself for the past twelve hours.

"Did you panic, Mel? Did you lose it and shoot Honeysett in some kind of . . . of unthinking knee-jerk reaction? Or did you wait until the bridge went up, so the noise would hide the sound of the gunshot? Which was it, Mel? Never mind, I don't care. Afterwards you lifted his body and set his head, with the bullet from your gun in it, on the bridge support and held it there while the bridge came down on it. Jesus, Mel, don't you have nightmares about that? What kind of sound does a man's skull make when a bridge comes down on it and crushes it like an eggshell and squeezes the brains into jelly? Sure works to hide a bullet, though, doesn't it? Sorry, a projectile. The pro-jec-tile becomes just another piece of junk off the bridge supports, like a flattened penny, and who the hell would look for that among crushed brains, right, Mel?"

He looked away and down, one hand squeezing the bridge of his nose.

"What's that, Mel? I couldn't hear you. Say it louder. I'm really interested in what you have to say."

He raised his head to look through the windshield again. "I

said you have no proof. And it was Gabe's gun that shot Dalgetty and Gabe's gun that he used to kill himself." He turned to look at me. "Because he discovered you had been screwing his partner."

Which might have been enough for me to shoot him there and then. But I didn't. I was too damn proud of myself to miss the chance to show him how clever I was. And how stupid I had been.

"I don't know if he knew that." I wanted to close my eyes, to lower my arms, and to think about Gabe, but I couldn't. Not yet. "But he knew you shot Dougal Dalgetty."

There's something else, Gabe had said when he called, wanting to make love on the blanket, and I said, *I know*, and Gabe asked me how I could know. He meant how could I know about Mel shaking down Dalgetty and Pilato and making up the story about Eugene Griswold, because that's what he wanted to tell me, that he believed Mel had killed Dalgetty.

"And Mike Pilato figured it out as well. That you shot Dougal. When I told him the forensics matched. The bullet that killed Dalgetty and the one that killed Gabe. They matched. Pilato knew Gabe hadn't shot Dalgetty, and now he knew you had. He suspected you all along, because you were the one shaking him and Dalgetty down. It fell into place with the forensics report, first with Pilato, then with me. So you take your choice, Mel. You get me sitting here, or you get Mike Pilato looking for your ass, ready to punish you for shooting his good buddy Dougal."

Mel actually smiled. "Mike Pilato doesn't scare me," he said.

"He'd better. And what were you doing at our house that night, anyway, Mel? Did you learn that Gabe knew who killed Dalgetty, and why? Were you looking for me? Never mind. Gabe went into the bushes, wrapped in a blanket, you followed him, maybe you talked to him while he was there on the blanket, trying to get him to go along with you, and Gabe wouldn't. He wouldn't cover for you, and he wouldn't have been on his knees when you shot him either. Not for you, not for anybody. I think he was getting up off the blanket, ready to kick your ass, and that's when you lost it and shot him with your gun—"

"It was Gabe's gun." Mel sounded tired, resigned. "Forensics says so. Hayashida signed the form. The paraffin test was positive—"

"No, no, no, no, no, Mel. You were so 'upset' about Gabe's death, so intent on 'investigating what really happened,' that you insisted on filling out the forensics forms yourself. You were the one who read the serial number of Gabe's gun aloud to Hayashida, who entered it on the form before the gun was fired. Except it wasn't Gabe's gun you fired into the water tank to get . . ." I couldn't resist saying it the same way again. " . . . the pro-jectile for the forensics lab. It was *your* gun. A Glock G22 identical to Gabe's, identical to the one carried by everybody else in the department. Boy, I hope they got a volume discount for all those ass-ugly guns. And you sure as hell deserve a medal for thinking fast in a tight situation, like Gabe said you could. You shoot Gabe, drop the gun in the right place, get the hell out from inside those bushes before anybody on the beach can see you, and walk through the garden and into our house, where you get Gabe's gun out of the kitchen. Then you put it together, slip it in your holster and leave by the front door, maybe already thinking about how you can convince Hayashida or whoever that your gun is really Gabe's until you get a chance to switch them again. Brilliant."

I waited for a reaction. There was none, except for a slight glistening on his brow. He was beginning to sweat. Good.

"Oh, and you shook his hand too, didn't you, Mel?"

He looked at me. I had surprised him again.

"You grabbed his hand, his right hand, with your own. Just a quick grab and release. Shaking hands goodbye, Mel, while Gabe lay dying? No, transferring some of the gunshot residue from your hand to his. Just enough, Mel, for the paraffin test to find some. Just a trace, that's all you needed. Where'd you pick that up, Mel?

At the police academy? Or from that case in Baltimore, where a suspect and his lawyer proved the residue on the suspect's palm came from shaking hands with the real killer? Nobody thought of doing a paraffin test on *your* hand, did they? Or even to check the gun for fingerprints. Why should they? Everybody believed Gabe had shot himself with his own weapon. Why waste time on finger-print tests? Boy, you were good, Mel. Really good. You almost got away clean, except that Wayne Weaver Honeysett was in the garden shed, waiting for me to come home so he could watch me undress in our bedroom—maybe I'd be near the window, where he could see me. He heard the shot and watched you instead. Watched you go into the house and get Gabe's gun. Poor Wayne. Jerking off among rusty rakes and a bag of topsoil."

I leaned forward, trying to look Mel in the eye.

"You also grabbed our notepad from the kitchen counter as you were leaving. What was in the notebook, Mel? Was there something in there about you and Dalgetty, maybe? Is that why you took it with you, why I couldn't find it? Or maybe he just wrote that he loved me. Is that what Gabe wrote on it?"

"Yeah, that's what he said." Mel sat up straight, his back against the seat. "Something like that."

"What did it say, Mel?"

"Go to hell."

"You know what I think? I think there was something about you in it that didn't add up with Gabe. Something my friend Dewey saw him writing a day earlier. Is that what it was?"

"Fuck you."

"Not anymore, Mel. Not you, not ever."

He looked over and actually smiled. "None of this matters. Either you shoot me now, which you can't, or you just get the hell out of here while you can."

"Or Walter Freeman and some other cops show up and take

over." The flashing red and blue lights appeared on the bridge. Bubble gum lights, Gabe used to call them.

Mel twisted in his seat to look at the cruisers on the bridge, the officers spilling out and heading along the canal toward us. "They'll shoot you when they see you with the gun," he said.

"Or I'll shoot you first," I said, and I took aim and pulled the trigger.

28.

Walter Freeman wouldn't look at me. He had avoided looking at me for the last hour while I sat in an interrogation room with him and Harold Hayashida and a female police officer who managed to look like a *Playboy* model with her blonde hair, blue uniform, black leather belt, gold badge, and silver bullets. What makes such a good-looking young woman become a cop, I wondered. Maybe good-looking young male cops.

Hayashida broke my thoughts by asking, for the third time, if I wanted a coffee. For the third time I told him no. He was sitting at a desk set at a right angle to me, flipping through pages in a red cardboard file. Walter had come and gone several times, conferring, I assumed, with whoever was behind the one-way mirror.

The mirror worked at blocking the view of the people watching me, but after a knock at the door took Walter out of the room, it couldn't block the sound of his enraged voice.

A minute later the door opened again, but instead of Walter Freeman, a tall man in his forties entered, dressed and groomed as though he had stepped out of a Brooks Brothers catalogue. I had never seen a better-fitted pinstripe suit or a better-coordinated Oxford shirt and striped tie. His Afro-styled salt-and-pepper hair was the result of genes, not a hairstylist, and his tortoiseshell glasses were so out of fashion they were avant-garde.

He nodded at me, set a leather briefcase on a side table, and walked toward Hayashida with his hand extended. "J. Michael Robinson," he said in a voice deep enough to deliver a good imitation of Barry White. "I have been appointed legal counsel for Mrs. Marshall, and I am requesting that this interrogation be suspended while I ascertain the charges against her and advise her of her rights. I am also insisting that I be present during any future interrogations."

Hayashida ignored Robinson's handshake. Instead, he shrugged, closed his file, and stood up. "Sure," he said. "You want to talk to her here?"

"Absolutely not." Robinson turned to me with his rejected handshake. I accepted it. "I insist on a counsellor's room and full privacy." He smiled at me as he spoke.

Standing in the open doorway, Walter Freeman's face was as blank as an empty plate.

I left the room, guided by the lawyer's hand at the small of my back. Three doors down the hall, past some knots of uniformed cops watching me and whispering among themselves, we entered a room about the size of a walk-in closet, with two chairs and a lamp table. Robinson closed the door behind us and set the briefcase on the table.

"Who the hell are you?" I said.

"I'm your lawyer."

"I didn't ask for one. I don't need one and I can't afford one."

He took a deep breath and let it out noisily while staring at the ceiling. Okay, he was exasperated. I got the message. "You didn't ask for one, correct," he said. "You tell me to leave and I will. But before you do, understand that you need a lawyer desperately. It doesn't matter if you can afford one or not. You either get me or you get somebody listed with legal aid who is probably sitting in a bar on James Street right now."

"It matters to me. Whether I can afford a lawyer or not."

"But not to Mr. Pilato."

"He sent you here?"

"He says he owes you."

"Then he can fix my car, the one his guys smashed with a sledgehammer. I don't need a lawyer."

He withdrew a sheet of paper from his briefcase and began reading from it. "It appears you are facing a charge of obstruction of police, theft of police property, possession of a firearm, resisting arrest and . . ." He moved the paper aside to look at me. " . . . attempted murder of a law enforcement officer, which carries a penalty of up to twenty years in prison."

"That's garbage."

He dropped the paper on the desk. "Of course it is. It's also legitimate. Do you want to spend twenty years in prison?"

"What do you think?"

He smiled and leaned back in the chair. "I think," he said, "that you have set a new record for embarrassing a major metropolitan police force in this country, and they are so upset with you that they are ignoring, for the moment, the reality that they have a rogue cop in custody facing a triple murder charge."

HALF AN HOUR LATER we gathered in Walter Freeman's office. Walter sat behind a desk as big as my dining-room table. Two uniformed officers stood behind him, their feet apart, their hands behind their backs, as approachable as bookends. Hayashida, Robinson, the blonde policewoman, and two guys from internal affairs, wearing cheap suits and faces that desperately needed shaving, flanked me in chairs arranged in a semicircle. An overweight guy Walter introduced as a Crown attorney stood to one side, like a referee.

Walter wouldn't look at me. His head down, he read aloud in a flat voice from a sheet of paper on the desk in front of him. "We will withdraw the charge of obstructing police on the basis of Mrs. Marshall's telephone call earlier today to Sergeant Hayashida, who confirms that she offered information she legitimately believed would assist us in our investigation."

"It sure as hell did, Walter," I said. Robinson nudged me to be quiet.

"We will suspend the charges of theft of police property and illegal possession of a firearm subject to evaluation of the projectile fired by your client, the aforesaid Mrs. Marshall, this evening—"

"The one you recovered from the sandbank, right?"

Walter's eyes flicked from the paper to me for a heartbeat, then back to the paper again. "Subject to evaluation of the projectile fired by your client this evening by the provincial forensics laboratory. We are also suspending the charge of attempted murder of a police officer pending the same forensics report and, as requested, will issue a document to the administrator of Trafalgar Towers confirming that our suspicions of possible fraud committed by Mrs. Marshall have no basis in fact."

"I am requesting that all criminal charges be dropped as of now," Robinson said, "on the basis that the alleged acts were conducted by Mrs. Marshall as a means of obtaining an exhibit that the forensics laboratory could use to confirm that the weapon was used in three unsolved homicides—"

Walter couldn't take it anymore. "Citizens are not permitted, are never permitted, to seize possession of a law officer's weapon and fire it in the direction of a member of the police force," he partially shouted, partially spat—I could see the spittle flying like water from a lawn sprinkler—"no matter what her motives might have been!"

Things turned into a verbal food fight after that. I screamed that no cop was likely to compare rifling marks on a bullet from Mel's gun with the ones that had killed Gabe and Dougal Dalgetty unless I gave him good reason to, and I had. Robinson quoted some statute supporting a citizen's arrest, Walter told me to keep my damn mouth shut and ordered Robinson to stick to the facts, Hayashida asked somebody to close the door and turn off the digital recorder, and Robinson said he would consider requesting a judicial inquiry into the operations of the police force. The two bookend cops looked at each other with confusion, especially when Walter Freeman lost it and stood up, crumpled the sheet of paper he had been reading from into a ball, and threw it at J. Michael Robinson, striking him squarely in the tortoiseshells.

I laughed. I couldn't help it. It was midnight, I was running on distilled adrenaline, Mel Holiday was being interrogated in a room down the hall, and the chief of detectives had just hurled an oversized spitball at my lawyer, who had been hired by the most notorious gangster in the city. What wasn't there to laugh at?

The Crown attorney walked behind Walter's desk, placed a hand on Walter's shoulder, turned him and his swivel chair around, and began speaking to him in a low voice while Robinson made notes in a binder pulled from his briefcase. Hayashida buried his face in his hands. I couldn't tell if he was crying or laughing.

Robinson leaned over and whispered to me while making his notes. "The Crown is telling Walter to free you on your own recognizance, with charges pending," he said. "When they confirm the forensics that prove Sergeant Holiday's gun killed your husband and Honeysett, all charges will be dropped."

I asked him how he knew that.

He closed the binder and slipped his Montblanc into his jacket pocket. "It's been previously discussed," he said, "between me and the Crown. Freeman is just learning about it now."

Let's have a cheer for our legal system, I thought.

"HOW CLOSE DID YOU COME to shooting Holiday in the head when you fired the gun?" Robinson asked. He was driving me back to the beach strip. His car was expensive, quiet, dark, warm, and smelled of Italian leather. I could marry a car like that.

"I don't know. I aimed for the open window. Missed him by maybe three or four inches."

"Clever of you to fire the bullet into the sand, to preserve the rifling marks."

"I'd rather have buried it in his head."

"Why not let the police do the test, once you explained it to them?"

"Who would believe me? Who would even *listen* to me? Who would ask for Mel's gun to do forensics on it on the basis that I, Gabe's crazy widow, was claiming that Mel Holiday had murdered three men, including my husband? I was sure I'd worked things out. How Mel had switched guns after shooting Gabe, substituting his own for Gabe's, and when they were getting the bullet for the forensics lab, how he told Hayashida the serial number of Gabe's gun, then in Mel's holster, rather than reading him the serial number of the gun in evidence. And how Hayashida trusted Mel enough to record it without inspecting it himself. Then Mel switched guns again, putting his own gun back in his holster and filing Gabe's in an evidence locker. Someday, somebody might have tested both guns, compared the results with Gabe's and Dalgetty's autopsy reports, and realized what Mel had pulled off, but it wasn't likely. And nobody was ever going to get anything from what was left of Honeysett's head."

"Walter Freeman said he suspected all along that the metal they found in Honeysett's remains had been a bullet."

"Walter Freeman would say he suspected the sun would come up in the morning if it made him look good. How could he stand it?"

"Freeman? Stand what?"

"Not him. Mel Holiday. How could he stand holding Honeysett's body like that, waiting for the bridge to come down on his head?"

"You'd be surprised what some people can do in desperate

straits." We were approaching my house. "Besides, he was a homicide detective for how many years?"

"Ten. Maybe more."

"Would you care to guess how many mangled bodies he encountered in ten years? How many autopsies he attended? Holding a body until the skull is crushed wouldn't be a picnic for anybody, but if it were necessary, a guy like him could do it. You can get used to anything, Mrs. Marshall."

I could get used to being in the company of a man like Robinson very late at night, every night, but when he stopped outside my door, I simply thanked him, stumbled inside, and climbed the stairs to my bed. The peeper in the garden shed was long gone. Mel Holiday was locked up, probably for life. I had a high-powered lawyer retained by an influential gangster to defend me. When Tina heard the news, she might actually admit that I have more intelligence than a string of barbed wire.

I hadn't slept so well in weeks.

MOTHER, OF COURSE, WAS SURPRISED to see me the next morning. She had finished her breakfast and was sitting at her window, watching the strollers on the boardwalk and along the canal. I startled her when I entered, and I hugged her longer and more firmly than normal, which made her reach for her chalk and blackboard and write, *Why are you here so early? Is something wrong?*

I assured her that nothing was wrong, and told her that the police had solved Gabe's murder. It was another police officer, I said. In fact, it had been Gabe's partner.

Mother's hand, gripping the chalk, flew across the blackboard like a drunken insect, writing, *Mel Holiday?*

"Yes," I said. "How did you know? Has it been on the news?" Walter Freeman had told Robinson that nothing would be revealed until the forensic examination of the bullets from Mel's and Gabe's guns was completed and charges laid.

She wrote, *He was here.* Then she added, *You slept with him, didn't you?*

I sat on the edge of the bed. I think it is a wonderful thing for a daughter to be surprised and impressed by her mother, no matter what their ages. At the moment, I just wished it were some other daughter. "When was he here?" I asked.

She wrote, *The day before yesterday. The day you left for Tina's. In the afternoon.*

"Why didn't you tell me?"

She wrote, *I didn't want to upset you.*

"What did he want?"

She erased everything she had written earlier and wrote, *He wanted to talk to me. He wanted me to talk to him.* She looked up and smiled at that.

I had mentioned Mother to Mel, I suppose. Only that I visited her now and then, and I had named the retirement home. I'd told him she had suffered a stroke, but I had not explained that she was unable to speak. "What did he want to talk about?"

Mother wrote, *What I knew about Gabe's death. What you had told me about it.*

"Did you tell him anything? By writing it down?"

She shook her head, erased the blackboard again, and wrote, *I told him to leave and asked for a nurse to take him out.*

"Did he tell you . . ." I had to start again. "Did he say that he and I . . . that we . . ." Damn. Then, in a torrent, "Did he say that he and I had slept together?"

Mother smiled and shook her head.

"You could tell, couldn't you? You figured it out all by yourself."

She nodded.

Harold Hayashida arrived at my house after lunch. I made tea, and we sat in the living room, not fully comfortable in each other's presence, like two patients waiting to see the same doctor.

He pulled a small sheet of paper from his inside jacket pocket and read from the notes. "Couple of things," he said. "First, forensics says there's no doubt that the projectile from the Glock G22 with serial number HPD7083, which is Mel's gun, matches the one that killed Dalgetty and Gabe and probably Wayne Weaver Honeysett." He looked up at me, his face downcast. "I trusted Mel, Josie. He read the serial number to me, I wrote it down, and we both signed the investigation document. I didn't think I needed to examine the weapon myself. I was supposed to, but I didn't. That was a mistake."

"I made a much bigger mistake a couple of months ago," I said, and Hayashida nodded. I had no secrets now.

"Gabe's gun was serial number HPD7836, in case you were interested."

"Has Mel confessed?"

"He's told us some things, things he can't refute. He's being charged with three homicides."

"Do you think Mel showed up at our house intending to kill Gabe? Or was it a spur-of-the-moment thing, maybe when Gabe tried to get at him?"

"This much he told us. He said Gabe came at him. He didn't plan on killing him. Mel says the gun went off and he dropped it there. Claims he didn't wipe his hand on Gabe's. Just got the hell out of the bushes."

"And Honeysett watched him go."

"Apparently. Mel knew where Gabe's gun was in the kitchen, took it, and went out the front door." Hayashida smiled and shrugged. "Of course . . ."

"Of course what?"

"Saying it happened that way makes it second-degree murder, not first-degree. Reacting instead of planning. Might get paroled, someday."

"He's facing two other murder charges, right?"

"If his statements hold up, he'll be sentenced for second-degree on those, as well. In both cases he said he hadn't planned anything in advance. Blamed it on his hot temper. Makes it hard to get a first-degree conviction. Not that it will make much difference for twenty-five years or so. And there's more. We got a tip that he received around a hundred thousand dollars in payoffs from street criminals over the past year."

"Who told you that?"

"Can't tell you."

"I'll bet his name ends in a vowel."

Hayashida smiled and looked down at his notes again. "Mickey Court sends his regrets. He says he's sorry he frightened you."

"What's a Mickey Court? Sounds like the Irish justice system."

"Constable Michael Court. Undercover officer from Toronto, posing as a drug buyer."

"The guy who showed up looking for Grizz."

"We had nothing on that person except Mel's claim that he'd heard Dougal Dalgetty had been shot by a heavyweight dealer, the Griswold character known as Grizz. Nobody on the street admitted to knowing anybody named Grizz, which isn't unusual. We had to flush him out, which was Court's job. It was trolling, is what it was. Enough people hear somebody's looking to buy, the dealer responds. Usually. When nothing came up, we started getting suspicious of Mel."

"Not suspicious enough. And not soon enough." Then a thought. "Did Gabe know? About Mel and this guy supposedly known as Grizz?"

Hayashida nodded. "The day he was killed, Gabe scheduled a meeting with Walter Freeman. They were going to get together the next day. Mel heard about it and knew he had to talk to Gabe that night. Which happened to be the night Gabe wanted you to meet him in the bushes. Nothing came together until after Honeysett's funeral. Walter had already heard that somebody in the department was shaking down a couple of street dealers—"

"And thought it might be Gabe." You stupid son of a bitch, Walter. "That's why he asked if Gabe had given me any expensive gifts."

Hayashida smiled and reached inside his jacket again, withdrawing a small piece of paper towel wrapped around something the size of a raspberry. "Nice timing," he said, handing me the ring Wayne Weaver Honeysett had made for his wife and given to Gabe for me. "Honeysett's daughters say you might as well have it. They've got lots more of their father's jewellery, and they're trying to respect their father's wishes. They've also found three other women who received jewellery from their father. He was basically a harmless, lonely guy. Just wanted women to like him, but was too afraid to approach them directly. They're sorry about accusing you." He folded his notes. "If it's any consolation, the ring he gave Gabe for you is the most expensive piece."

He stood up and shook my hand.

"By the way," he said, heading for the door, "no charges will be laid against you. Robinson's getting the official word this week. And you shouldn't have to testify at Mel's trial. Oh, and Walter is still pissed at you."

THAT WAS MORE THAN THREE MONTHS AGO. Now it's late November and everything is grey. The water, the sand, the sky. The lake, which is warm only in August, is getting colder, and in a few weeks I'll wake up and find thin ice on the shore where the water meets the sand. Nobody rollerblades on the boardwalk between my house and the beach anymore, and few people pedal their bicycles along it. They walk briskly, wrapped in woollen sweaters and leather coats. I'm starting to think like a bear: I just want to put on weight and curl up in a warm place for a few months.

Some days are golden for a while. Not July golden, of course, just golden with the sunlight. Nobody is fooled. Winter's somewhere north of Toronto, heading our way. Sweaters smelling like mothballs have been hauled out of closets, people are looking at brochures with pictures of Caribbean resorts they can't afford to visit, laggard birds are flying south, and tans have faded. Yesterday I made a pot roast for me and the Blairs. Gabe always liked pot roast.

Maude Blair still natters at her husband, Glynnis Dalgetty no longer walks the boardwalk glaring in anger at our house, and Hans and Trudy, who built their home in the style of a castle, sold it to a company that plans to convert the place into a schnitzel restaurant. Tuffy's still serves cold beer and hot chili to the biker crowd, and the sun still rises over the lake each morning, although farther to the east and much later.

Mother hasn't changed, nor will she, except she knows I love her more than ever. Tina thinks Mother's next stroke may arrive with the next cup of tea or the next sneezing fit. Mother is determined it won't. We may underestimate the power of love. We should never underestimate the power of a determined woman.

Tina rummaged through every site on Google about Mel's arrest, learning the details on the three murders, including Gabe's. She now knows more about it than I do.

The day after Hayashida and I had tea, Helen Detwiler called, her voice warm and sweet. She apologized for her unthinking response to Walter Freeman's suggestion that I might be stealing money from the retirement home and told me I could have my job back whenever I wished. In fact, they hoped it would be very soon, because the replacement woman wasn't . . . well, she just wasn't as efficient or as well-liked among the staff as I was.

I told her I would think about it.

Dewey Maas called. I told him I was considering getting a dog to keep me company when I went for walks on the beach. He said that sounded like a good idea. Then he had a better one: he needed someone to work the front of his business for him, handling appointments, selling dog food and toys, keeping the books, all of that. "We would have so much fun working together," he pleaded.

I said I would think about it.

Mike Pilato called twice, the first time to congratulate me on my detective work, prompting me to thank him for the services of J. Michael Robinson. The second time, he was more direct.

"Now that you know I'm not such a bad guy," he said, "maybe we can have dinner sometime, a little veal Marsala, nice wine. You know, not right away. When you get over all this stuff, your husband and that *testa di cazzo* Holiday. You never asked me about him, Holiday. You should have. That's the question you never asked me. I would have told you what I thought about him, what I knew about him. I knew lots. Not as much as you found out, maybe, but lots."

I asked why he didn't just volunteer the information, why he didn't tell me what he knew without me asking.

"Volunteer?" I might have asked him to kiss the pope. "Hey, listen to me. Nobody volunteers anything, okay? Nobody but an *idiota*. You ask, maybe I answer. You don't ask, you get nothing. That's how the world works. I think a woman like you, been around the block a few times, right? I think maybe a woman like you should know that."

"Been around the block a few times?" I was prepared to scream at him from a safe distance.

"Relax, relax. I mean you're a woman as tough, maybe as smart as a man. Don't meet many women like you anymore. You know your way around, you can still be a lady. Doesn't mean you're a *puttana*. You think maybe I invite a whore to have dinner with me? I like nice women. Nice sexy woman like you, maybe have dinner with me. You heard of a restaurant called Omera?"

"Is it a local place?"

"No, no, no. It's in Positano. On the Amalfi Coast."

"You want me to go to Italy with you."

"That's right."

"For dinner."

"And a little longer. When you're ready. When you're feeling ready."

I said I would think about it.

Two days later, Tom Grychuk called. It was Grychuk who had phoned Walter Freeman's office when he saw me get into Mel's car, as he had agreed to do when I called him from Vancouver that morning. When the police arrived at the lift bridge, it was Grychuk who told them to listen for a gunshot, which was enough to send them running toward the car just as I fired the Glock, aiming behind Mel's head.

Grychuk reminded me that his wife had died a year earlier, which made it easier for him to ask if I would like to discuss the case, we two law-abiding conspirators, over dinner some evening. Not in Italy. Right here in town.

I said I would think about it.

LAST WEEK, J. MICHAEL ROBINSON PHONED to say I might have to come to his office and make a deposition for Mel's sentencing hearing. "I understand he has told the police just about everything they need to know," he said. "The Crown will probably want a statement from you to corroborate things and ensure that he is not leaving out information vital to the case or vital to similar cases. But you shouldn't need to appear in court."

"What does a deposition involve?" I asked. I already knew. I just wanted him to keep talking.

"For the most part," he said, "it will be a matter of you and I discussing the case, recorded on video. This will be submitted to the Crown. If necessary, a second deposition, with the prosecution in attendance, may be required to settle their concerns."

I asked him what the *J* stood for.

He said it stood for Jonathan.

I asked him if there was a Mrs. Jonathan Robinson.

He said there was. His mother.

"Tell you what, Jonathan," I said. "I'll show up for the deposition on the condition that you let me call you Jonathan from now on, and that sometime in the new year you take me out for dinner twice. Once at a local Italian restaurant and, if the night goes as well as I hope, a second time at a restaurant I've heard about on the Amalfi Coast."

He said he would think about it.

ACKNOWLEDGEMENTS

A fter being absent so many years from writing mystery fiction, I needed something of a support system to complete this tale, especially because I chose to write in a woman's voice. I found it in a number of people, including the usual suspects—my darling wife, Judy, and my illustrious agent, Hilary McMahon. The professional and caring assistance offered by Iris Tupholme, Noelle Zitzer, Lorissa Sengara, Allegra Robinson, and the balance of the editorial staff at HarperCollins Canada made the entire experience a delight. Others were both helpful and encouraging, especially Deborah Grey and James McMahon. I am grateful to them all. As I suspect Josie would be.